MEDDLING AND MURDER

Ovidia Yu is a Singapore-based novelist and award-winning short story writer and playwright with over thirty plays staged by theatres in Singapore as well as Malaysia, Australia, Hong Kong, Edinburgh and San Francisco. Ovidia has received several awards and attended the University of Iowa's International Writing Programme. Her latest novel, *Meddling and Murder*, features best-loved amateur sleuth and restaurant proprietor Aunty Lee, who appeared in her previous *Aunty Lee's Delights* series. Ovidia has also written a new historical series, *The Crown Colony Murders*, which will be published by Constable and Robinson in summer 2017.

@OvidiaVanda
OvidiaYuDoggedAuthor

Previous books in the Aunty Lee series

Meddling and Murder

An Aunty Lee Mystery

OVIDIA YU

A division of HarperCollins*Publishers*
www.harpercollins.co.uk

This novel is entirely a work of fiction.
The names, characters and incidents portrayed in it are
the work of the author's imagination. Any resemblance to
actual persons, living or dead, events or localities is
entirely coincidental.

Killer Reads
An imprint of HarperCollins*Publishers*
1 London Bridge Street
London SE1 9GF

www.harpercollins.co.uk

This paperback edition 2017
1

First published in Great Britain by
HarperCollins*Publishers* 2017

A catalogue record for this book is
available from the British Library

ISBN: 978-0-00-822242-0

Set in Minion by Palimpsest Book Production Limited,
Falkirk, Stirlingshire

Find out more about HarperCollins and the environment at
www.harpercollins.co.uk/green

To Rasu Ramachandran and in memory of his beloved
wife, Premavathy Ramachandran

PROLOGUE

Of course the stupid woman had been living in a dream, a fantasy. Look at that too short dress (now hitched up, exposing cheap polyester panties) and the way that silver belt and fake gold necklace clash. Those pointed narrow shoes look like torture to walk in. All things considered, putting her down had been a mercy.

She had dressed up like an actress on opening night, ready to be the centre of attention. But the worksite was deserted by the time her big moment came.

Rolled up in blue plastic sheeting then stuffed into the disposal container, she made a surprisingly small bundle. The day's garbage went back in over her, then the wooden planks over the dumpster pit.

Tomorrow the remaining construction debris would be shovelled in before concrete was poured into the foundation. This was the accepted way of cutting down on disposal fees in land starved Singapore.

CHAPTER ONE

Aunty Lee's Life of Crime

'This is a big emergency! There is a human body in the drain next to our house. It is a very big body. Please to come fast.'

That was as much as Staff Sergeant Neha Panchal could make out from the panicked caller whisper-shouting in a mix of Mandarin and English.

'I'll be right there.'

Panchal got the address and set out immediately, calling to notify her boss, Inspector Salim Mawar, on the way.

The Bukit Tinggi Police Post was mainly responsible for the Binjai Park residential district. Some of Singapore's wealthiest residents lived in the area and the Bukit Tinggi posting was considered both a career breaker (for its lack of serious crimes) and career maker (from exposure to Singapore's most influential people). The last few emergency calls from Binjai Park had been triggered by badly parked cars and monkeys stealing fruit.

SS Panchal's first thought had been to qualify for a new posting as soon as possible. Now she had to admit she had learned a lot from this posting about how understanding people helped untangle the crimes they got caught up in. But Panchal would never understand why Inspector Mawar, who seemed like an intelligent man, would reject offers of promotion to remain in charge of the Bukit Tinggi NPP.

There was indeed a body in the big storm drain next to the caller's house. Fortunately, it was a live body. It was also very familiar and wearing a bright yellow Curry Up! tee shirt over pink and green batik pants. SS Panchal winced just a little before she leaned over the drain barrier's green metal railings and called: 'Aunty Lee! What are you doing down there? Are you all right?'

'Panchal!' Aunty Lee looked up, squinting against the sun. She did not seem hurt and was clutching clumps of weeds. 'Good, you are here. Come down and help me!'

Suspicious heads were watching from the windows of the house. That would be Mr and Mrs Guang who had phoned the police, Panchal guessed. They had to be newcomers to Singapore as well as Binjai Park, or they would have recognized Rosie 'Aunty' Lee of the famous Binjai Park café, Aunty Lee's Delights.

Thanks to her *kebaya*-clad image beaming from jars of Aunty Lee's Amazing Achar and Aunty Lee's Shiok Sambal, Aunty Lee was familiar to food lovers in Singapore and beyond.

And Aunty Lee was familiar to Panchal and the rest of the police force, thanks to the murders she had been involved in. But Aunty Lee was seldom out without her faithful Filipina helper. For an instant Panchal wondered if something was wrong.

'Aunty Lee, what are you doing in the storm drain? Where is Nina?' Panchal did not want to be the one to tell her boss that something terrible had happened to the main reason he chose to stay stuck in this backwater posting. 'Is Nina all right?'

'*Hiyah*, everybody only interested in Nina,' Aunty Lee said grumpily. 'Why should I care where is Nina?'

Nina Balignasay was Aunty Lee's domestic helper. Nina, whose nursing degree was not recognized in Singapore, had started as a home caregiver to Aunty Lee's late husband. Seeing she was smart and hard-working, the Lees had sent her for computer classes and business courses and even driving lessons. This last had required intricate bureaucratic wrangling since foreign domestic workers were forbidden from driving in Singapore. Permission for Nina's driving licence had only been granted after two doctors and an MP testified she was the sole caregiver for two old people who *might* need emergency medical treatment.

The Lees' intention had been to equip Nina for a profession after she left them. Instead, she had become invaluable to Aunty Lee's business as well as her closest friend and companion after M. L. Lee's death.

Aunty Lee was the ultimate snob when it came to durians and spices, but she was egalitarian when it came to people.

It was only today that Aunty Lee was cross with Nina.

Back in Aunty Lee's Delights. Nina was also cross with Aunty Lee. She knew her boss meant well. But why did she have to keep trying to interfere with her personal life?

Nina had already taken care of everything. She had told Salim she would not go with him to meet his mother; made it clear that she would not go anywhere with him, they could never be anything more to each other than customer and waitress. This was slightly complicated by the fact that the customer was a police officer and the waitress was violating her domestic work permit. But if Salim had accepted it, why couldn't Aunty Lee?

Singapore was a multiracial, multicultural city largely run by English educated Chinese people, and Aunty Lee was a very wealthy English-educated Chinese woman. Fond as she was of her boss, Nina suspected Aunty Lee was barely aware how differently the island's rules and regulations looked to those below and from the outside.

After Aunty Lee's last tirade on love and the rarity of 'Good Men', Nina was not sorry the older woman had gone out. She only hoped Aunty Lee was not headed to the police post to tackle Salim. Again.

'What's wrong with Nina?' SS Panchal asked. She wondered if it had anything to do with Inspector Salim's subdued mood over the last week. You didn't have to be a *kaypoh* – a busybody – as Aunty Lee was to see how much Salim liked Aunty Lee's helper. Aunty Lee had not seemed to mind, but her *kiasu* side might have kicked in. Had she, afraid of losing Nina, banned Nina from seeing the police officer?

'What's wrong is that stupid girl won't listen to me! I told her they should quick quick make up their minds and get married now that the property prices are down. Then they can get a flat near here … Clementi perhaps, or Bukit Batok. Then Salim can go on working at his police post and Nina can go on working for me.

'I told Nina I was going to tell Salim to faster faster apply for permission to marry her. Do you know what she told me?'

'That it's very difficult for foreign domestic helpers to get permission to marry locals?' Panchal guessed. That was well known. 'Aunty Lee, can I help you get out of the drain?'

'Difficult is not impossible. Foreign domestic helpers also not supposed to drive, *what*? But I got permission for Nina to drive. You just got to apply and apply and apply until they see you are serious. But Nina told me "No". She and Salim never getting married. Good bye! Finish! Chop-chop!'

'Ah.' Panchal could not remember anything about talking people out of drains. But she had attended a seminar on talking suicides off balconies. 'If you come out of the drain we can talk about it?'

Just then, her phone buzzed.

'Inspector? No, not another burglary. It's Aunty Lee. She's in a storm drain. No, she's not hurt.'

'Tell Inspector Salim I said Hello!' Aunty Lee called up.

Despite having been involved in several of Salim's murder

cases, Aunty Lee was still somewhat in awe of the Inspector. She had been on her way to tell him what cute and clever children he and Nina could have together. And how true love would be enough to overcome any differences in their Muslim and Catholic backgrounds. But remembering Nina's refusal to listen to her, Aunty Lee's steps had slowed … that was when she had seen the wild *kesum* growing on the slope by the storm drain next to the house that had been under construction for so long.

Daun kesum or *kesum* leaves were such an essential ingredient in making *laksa* that many people referred to them as *daun laksa* or *laksa* leaves. The oils of the young *kesum* leaves gave just the right aroma to spicy *assam laksa*. In the old days the creeper with its tiny purple flowers had been easy to find in muddy roadside ditches or growing along shallow drains. When you wanted to cook you went outside and plucked what you needed. But today's Singapore lacked muddy ditches and shallow drains. As a weed rather than a cash crop, *kesum* was seldom found in markets and never in supermarkets. Too often Aunty Lee had been reduced to using mint leaves as an alternative. Though no one had complained, the compromise galled her. Forget love problems. Make good *laksa*, she had decided. That renovations had damaged the protective barrier around the drain made it easier for her to climb round to the weed-filled slope.

'Inspector Salim would like you to get out of the drain, Aunty Lee,' SS Panchal said. 'And I need to let Mr and Mrs Guang know you are not at risk.'

By now the Guangs had come downstairs and were watching from just outside their gate. 'How did you get down there? Can you get out?'

'There's a path on that side behind the bushes. Here, hold for me first.' Balancing against the stone side of the drain, where it ran underground beneath the road, Aunty Lee reached up with a bunch of leafy stalks which SS Panchal squatted to pull through the railings.

'Please be careful, Mrs Lee.'

'You please be careful of my *kesum* leaves!'

Once her hands were free, Aunty Lee scrambled up the over-grown slope on her hands and knees as a child might. Though undignified it was effective and she was soon standing by Panchal brushing herself down.

'You should apologize to these people for worrying them.' SS Panchal smiled at the Guangs. They nodded back cautiously.

'I don't see what the big fuss is about. Nobody was going to use the *kesum*. Anyway it will grow back. I didn't pull up the roots. Why shouldn't I take it?' Aunty Lee grumbled.

'Outside of community gardens of which you are a registered member, the plucking of fruit and flowers in public spaces without permission is an offence which carries a fine of up to $5,000,' Panchal recited dutifully. Now it was time to Defuse Neighbourhood Tensions. She handed Aunty Lee's leafy loot back to her before waving to the new neighbours. Mr and Mrs Guang came over, still looking suspicious. No doubt they had expected Aunty Lee to be removed in handcuffs.

'So sorry I frightened you! I wanted to get these leaves to cook my *laksa*. Later you must come to my shop and try my *assam laksa*. My treat. I hope you will come and try?' Aunty Lee beamed hopefully at the Guangs, and to Panchal's surprise they melted. Aunty Lee was so plump, positive, and genuinely good-natured.

'Sorry, sorry,' they repeated, bowing. 'We hear there are many house burglaries in Singapore, that's why we are worried,' Mr Guang said. 'And the police signs say we must report suspicious activity.'

'Oh I totally understand!' Aunty Lee said. 'One of my old school friends *kenah*. So terrible *hor*!'

They launched into an animated discussion of burglar alarms and guard dogs till Panchal said: 'You want me to phone Nina to come and get you?'

'No! I don't want to see Nina!' Aunty Lee winced at the thought of facing Nina with nothing resolved. 'Don't you have to take me to the police station to question me?' Perhaps she could still have a quick word with Inspector Salim.

'We know where to find you if we need to ask questions. Don't you want to get your leaves back to your house or to your shop?'

Aunty Lee's bungalow was deep in the right branch of the housing estate, about ten minutes by foot beyond the row of shop houses where her café was.

'You better bring me back to the shop,' Aunty Lee sighed. She got into the police car then lowered the window to call out to her new friends: 'You must come to my shop to eat!'

Truth be told, it was not just because of Nina that Aunty Lee was feeling a bit out of place in her own shop these days.

Aunty Lee's new partner, Cherril Lim-Peters, was a very skinny, very smart, young woman who never seemed to get tired. Aunty Lee liked Cherril's energy. What she found difficult to deal with was Cherril's constant need for change and improvement. She was always coming up with ways to do things faster, better, and to greater profit.

Selina Lee, Aunty Lee's stepdaughter-in-law, said Cherril was compensating for growing up in a Housing Development Board flat and studying in a government school. Selina never missed a chance to correct Cherril's pronunciation or grammar. But Cherril knew far more about business productivity.

Given that Cherril's determination was directed towards building the business and making more money, taking Cherril on as a partner had certainly been good for the business side of Aunty Lee's Delights. It also made Nina's temporary absence possible. (Aunty Lee had picked out several honeymoon packages to start off the marriage Nina was rejecting). Before Cherril came on board, Nina had taken care of Aunty Lee's accounts, ordered supplies, and planned menus as well as helping with the actual cooking and serving.

Initially, Cherril had only taken over the drinks side of the business that Aunty Lee's stepson, Mark, had started and given up. But lately Cherril had been talking about introducing new healthy alternatives. She had also taken over the accounts and balancing the books after taking an online course on cost-effective business accounting. Nina was just Aunty Lee's assistant in the kitchen again. And not even the sole assistant, now that Cherril had hired two Chinese nationals to help in the shop during peak hours. Avon and Xuyie were both fair, pretty girls who claimed to speak English.

Aunty Lee could not understand their English any more than they could follow her Singlish. Luckily Cherril could give them instructions in Mandarin. Aunty Lee wondered if Nina felt left out, listening to the three Chinese girls chatting and giggling incomprehensibly. Aunty Lee certainly did. Both Aunty Lee and Nina were comfortable enough with Chinese dialects to do their marketing, food ordering, and scandal gossiping in Hokkien, Teochew and Cantonese. But neither had studied the government-sanctioned Mandarin. In the old days, newcomers to Singapore had learned English to integrate. The recent influx of Mandarin speakers no longer seemed to find that necessary.

CHAPTER TWO

Aunty Lee's Delights

'All residents are encouraged to report any suspicious persons to the authorities immediately.'

'Turn off the radio,' Aunty Lee grumbled. 'Frighten people for nothing, only.'

Normally, Aunty Lee loved public service crime announcements, but not when she had just been reported as a 'suspicious person' herself.

Obligingly, Panchal turned off the car radio.

'You were telling them one of your friends got burglarized?'

'My friend, Helen Chan. They took her jewellery, a television, and two computers!'

But even Helen's losses didn't interest Aunty Lee very much today.

'Did you have home security put in? You should think about it, you know.'

Aunty Lee shrugged. The most precious things in her house were the photo portraits of her late husband she had in every room. Housebreakers were hardly likely to take them, and even if they did, Nina had digital copies of all the images. Aunty Lee appreciated Nina even when she was cross with her. And she had not given up yet.

'Here we are,' Panchal said, pulling up across the road from Aunty Lee's Delights.

Nina was watering the row of potted plants in front of the shop. Their branches were heavy with tiny green limes, the larger *limau purut* or kaffir limes, kumquats, and chillies in various shades of red to be plucked as needed. Until then, they provided good *feng shui*.

A familiar car was parked in front of the 'no parking' sign.

'Shouldn't you fine them for parking in front of the fire hydrant?' Aunty Lee asked hopefully.

'I'll leave that to the traffic wardens.' SS Panchal knew the car belonged to Aunty Lee's stepson, Mark, and his wife, Selina. Like almost everyone else except Aunty Lee herself, Panchal preferred to stay clear of Mrs Selina Lee.

Selina was expecting her first child, and stressing over what schools and colleges he or she should someday apply for had made her even more tense and terrifying.

Nina stared at the police car, looking worried. She had been looking worried a lot lately, Aunty Lee thought, feeling a stab of guilt. Well, once Nina was safely married to her policeman she would be happy again. And she would thank Aunty Lee.

'You went to the police post?' Nina asked suspiciously after Panchal drove off. She could not bring herself to ask if her boss had spoken to Salim.

'I found *daun kesum*!' Aunty Lee held up her leaves like a peace offering. 'The construction people finally took down the hoarding over the drain and I saw the plants, so big already, so I went and grabbed. We must make a *laksa* special today! I invited people to come and eat! China people, I think. Must let them try real Singapore *laksa*!'

Nina Balignasay was the opposite of Aunty Lee in many ways. Aunty Lee was a fair, plump, busybody while Nina was thin, dark and wished everyone would mind their own business as she herself preferred to do. She was not, however, as skinny as she had been when she first came to work for Aunty Lee and her late husband all those years ago. Whatever the complications of working with Aunty Lee, she was as generous with food as with her advice. And Nina was no longer the scared, inept girl who had arrived hopeless at something as simple as separating egg yolks from whites. Now she was competent in the kitchen, powerful on the computer, and financially stable. She knew how much she owed Aunty Lee but she was not going to listen to her and let Salim destroy his future.

'Master Mark and Madam Selina are here.'

'*Alamak,*' Aunty Lee groaned dramatically.

Nina knew Aunty Lee found Selina entertaining rather than offensive.

'Silly-Nah is just Silly lah!' was one of Aunty Lee's favourite sayings. But with Mark and Selina expecting a baby, Aunty Lee was on her best behaviour. Her stepdaughter, Mathilda, had two children who Aunty Lee adored. But Mathilda and her family lived in the UK, well out of range of any culinary grand-mothering. Aunty Lee fully intended to be involved with the new grandbaby when it arrived.

The front entrance was locked since Aunty Lee's Delights was officially closed on Mondays. Regulars in search of food knew to go round to the kitchen entrance, as Aunty Lee did now.

Inside, the industrial sized cooker set on low was simmering and scenting the air with a promise of cloves, peppercorns, tender curried chicken, and soft spicy potatoes. Aunty Lee could hear Cherril's voice but there was no sign of Avon and Xuyie. The girls were in Singapore as students and there was a limit to the hours they were allowed to work. But Xuyie often hung around the kitchen even when she was not on duty. She seemed genuinely interested in Singapore food and enthusiastic about practising English. Avon on the other hand preferred to go out dressed in short skirts and high heels.

Aunty Lee's Delights specialized in brunches, lunches, and high teas. In the old days Aunty Lee had simply put up a 'Closed' sign when she was booked to handle the catering for a party. Her husband had left her sufficiently well provided for, and the café had been started more as an outlet for her love of cooking (Aunty Lee had been selling *pandan* and peach cakes, pineapple tarts, and fried curry puffs out of her kitchen) than as a business venture. Indeed the late M. L. Lee had liked to joke that while other husbands had to buy their wives diamonds and Prada he had to buy his Rosie dishwashers and pan holders. Not that he had seemed to mind. He had been very proud of her.

Now Cherril was actively pursuing catering jobs and talking about buying advertising in lifestyle magazines. A recent attempt at franchising hadn't worked out, but that hadn't kept her down for long. Aunty Lee liked Cherril. Since they'd got to know each other over the murder of Cherril's sister-in-law they had become closer than Aunty Lee was to Mathilda or Silly-nah.

Still she found Cherril's youthful energy tiring at times. Aunty Lee knew she must have once been as young, but she could not remember ever having been as eager. She was certainly not as eager now.

Cherril had her mobile phone clamped between ear and shoulder saying: 'No ... I mean, yes, of course. But are you sure? Yes. Of course but ...' as she made notes on her iPad. Seeing Aunty Lee, she rolled her eyes and jerked her head in the direction of the dining room, warning her they had visitors.

The spicy fragrance of a good chicken curry ... especially one cooked in Aunty Lee's rich, golden gravy ... should have been enough to make anybody feel good but Cherril looked ill. She had taken on a job catering a high tea for a friend that afternoon and, from the tension in her voice, Aunty Lee could tell the news was not good.

But then again, Selina might have just said something to upset her. Cherril had been a stewardess on Singapore's premier airline before her marriage and was trained to deal with emergencies ranging from drunks and heart attacks to babies and food allergies without smudging her mascara, but even she was not immune to Selina Lee.

'Don't worry, lah,' Aunty Lee whispered to Cherril as she passed her. Even if Cherril's plans for expansion didn't work out, Aunty Lee would still have her little café shop – and the best traditional home-cooked Peranakan food in Singapore.

Aunty Lee put her *kesum* leaves in a glass bowl which she placed on a shelf inside the cool room. Aunty Lee loved her cool room. Mark had installed it for wine during his (failed) attempt at running a wine business. Now it stored all the ingredients that did not need refrigeration but could not survive long in Singapore's hot, humid environment. Aunty Lee thought the cool room was one of the best things Mark had ever done. Backing out of the room as she carefully pulled the door shut behind her, Aunty Lee yelped as she bumped into someone.

'We've been waiting for you.' Selina was smiling but her eyes remained aggressive. 'I was hoping to have a word with Nina first, but she disappeared outside somewhere when I tried to talk to her. She's so shy, isn't she?'

Aunty Lee knew Nina was not at all shy. She also knew Selina usually ignored Nina unless she was telling Aunty Lee off for paying Nina too much ('Spoiling the market') or giving her too much freedom ('You let her use your computer, you let her drive your car … you don't know what she's getting up to!') But Aunty Lee reminded herself of the coming baby and said: 'Hello. Have you eaten yet?' It was her way of saying nothing.

'Hi,' was all Mark said as he followed his wife into the kitchen.

'I want to talk to you. It's about the nursery school we are helping to set up,' Selina said. 'I need some help.'

'What nursery school?' Aunty Lee winced and steeled herself for another of Mark's moneymaking schemes. Since M. L. Lee left the bulk of his estate to Aunty Lee, Mark and Selina had already persuaded her to finance several disastrous projects. But as Aunty Lee was intending to divide her own money between her two stepchildren, she thought it unfair to Mathilda to continue. Mark and Selina had already 'borrowed' far more than his share.

'If you want money you have to talk to Darren.' Darren Sim had been M. L. Lee's investment officer at the bank. Aunty Lee had inherited his services along with her husband's money. 'I cannot invest any money without talking to Darren.' Aunty Lee had already told Darren to say 'No' to any investments Mark came up with.

'We're not asking for your money!' Selina snapped in her usual voice. Mark looked worried and started to say something, but Selina put a firm hand on his arm and reassembled the smile on her face. 'We need your help with a problem, that's all.'

'Of course we will come and help you, Silly-Nah!' Aunty Lee loved solving other people's problems almost as much as she loved cooking, which was saying a lot. Friends and customers often brought her little puzzles and conundrums. As the late M. L. Lee had said, his *'kiasu, kaypoh, em zhai se'* (tireless, fearless busybody) little wife was happiest when digging clues out of problems and marrow out of bones.

Of course, not everybody appreciated Aunty Lee's advice. Indeed, Selina had described Aunty Lee's previous attempts to help as 'bossy interference'. This was the first time Selina had come to her for help, and Aunty Lee intended to enjoy it properly,

'Come and sit down with me in the dining room. Tell me about your nursery school. How can we help?'

'I don't need you, just Nina. I want to borrow Nina for a few days. For a couple of weeks, at most. Just until Beth's maid turns up or she gets a replacement from the agency.'

Nina had come in and was silently slicing and deseeding tomatoes. She looked up on hearing her name. Selina threw her one of what Aunty Lee called her 'condensed milk' smiles (thick, sticky, and over sweetened), and Nina looked alarmed.

'Nina, my friend Beth's maid disappeared two days ago. The early education nursery school we're setting up is going to be run out of her house. It's a very bad time right now because of all the renovations going on and deliveries and workers, and we need to get everything ready in time to show parents to get them to sign up for next year. Aunty Lee is always saying how much you helped her set up this place, right? Beth just needs somebody to clean up the mess and be there to keep an eye on the workers.' Selina turned back to Aunty Lee. 'I told her that Nina has been working for the family for years and is completely reliable. Look, I never ask you for favours. Don't let me down.'

'Hiyah, Silly. Your baby not even born yet. Why are you already worrying about what school to send it to? Anyway, Singapore got so many schools, what for want to start your own?'

'Selina isn't just trying to get our baby into KidStarters, she's helping to set it up,' Mark explained. 'She's one of the partners, and she's going to be on the school board. We were considering homeschooling but there isn't really a homeschooling network in Singapore. This way it will be like homeschooling only other people will be paying for it!'

'We were looking at value-adding nursery schools when I met Beth Kwuan, and she told me she was setting up a playschool. Mark asked her whether it was going to be one of those Montessori places, and Beth said that in an environment as competitive as Singapore there's no point wasting time on playing. Right from the start, while children's minds are still open, they should learn to learn by learning! Otherwise how are they going to get ahead and stay ahead? They need to learn self-discipline and how to obey rules!'

From the fervent respect in Selina's voice, Aunty Lee suspected she longed to have attended such a school herself.

'Beth and I agreed on all points. I'm going to help set up the curriculum. Beth knows the Singapore education system inside out. She's been a private tutor to the top students from all the best schools in Singapore, including the Anglo Chinese School and the Raffles Institution. I've been researching the psychology of gifted children, and how to support them and teach them to create safety boundaries. Gifted children are often sensitive and get bullied ... like Mark was, for example ... and it's very important for them to learn to create boundaries. Of course we will have to make sure the parents are going to commit to this also. Children can start as soon as they are toilet-trained, so children who learn faster can start earlier.'

'And Beth has got a native Mandarin speaker to set up the Chinese syllabus. You can't start learning languages too soon. You know how much students here are always having trouble with Mandarin, right? Well, we won't waste time with stories and conversation, we'll just teach them to take exams! Instead of children's storybooks they'll take assessment quizzes for fun!'

It sounded terrible to Aunty Lee. She did not remember any of the lessons studied in school but she had fond memories of jokes and games and sweets passed around during boring classes. And some of her closest friends now were friends she had made then. None of them would have found assessment quizzes fun.

'Who is this friend of yours? This Beth woman? What happened to her helper? Some people treat their helpers very badly, you know, work them non-stop and don't give them enough to eat. If she abused her helper until she ran away, you shouldn't go into business with her! Next thing you know she is getting arrested and you are in the newspapers trying to cover your face!'

'Of course she didn't abuse her helper!' Selina raised her voice. 'She told me that the maid had a boyfriend and, when Beth stopped her from seeing him, she ran away.'

'Did your friend report it to the police? *Aiyoh*, if she ran away with the boyfriend, maybe she got pregnant; your friend is going to lose her deposit!'

Selina waved Aunty Lee's deposit worries away and turned her focus back on Nina.

'Nina, I need your help for a few days. I told my friend that you can speak English, you can handle workmen, and you can be trusted with money. You can be trusted, right?'

'Of course, Madam.' Nina's words were automatic but cautious. 'But Aunty Lee needs me here. I cannot leave Aunty alone. If I go to help your friend, Aunty will be alone by herself in the house at night. Old people should not be alone at night. If she falls down at night, then nobody will know.'

'We'll come and check in on her—' Mark began, but was cut off by his wife.

'Aunty Lee is not that old,' Selina interrupted. 'My mother is older, and she's so independent she doesn't even want my father in the room at night—'

But they were both drowned out by Aunty Lee. Aunty Lee was only slower off the start because her indignation needed time to swell up to full force at being lumped in with 'old people'. Her eyesight and hearing might have *slightly* weakened over the years, but her sense of smell and taste were still sharper than most women half her age!

'I never fall down!' Aunty Lee spluttered like chilli oil in a hot pan. 'My father always told people I am as agile as a mountain goat!' That was true, though said over fifty years ago by her fond father who was now long dead.

'Madam, you remember you fell down that time? For so long you had to walk with that stick … '

In fact the walking stick from that fall was by Aunty Lee's chair now, though her ankle was quite recovered. She had discovered that walking with a stick meant nice people gave way to you in queues. Plus, if they didn't, you could use your stick to push them aside. Aunty Lee picked it up and thumped it on the floor for emphasis.

'That was not at night, what! That was a workplace accident! Anyway, you young people have workplace accidents all the time! More often than us old people! Is that why you don't want to leave me to get married? Because you think I am old?'

'I never say you are old, Madam.' Too late Nina saw her mistake. 'Just older than me. That's why you need me in the house to make tea for you at night. And to help you in the shop in the daytime.'

'I can make my own tea. I was making my own tea before you were born!' Aunty Lee huffed. That did not really help her case, but sounded too good to waste. 'If you want to go and help Selina's friend then go and help them. Don't worry about me, I don't need you!'

'It's just until Beth's maid turns up or she arranges to get someone else to help,' Mark said comfortingly. 'And we'll check to make sure Aunty Lee is all right.' He patted Aunty Lee on the arm and nodded encouragingly to Nina. 'Why don't we try this for one week and see how it goes?'

None of the women paid any attention to him.

'Where does this friend of yours live, anyway? What's her full name? What does her husband do? Did she report to the police that her maid is missing yet? What's her maid's name? Where is she from?'

'Her maid's name is Julietta, from the Philippines, I think. Beth lives in Jalan Kakatua, in the Bukit Batok area. She's not married. It's her family house that she's renovating for KidStarters. I met Julietta there once, and she looked fine to me. If anything I think Beth treated her too well, gave her too much freedom, that's why she got so spoilt. Beth said that she told her to stay at home to wait for a delivery when she had planned to go out with her boyfriend, and Julietta got angry and ran away.'

'Do you know a Julietta?' Aunty Lee asked Nina.

She seemed to think all the Filipina helpers in Singapore knew each other. Nina shook her head without saying anything. She knew a great many other domestic helpers in Singapore. She also knew some bosses refused to let their maids have any contact outside the home. Working for such people was like being sentenced to heavy labour in solitary confinement.

'Jalan Kakatua ... I used to know a Patricia Kwuan-Loo who lived in Jalan Kakatua,' Aunty Lee said thoughtfully. 'She was Patty Kwuan when she was in my class in school, and she married a doctor, Ken Loo. Then after Ken died, Patty went on a tour to China. Instead of buying fake handbags and watches, that woman ended up bringing back her Chinese tour guide and marrying him!' Aunty Lee chuckled in gleeful approval but sobered to continue. 'Patty just died quite recently. I saw there was a notice in the newspapers. "No wreaths", "no donations", no other information. I didn't even know she had been sick. I asked around some of the other old girls but nobody had seen her for some time. If only we had known that she was sick or in hospital, we would have gone to see her.'

If the late Patty Kwuan-Loo had been sick, she might not have been up to receiving her old classmates, Nina thought. The class reunions Aunty Lee occasionally hosted at the café grew more gleefully raucous and uninhibited as the ladies' inhibitions retreated with their schooldays.

'One of my friends phoned the house to ask about the funeral service and was told "no wake, no service". So funny, right! Usually such things they list all the family members to show people who is dead and who is still alive. Nina? Do you remember if Patty Kwuan-Loo had a sister or cousin called Beth living in the same area?'

Reading obituaries was one of Aunty Lee's favourite daily rituals. At her age, it was a more effective way of keeping track of old friends than Facebook or Twitter.

'Beth is Patty Kwuan-Loo's sister,' Selina said. 'Patty's second husband, Jonny Ho, is Beth's partner in the KidStarters project. He is the Mandarin expert who will be working with the children.'

'Oh, so he's a teacher?'

'He's a native Mandarin speaker. And he speaks Standard Mandarin, not like the Singapore Mandarin people here speak. He says that the people in China would laugh at how people here speak Mandarin.' Selina was sensitive about not speaking Mandarin at all, having studied Malay as her second language in school.

'Jonny Ho inherited Patty's house at Kakatua. But she didn't leave him much else, that's why he and Beth are turning it into a school. Did you know Patty Kwuan well?' Selina seldom encouraged Aunty Lee's stories, which tended to meander without a point. But there was always a chance the old woman knew something that might be useful. After all, you couldn't know too much about people you were going into business with.

'I always wondered what happened to that man. They say he is very good-looking. I never got a chance to see him. When Patty first got married again, Helen Chan threw this big dinner party for them so that we could all get to meet her new husband. I couldn't go. That was around the time when those stupid people were blaming my chicken *buah keluak* for poisoning them, remember? But Helen told me, *wah*, that one is a real *leng zai*.'

'That means "pretty boy",' Mark told Selina.

'I know that!' Selina snapped.

'Anyway, I was waiting for a chance to look at this handsome man Patty had married. But then right after that Helen and her husband went to Glasgow to get a flat for her son. Her son is studying medicine there. And then, so terrible, while they were away their house got burglarized! That's when the house break-ins just started, remember? The insurance still hasn't paid up for everything; don't know why so slow.' Aunty Lee's eyes shone with remembered excitement. Even Patty's handsome new husband had been overshadowed.

'And then after that Patty just stopped seeing people. She wouldn't accept any invitations, didn't even join us for the Founder's Day reunion dinner. I told Helen one of them must have said something to offend her or her husband but she swore they never said anything. Then the next thing we knew, Patty was dead. Must have been one of those sudden cancers or heart attack or something. Maybe she found out about it and didn't want people to know. She should have told us she was sick, but maybe she lost her hair and didn't want us to see her. Patty was always very proud of her hair.'

'So you don't remember Beth Kwuan?' Selina said with emphasis on the name.

'Oh, of course I remember that Beth: Elizabeth, she was in school; now I know who you are talking about. Elizabeth Kwuan was one year ahead of us in school. She was a school prefect, always very fierce. She went with Patty on that tour to China where Patty met the PRC tour guide that she went and married.'

'So will you help Beth out? She's your old friend's sister after all. I'm sure you can trust her—'

'The mushrooms haven't come yet.' Cherril, finally off the phone, dashed into the dining room looking desperate. She was followed by Avon and Xuyie. 'Can you believe how many things can go wrong at once?'

'What? What? What? Quick, quick tell me!'

'That was Elena Lim-Garibaldi on the phone. About this afternoon's do. About the curry chicken.'

'*Hiyah*, I told you those skinny dieting people wouldn't appreciate curry chicken ... so what do they want you to change it to?'

'Oh no, they want the curry chicken. The spices are supposed to be good for stimulating the digestion or something like that. But they want only thigh meat without skin. And they don't want any potatoes in the curry.'

Aunty Lee could have told Cherril that catering a party for a group of skinny businesswomen celebrating corporate weight loss was not a good idea ... indeed, Aunty Lee had told her young business partner several times, though without any real intention of cancelling the job. Aunty Lee liked giving advice almost as much as she liked cooking.

'But the potatoes are the best part of the curry!' By the time of the party the soft chunks would have absorbed the perfect essence of curry and chicken. 'And organic, some more!'

'Can we take out the potatoes?'

'I can take out the potatoes,' Xuyie offered helpfully.

'Of course you can,' Aunty Lee was surprised but pleased by the girl's offer, 'but not yet. Leave them inside until three o'clock, otherwise the gravy will be too salty and too thin. Then we can use and make something else. At least they didn't tell you to take out the coconut milk from the gravy!'

This suggestion drove Cherril into another minor panic. 'Can they do that? I mean, can we do that?'

'Look, we're short of time,' Selina said. 'I told Beth that we would bring Nina back to talk to her. Unless that policeman of hers is still hanging around.'

Cherril turned to Nina. 'Inspector Salim likes curry potatoes, right? We can use these potatoes to make something nice for the people at the station. If they like them, maybe they'll even offer to pay and order more next time! How many people at his office today? Do you know?'

'I don't know. I don't talk to Inspector Salim.' Nina kept her eyes and hands focused on scraping thin strips down the length of a cucumber. But her expression hardened, and Selina picked up on this immediately.

'If that man is still bothering her, it may be just as well to get her away from here for a bit. Nina's not stupid. But men can be so persistent.'

'I don't think Salim will give up so easily,' Aunty Lee said thoughtfully. 'He's not the sort to give up. But good for him to have to work harder to get her. Then he won't take her for granted!'

If I go away for one week she will see she cannot do without me, Nina thought, then she will have to stop trying to get married off.

Working for somebody else will show her what a

am, Aunty Lee thought, then she will do what I tell her to do. And maybe spending one week far away from Salim will make Nina appreciate him more. Just to push things a little further she said: 'You say you don't want to see Salim any more, just close your eyes, *lor*. What for you want to go so far away?'

'Okay, one week,' Nina said to Selina.

'Okay your head,' said Aunty Lee almost amicably. She had turned away from them and was rummaging in one of the cabinets beneath the counter.

Cherril made a sound that was half squeak and half moan. Having been with Aunty Lee far longer than her, Nina was far more efficient at practical cooking than she was.

'I will help,' Xuyie told her softly.

'So can we bring Nina over to meet Beth?' Mark's voice was high in his disbelief. 'Now?'

'Sure!'

'Well, what are we waiting for?' Selina all but clapped her hands.

Nina was the only one who was not surprised when Aunty Lee, clutching her bag and two pineapple tarts, led the way to Mark's car.

'Wait, Aunty Lee, you're going too?' Cherril cried out. 'What are we going to do with all these potatoes? Throw them away? Such a waste! I should charge them anyway. It's their fault for not telling me sooner. Can you tell them that we can't take out the potatoes because without potatoes it won't be Peranakan Chicken Curry?'

Aunty Lee was nothing if not flexible. Anyone who had tasted food experiments could testify to that. As far as she was ʾned, anything cooked with local ingredients was local food: ʾe I am Peranakan, everything that I cook is Peranakan ʾs the waste nothing, adapt everything spirit of the ʾk that Aunty Lee embodied, rather than any set of ʾd find some way to put those potatoes to good use. But not while Cherril was in full emergency mode. Cherril had Avon and Xuyie to help her take care of what Aunty Lee and Nina could have handled between them.

'Leave them there!' Aunty Lee called over. 'Leave them to Nina and me. We'll come up with something when we come back!'

CHAPTER THREE

Beth and Jonny Ho

Beth Kwuan stood at the upstairs window looking down on Jonny Ho talking to the new contractor. She'd had to come up to change for a meeting at the Early Childhood Development Agency (ECDA) which oversees the setting up of child care centres in Singapore. Those bureaucrats had demanded to see her plans for soundproofing and toilet facilities. All the rules and regulations, requirements, and inspections were ridiculous, Beth thought. In the old days all you needed to train children were rattan mats on the floor and a tin potty in the corner. And hadn't those children turned out much better than the youth of today?

When it was not raining the children played catching and hopscotch and jumped rubber bands outside, and if it rained they played Happy Families or five stones inside. Part of her wanted to throw up this whole idea of running her own preschool.

Jonny had worked on the figures with her. There was no way she could keep this house. She tugged at the blue and red knit dress she had changed into. It was a bit tight all her late sister's dresses. But they still looked better than any of her own clothes.

She should leave soon if she didn't want to waste

money booking a taxi, but still she stayed at the window, watching Jonny Ho wave his arms around as he talked. She wished Jonny would come with her to the ECDA. He was so much better at charming people than she was. And he could impress them with his Mandarin. But Jonny despised Singapore's rules and regulations. He was convinced their permits were taking so long because Beth was too stingy to hand over the necessary bribes, and refused to believe that was not how things were done in Singapore.

'That's how things are done everywhere!' he had said.

Beth didn't want to think about how Jonny was managing the renovations. The new batch of foreign contract workers Jonny was working with were all Chinese nationals. He had fired the first lot of men and demanded only Mandarin speakers this time. At least he wasn't hitting them like he had hit that Indian welder. Jonny got very angry when people didn't follow his instructions exactly and immediately. He had thought the Indian workers were making fun of his English when they tried to ask him questions. Their first contractor had quit after making a huge fuss about Jonny breaking that welder's arm. Luckily Jonny was good at handling people like him. After Jonny threatened the contractor with all kinds of things from invented violations to Jonny's close friends in the permits department to broken legs, the first contractor had quit the job and taken his workers with him. They were already behind schedule, and they left walls half hacked and stacks of child-safe railings propped on piles of padded play area squares. But Beth hardly had time to panic before Jonny announced he had got them a replacement contractor.

'Even cheaper! The first bugger was trying to swindle us!'

Of course Beth still worried. But then Beth worried all the time about everything. That was how she had always been. It was wonderful to have someone like Jonny Ho around to say: 'Le everything to me!' and take over.

'Leave the building renovations to me!' he had to

she did. Jonny had so much more business experience. Despite being younger, he had so much more experience in everything, and when he said: 'Everybody will always try to cheat you if they can. But don't worry! I will watch out for you!' Beth knew she could trust him. It was what she had always believed.

That didn't mean she didn't worry about him, of course. Beth worried about what Jonny had thought of Julietta, and how he would react to Fabian. Julietta had disappeared after her nephew Fabian turned up at the house and made a scene.

'If you can't show some respect to your elders you'll have to leave!' Beth had told Fabian. To her relief, he had left. But she had seen Julietta slip out after him. Should she have stopped her? Beth had no idea what Fabian might have said to Julietta; what he might have tried to get her to do.

Well, there was no point wondering about that now. There had been no sign of Julietta, no queries from Julietta's family members or friends, which Beth took as a good sign. It looked as though Julietta had been in touch with them even if her employer didn't know where she was.

The only person who kept bringing up the missing woman was that stupid Mrs Selina Lee, who asked: 'Where is Julietta?' every time she came by.

'I don't know.' Beth had finally told her.

This was difficult for Beth, who liked everything and everyone to be in the right place all the time. Surprisingly, Selina Lee had not seemed surprised. Nor had she seemed surprised that Beth had not reported Julietta as 'missing'. Why get the government involved unnecessarily? Beth said. It would just mean more red and more delays and they could not afford more delays right

probably show up when her boyfriend gets sick of her out of money,' Selina had said, making Beth feel her. Beth liked Selina's shy husband, Mark, though s clearly under his wife's thumb.

Beth liked having a man around to handle things. If she had her life to live over again, there was only thing she would have done differently. She would have worked harder to get married. She would have liked to have had a man around. One who could earn enough for her not to have to work. It was another thing she blamed her late mother and sister for. The two of them had talked clothes and shoes and make-up together but they had never included her, never shown her what to do. Even though Beth had despised them for being superficial, they should have helped her. Her life would have been so much more comfortable now. Instead she was still the spinster sister. With all her things from her flat, she was squeezed into the small room that had once been her nephew's while Jonny still occupied the much larger master bedroom he had shared with Patty. He insisted on cleaning the room himself. Though he let Beth do his laundry, he asked her to leave it on the little cupboard at the top of the stairs. Of course Beth had gone into his room to look around when he was not in. She had been half afraid of what she might find ... a shrine to her sister, perhaps. But fortunately there was nothing of the sort.

'What are you doing in here? How dare you spy on my things!' Jonny had demanded when he came home unexpectedly and found her in his room.

Beth could not tell him that she had been lying on the bed enjoying the scent of his shampoo and aftershave on his pillow. Embarrassment turning into anger; she had lashed back at him: 'Why shouldn't I? This is as much my house as yours!' and, for an instant, she had been certain he was going to hit her. 'My sister's dresses,' Beth had said. 'I need something to wear to the Ministry. I thought since Patty has so many dresses I could borrow something.' The lie was convincing because her sister had always had too many dresses.

Jonny had glanced towards the walk-in closet, and the rage that had flamed up in his eyes lowered to a pilot light. 'You should take all of them,' he told her. 'Give me more space.'

And the next day Beth had found all of Patty's dresses, skirts, blouses, scarves, and winter wear piled on her bed and in heaps on the floor of her bedroom.

The loud grinding of poorly maintained gears drew Beth's attention outside again. The contractor's lorry had backed up noisily to the gate, and the new contractor was directing his men to load on what looked like bags of cement. The workers climbed in after, and the lorry groaned off. Why were they leaving? There was still so much work to be done ...

'Jonny!' Beth shouted. 'Why are they leaving? Stop them! Don't let them go!' Oh no, she thought as she headed for the stairs, had Jonny fired this contractor too?

Jonny Ho was the tour guide assigned to the Kwuan sisters on their tour around China. Beth had arranged everything without any help from her sister. Patty had not even wanted to go, but Beth had insisted. The shopping and sightseeing in China would be good for the new widow, she pointed out. Now her husband was dead, Patty ought not to go on spending so much on designer handbags, scarves, and shoes, and China was the best place to buy fakes.

More importantly, Beth had meant to use the time to persuade Patty to sell her large, inconvenient Jalan Kakatua house and buy an apartment, in both their names, where the two sisters could grow old together. The tour was really to get Patty out of Singapore and away from her friends with their bad advice and, more importantly, away from the demands of Fabian, Patty's useless, spoiled, son.

Patty wanted to leave the house to her son.

'Fabian's not coming back to Singapore! What is he going to do with a house here?' Beth had demanded.

'Then he can sell it after I'm dead.' Patty, always romantic and impractical, had said.

'And what will happen to me if you die first?' Beth blurted out her deepest fear of ending up alone and homeless. It was not fair. Beth, who knew the value of money and had worked so hard all her life, could barely afford the payments on her Housing Development Board flat. And Patty, who had drifted through school and life adored by her parents and her husband, knew nothing and had everything.

Of course, that was before Jonny Ho came into their lives.

Through all the wining and dining and flirting, Beth had thought that Jonny Ho was just doing his job exceptionally well. She had taken him aside and explained that the point of their trip was to help her sister get over her husband's death. She had been pleased to see how much Patty's mood and temper improved when Jonny was around. Patty stopped, saying: 'I wish I hadn't let you talk me into this,' and 'We should have gone to India instead!'

Beth had dreamed of making another trip to China. Once she had Patty settled she would go back to China alone and get in touch with Jonny Ho and ask him to show her around the cultural landmarks that Patty had shown no interest in … he would see she was much more interested in history and culture than her sister.

But less than two months after their China tour, Jonny Ho had come to Singapore on a tourist pass. On Patty's invitation, he had extended his stay and moved in with them. Then Jonny Ho and Patty had announced, so casually, that they had gone to the registry that day and signed papers. They were married.

This had stung Beth painfully. Why hadn't Patty told her? After all, she was her sister and she would have told her exactly how ridiculous it would look, her marrying a man so much younger and so soon after her husband's death. It didn't occur to Beth that that was exactly why Patty had said nothing to her. But it was Jonny Ho she felt most betrayed by. Beth had thought that she and Jonny were a team, working to cheer Patty up and get on with her life. Once Jonny was married to Patty he agreed that she should keep the house: 'landed property is always more valuable'. At least he had seemed to like the idea of Beth continuing to stay in the house, so Beth did not have to kick out the tenants who had sub-leased her flat.

All these thoughts were far from Beth's mind as she hurried down the stairs carefully. This was no time to fall and end up with a broken leg.

'Why are the workers leaving? Why did you let them go? Call your contractor at once and make him bring them back. Do you have his mobile number?'

But Jonny Ho, standing by the dusty wreckage of what had been the wall between the living room and dining room, laughed at her. 'Why do you worry? Why don't you trust me? They have another project, big emergency project to fix now. They will earn big extra money and they will come back to finish the work here tonight. No problem. Why do you not trust me? You must trust me, pretty lady!' He put his arm around her shoulders and squeezed her against him.

The physical thrill of being so close to him made Beth forget her renovation worries.

'I just want this to work, that's all. It's got to be finished before the building inspectors come.'

'Of course it is going to work. It is not just going to work; it is going to be a big enormous success!'

Beth wanted to agree with him, to believe him. But the school-teacher in her surfaced. '"Big enormous success" doesn't sound right.' She regretted speaking as soon as she started, but once started she had to finish. 'You should say a "huge success" or just "an enormous success".'

Jonny Ho's English was good. Good enough for Beth, who could not stand being around people who spoke English badly. Because of his dream of getting to America or England or Australia, Jonny had worked hard at improving his English for years, long before the opportunity to come to Singapore. But he still used phrases like 'big enormous success' that shouted non-native speaker to Beth's ear.

Beth was very proud of having been classed a 'Native English Speaker' in an English Proficiency test. That test had been part of the admissions criteria for getting into a teaching course years ago but the precious label had grown in her memory. Beth had lived in Singapore all her life and had never studied overseas, but she always remembered to speak the proper English that had become part of her identity.

'Same difference,' Jonny said with a teasing grin. That had been one of her sister's favourite phrases, and he should have known how much it annoyed her. 'Come on now. Everything also you want to worry about. Success too big also you want to worry. Relax! Go with the flowing!'

Biting back the urge to correct him again, Beth looked at the man and felt herself starting to relax. It was easy to look at Jonny Ho. He did not have the soft, overprotected good looks of young Singaporeans his age, the easily bruised 'strawberry' generation. Look at Fabian, for example. All Fabian was good at was complaining and whining till someone else got fed up enough to sort things out for him. After all the money his parents had put into sending him to study in America he had never got a real job. Beth had seen that coming for years. She would have whipped Fabian into shape given half a chance but Patty and Ken had a blind spot when it came to that boy. He had turned out much like his mother, as a matter of fact. Patty had always got what she wanted without working for it. Ever since they were girls, that was the way it had been. And that was why it had been so unfair of Patty to decide she wanted Jonny Ho too.

After all, Beth had seen him first.

And she had watched the young man with far more attention than her sister. Beth had seen how offended he was when Patty asked: 'Are you a farmer?' Beth had been all ready to reproach her sister for being rude. But then Patty said: 'You look like a man who is strong enough to solve all his own problems.' And

Jonny Ho had beamed and said: 'Exactly. I always solve my own problems. I am independent.'

'I like that in a man.' Patty had told him. That was Patty all over. Why should it matter to the man whether or not she liked him? He was there to do his job as their tour guide. And since Beth had made all their tour arrangements, any flirting with the tour guide should have been done by her, the unmarried sister, not the grieving widow. It was all part of the unfairness of life. Women who wanted to get married never got a chance, no matter how hard they tried, while other women barely waited to collect one husband's ashes from the crematorium before picking up another.

Well, Beth Kwuan was going to show everyone that once she was no longer in her sister's shadow, she could shine and do better than Patty ever did. Jonny Ho would have to admit that he had chosen to marry the wrong sister. And maybe, just maybe, he would see that it was not too late to put things right. Of course, Beth would never propose such a thing to him. Beth's moral standards were higher than that. She had always held herself to far higher standards than Patty in everything. She had even done better than Patty at her O-levels, not that anybody had paid much attention. Well, Patty had never taken on a business project like KidStarters. That was why Beth had to make a success of it.

Beth knew she would have been a far better wife and mother than her sister. KidStarters would show all the men who hadn't given her a chance how good she was at bringing up the best and smartest children. KidStarters had to succeed.

She had almost forgotten that it was Jonny who had been the drive behind KidStarters. Beth had talked about her child training theories for so long that she didn't immediately realize Jonny was taking her seriously. But once the details started to fall into place she saw it was the perfect plan. They could both keep the house and have something to live on.

Beth pulled her thoughts back and looked around the mess that was the ground floor of the house. The old wire fencing had been dismantled but the wood planks for the new privacy barrier lay in unassembled stacks next to the bundles of stickers (showing cartoon children playing ball, reading books, chasing ducks) meant to decorate them. Jonny had got a huge discount for the stickers, just as he had for the shiny dark wood planks. Beth had been delighted by how classy the planks and stickers looked. But the stickers had been delivered without the waterproof, smudge proof protector sheets and the dark wood planks without any end posts. Work had halted till these could be delivered. Until then nothing separated the house from the drain and pavement except the ugly gash of upturned earth and broken roots where Patty's ornamental hedge had once stood. It had been a stupid low hedge that only reached halfway up the fence as though the residents wanted to show off their perfect lawn and perfect house. Even in her panic over deadlines the sight of the lawn now dug up (for the children's outdoor play area) and the front walls of the house hacked through (to install the required soundproofing insulation) gave Beth some pleasure. She had loved and hated this house for so long – this house that Patty had taken for granted filled with such pointless decorations.

'The insulation materials still haven't arrived yet,' Beth said. But Jonny was not listening. He was on his mobile phone again, shouting instructions in Mandarin too swift and colloquial for her to follow. Jonny always shouted at his business contacts so Beth was not worried. She just hoped that it was their supplies he was shouting about. Jonny Ho had so many projects all going at the same time.

Beth had naively assumed that all it would take to transform this family home into a child centre was childproof locks and toys and children's books. That was all her nephew Fabian had needed growing up there. Beth knew, because she had helped bring him up. She had probably spent more time with her nephew than his parents had, Patty had never been very hands on as a mother and Ken had seldom been home. It had been Beth who made sure his homework was done and that he studied for his tests. But of course that just made the ungrateful little boy take her for granted and walk all over her while worshipping his parents.

'You said the new insulation was going to arrive today. Shouldn't you make sure it's here before the workers come back?' Beth asked as soon as Jonny ended his call.

Regulations called for soundproofed playrooms. Unfortunately, it was only after the walls had been hacked that the bales of insulation material had been cut open and were discovered to have been soaked; the insides were foul-smelling and rotting. Very likely they had fallen into the sea at some stage and then sunned till the outside was dry. Beth had been furious, certain that they had been cheated and wanting to complain and sue, but Jonny Ho calmed her down and said it was more important to get them replaced fast than win a lawsuit years too late. He was smart like that, Beth thought fondly. That was what made him such a good businessman. She just wished he would notice what a good businesswoman she was becoming ... she wished she had a chance to show herself that. After all the excitement and noise of the hacking this waiting was so frustrating.

'Come and meet the ECDA people with me,' Beth suggested again to Jonny. 'Maybe after the meeting we can look at some non-slip tiles for the paddle pool area.'

'Somebody has to stay here,' Jonny said. 'Look, anybody can walk in and steal everything!'

He was right. It would have been all right if only Julietta had been there to watch the house. But Beth did not want to think about Julietta.

A car slowed down and stopped outside. Beth looked out and saw that Mrs Selina Lee was back. Beth met her at the ECDA where Selina had been trying to get information on local school resources. Beth had talked to her at length, hoping Selina would register her children with KidStarters and also get her friends to. She had also hoped to talk her into becoming an investor. The renovations were coming to much more than Beth expected. Selina had been interested but stingy. Still, Jonny said she might turn out to be useful so Beth didn't mind. As long as it wasn't Jonny that Selina was interested in, Beth didn't mind her sniffing around.

'I really should go,' Beth said again. Jonny did not answer. She made no move to leave.

Aunty Lee looked at the large, detached bungalow. She remembered a gracefully landscaped lawn with sloping side gardens. Today it looked like a bomb had gone off, destroying the windows and some walls and wrecking the garden.

The last time she had been here was years ago when both her husband and Patty's first husband were still alive. It had been during Chinese New Year and Aunty Lee had been awed by the driveway lined with large traditional glazed dragon pots containing kumquat trees heavy with plump, golden nuggets of good luck. Back in their Binjai Park house they had only had two 'golden auspice' kumquat bushes flanking their front entrance (and these had already lost several of their fruits to Aunty Lee, who loved the combination of thin sweet rind over sour pulp). Ken Loo had arranged for a lion dance troop and an impressive show of fake fire crackers with laser lights and sound effects. 'I thought only superstitious businessmen were so concerned about good luck,' Aunty Lee had said to M. L. 'These days, doctors have to be businessmen if they want to be successful,' her husband had told her.

'There's nobody here,' Aunty Lee said, returning to the present.

'Beth and Jonny will be here. They're living on the second floor, above the school. This way, no matter how late parents come to collect their children there will be somebody here.' As Selina spoke she was touching up her lipstick, eyes focused on a tiny mirror. She patted her hair. 'Wait here, Aunty Lee. This is important. This could make all the difference for the baby's future. I'm not going to let you mess this up for us!' Selina reached across Mark's lap and turned off the engine, taking the key with her. Then she left the car without waiting for a response. If she had had the decency to leave the car air-conditioning on, Aunty Lee might have stayed in the car for longer than the two minutes it took Selina to push through the half open gate and start up the driveway.

CHAPTER FOUR

KidStarters

'Come on,' Aunty Lee said to Nina, 'let's go and look!' She was glad she had brought pineapple tarts with her. No one had ever been accused of breaking and entering when carrying pineapple tarts.

'Selina said to wait in the car!' Mark protested.

'Then you better wait in the car,' Aunty Lee said sweetly.

There was no sign of Selina as Aunty Lee and Nina picked their way between the stacks of tiles and piles of foam sheeting that occupied the driveway. She must have gone inside. Then the door swung open and a man came out. Despite the heat he was wearing a dark blue shirt shot through with lighter blue lines over dark trousers and pointed toe shoes that always made Aunty Lee think of the elves in the picture books of her childhood. She knew, thanks to Cherril who was always trying to get her husband to dress more like a successful lawyer, that such high-gloss leather shoes were probably from a designer line. And she knew from Mycroft that they were hot and uncomfortable. They did look sleek and beautiful, though.

But it was not the shoes that made Aunty Lee stop and stare. The man was even more beautiful than his shoes. He stood there, just outside the shelter of the porch, squinting slightly in the sun which showed up the straight line of his nose, the high cheek-bones, clean jaw and smooth skin and perfect slightly slanting eyes and mouth. Despite her age and slightly aching knees, something deep inside Aunty Lee gave a shiver of delight. It was a purely animal response to the symmetry of the man's perfectly balanced features; the sensation of coming upon the first ripe durian of the season at the moment when the tough thorny fruit ripped willingly to expose its smooth virgin creaminess.

'Can I help you ladies?' the man said.

'Are you Jonny Ho?' Aunty Lee asked at the same time as Nina said: 'We are waiting for Madam Selina.'

'Ah, Selina Lee.' Jonny Ho smiled, and Aunty Lee heard Selina give a gurgling little giggle, coming out of the house behind him. She seemed to be having some trouble with the strap of her purse.

'Do you need a cough drop?' Mark asked, following his wife out of the house.

Selina walked around the man to stand next to Nina without answering Mark. 'This is Nina, Jonny. I told Beth all about Nina. She's worked for our family for years, and she's completely reliable. I told Selina that Nina could stay here and clean up and watch the house while we take care of all the other things.'

Selina was like a little dog, Aunty Lee thought, wagging its tail and trying to impress its master with a dead rat. Jonny nodded to her before turning back to Aunty Lee and Nina.

'Yes, I am Mr. Jonny Ho.' His English was so proper that it must have been studied as a second language. 'But you ladies can call me Jonny.'

As the man ran his eyes over them Aunty Lee was suddenly very aware that her Curry Up! tee shirt was curry stained, and her pink and green floral pants (such a bright, happy batik, she remembered thinking when putting them on that morning) were old, worn and a little faded. Most women would have been embarrassed, spending the rest of their visit awkward with embarrassment. But Aunty Lee chose to be intrigued instead. It was unusual for her to concern herself with anything beyond comfort when it came to clothes. Looking around for the cause, she realized it was the way Jonny Ho was looking at her. Now she studied him, she saw Jonny wore as much tinted face cream as a Korean movie star and was probably good-looking enough to be mistaken for one, but that wasn't it. Aunty Lee was more susceptible to a handsome plantain than a handsome man. No, it was because Jonny Ho eyed her like a man wanting to get his money's worth out of an eat-all-you-can buffet. He was trying to estimate the value of the prawns concealed in their fried batter casings. And that made the prawns feel the need to validate themselves.

Aunty Lee watched Jonny Ho run his eyes over Nina. Without saying or doing anything improper, he made it clear he was interested in her as a property worth acquiring. Aunty Lee felt worried. She hoped Nina would not try to forget Salim by falling for someone else. But Nina was looking bored and stupid. It was the look she wore when Selina was lecturing her. That was all right then, Aunty Lee thought in relief. She turned her attention back to Jonny Ho. He really had a very nice face, Aunty Lee thought, though she would have liked it better with less make-up. His skin was as smooth and white as a steamed rice flour bun and didn't seem to have any pores.

'I remember this house,' Aunty Lee said. 'I haven't been here for so long. *Wah*, you are doing big renovations here, *hor*? All this dust must be very bad for children, right? In the old days there was a fountain here, right?'

'We had to get rid of the fountain. Mosquitoes,' a woman said briskly, coming out of the house.

Aunty Lee recognized her at once as Beth, Patty's sister. In school they had all called Elizabeth Kwuan 'Bossy Betty'. Beth was wearing a smart dress and lipstick, but still looked like a strict, rule-bound schoolteacher. She would be the teacher schoolgirls made fun of while in school and remembered fondly as part of their girlhood – like acne. Now, though Beth smiled and nodded to Selina and her visitors, there were frown lines between her brows, and the sides of her mouth immediately returned to their usual down position. She looked like she was looking out for faults just to show she was paying attention. Working for this woman would not be easy. Beth looked like the kind of boss who had already driven one helper into running away and would soon make Nina realize that Aunty Lee, however meddling, was easier to work for.

She was the perfect temporary boss for Nina, Aunty Lee thought.

'Selina told me your helper ran away,' Aunty Lee said.

'Did she?' Beth looked surprised and disapproving. Selina, who had meant to surprise her but differently, glared at Aunty Lee and started to explain: 'You said you needed someone to clear away the dust and rubble before painting—' but Aunty Lee continued over her.

'I remember you from school. I was in the same class as Patty. Don't you remember me? I'm Rosie! Here—' Aunty Lee pushed the pineapple tarts at Beth, 'from my shop. My condolences about Patty. Poor thing. She was still so young.'

'At least she was still beautiful when she died. Oh Rosie, of course I remember you. Thank you. Jonny can take ... I'm sorry, I'm in quite a hurry right now. I have to go for a meeting with the ECDA. Planning permissions and regulations and all that. I've been phoning and phoning but there aren't any taxis ... '

'There's a taxi waiting at the end of the road,' Aunty Lee said. 'Maybe you gave him the wrong address.'

'No. I didn't even manage to get through. They kept putting me on hold. If there's a taxi there the driver is probably having a smoke and waiting for peak hour. I have to go now.'

'We'll drive you in,' Selina said quickly. 'Or Mark can drive you in. I'll stay here and help Jonny with the cleaning up.'

Aunty Lee saw Beth's eyes go from Selina to Jonny and back

to Selina. She thought Beth probably understood Selina better than Selina herself did. But then she had probably watched Patty go through more than her share of adolescent crushes and passions.

'If you and your husband stay here and start on the cleaning up, Jonny can drive me.'

'If you're going to see the ECDA people, I should come with you,' Selina said. 'I'm part of this, after all. Aunty Lee and Nina can start on the cleaning.'

'I have to get back to my shop!' Aunty Lee said firmly. 'Nina will come back with me until you get time to talk about who pays Nina's salary while she is working here. She can still come back and sleep in my house at night.'

Beth looked surprised. She turned to Selina and started to say: 'Aren't you the one who pays—?'

'We can discuss this later!' Selina seized Aunty Lee by the elbow and hissed: 'You mustn't spoil this for us! You know that it is actually illegal for Nina to be working at your shop, right? If we report you, you'll be fined and your café closed down and Nina sent home and never allowed to come back! But if she helps us get through this then she can go back to you after.'

Aunty Lee was taken aback to hear Selina put it that way, but not as taken aback as Mark was … though Selina was only repeating what he had told her. Mark looked shocked. Beth looked interested. Jonny Ho looked beautiful. He was also watching Selina with more interest than he had shown before.

'Dear … ' Mark said in alarm but nobody paid any attention.

'Well?' Selina's attention was fixed on Aunty Lee.

A combination of Peranakan pride and mission school upbringing meant Aunty Lee did not scratch herself in public whether the pain in her pants was due to bugs or blackmail. Instead she turned to Beth and said conversationally: 'What is Fabian doing now, by the way? The last I heard he was still in America.'

'Oh, Fabian is back in Singapore,' Beth said quietly, matching

Aunty Lee's tone and turning away from Selina. 'Last time he was here, he barely talked to me. He spent most of his time talking to Julietta outside.'

'He knew her?'

'Of course. She was working for his parents for years, since before he left Singapore.'

A helper who had been working for one family for years didn't sound like one who would run away without warning. 'You think he told her something that made her run away?' Aunty Lee asked with interest.

'Poor Fabian has always been excitable, high strung. He was upset about us setting up the school here. But Patty knew that I'd always dreamt of having a little school of my own. When we were children, Patty would always play at getting married. She was always the bride. I would play at being a schoolteacher. Setting up a school is a big dream for me. I know it's what Patty would want.'

Selina was furious. The woman she had tried to manipulate and the woman she wanted to impress were talking together like old friends and ignoring her.

'About your helper,' Aunty Lee said to Beth, 'you didn't report Julietta missing because you think she ran off with her boyfriend and you don't want to get her into trouble. What are you going to do with her if she comes back?'

Beth looked taken aback then hugely relieved. 'That depends what she says. I spent so long as a teacher I know how stupid young girls can be. You are so brave to go into the café business on your own, Rosie. I wouldn't dare to if I didn't have a partner who understands how these things work.' Aunty Lee sensed some gentle criticism there, as though it wasn't quite ladylike of her to be running a business, far less making a success of it. But having come from the same mission school as Beth she understood where she was coming from. And though Beth would have thought it presumptuous, Aunty Lee felt a little sorry for her. Starting a new business was terrifying as well as exciting, all the more so when you were using your own money but putting your confidence in someone else.

So somehow she agreed that Nina would start immediately on a trial month, helping Beth with the cleaning and supervising renovations.

'Mark can drive Jonny and me to town in his car for the meeting. And Selina and Nina can get started on the clean up here and wait for the workers to get back,' Beth decided in her flat, decisive schoolteacher voice, conveniently not hearing Selina object that it would make more sense for her to drive Beth, and Jonny and attend the meeting with them.

'And I will take taxi back to the house and pack up some clothes for you,' Aunty Lee told Nina.

Aunty Lee tried to hail the apparently free taxi at the end of the road, but was ignored by the driver. She could see him there, behind the wheel. She was thinking of photographing the taxi's licence plate with her phone so she could report the driver for ignoring an old lady when Beth said that Jonny Ho would drive Aunty Lee home to collect Nina's things.

'I will go with Jonny and get Nina's things,' Selina said quickly. 'Aunty Lee is better at cleaning.'

But Beth was even more used to getting her own way than Selina. Beth had also seen at once that the threat Selina used against Aunty Lee could easily be turned against her and her school. Besides, Beth did not like the way Selina was looking at Jonny Ho.

'Don't forget you are pregnant, Selina. You shouldn't be driving around in sports cars in your condition. I'm sure your husband wouldn't like it.' Beth smiled at Mark. 'Shall we go?'

Jonny Ho had a bright blue low, flat Subaru. It was a shiny, flashy car and Aunty Lee saw he was as proud of it as a woman with her first pair of Jimmy Choos. When it came to plump elderly ladies, designer cars were as uncomfortable as designer shoes. But when Jonny carefully helped her into the low front seat and leaned across her to lock in her seatbelt Aunty Lee couldn't help being flattered. Like dried lotus leaf soaked in warm water she felt herself relaxing. No wonder rich old men liked to go to massage parlours to be pampered by pretty young women. There ought to be spas specially for rich old women to be pampered by pretty young boys.

'So, where is this shop house of yours? You live above it, right? Selina told us you run a little cake shop. You will never get rich by making cakes. You should learn to cook real Chinese food. It is impossible to get good Chinese food in Singapore. You should let me take a look at your business. I am very good at turning businesses around. Give me six months and I can give you a profit!'

'No, not to the shop.' Aunty Lee decided, remembering Cherril and the curry potato crisis. 'Take me back to my house.' She directed him deeper into Binjai Park and told him he could leave his car on the grass verge outside.

'You want to come in and wait while I pack some things for you to take back for Nina?'

Jonny Ho was impressed by Aunty Lee's Binjai Park house, especially by its size and location. He had studied the wealthier housing districts in Singapore and could sum up its market value pretty accurately. Aunty Lee might look and sound like a low class, uneducated peasant, but she had obviously married into money. Jonny looked at the photo portraits of her dead husband while waiting for her to pack some things for Nina.

'You have a lot of pictures of your dead husband,' he said when she reappeared wheeling a cabin bag with a large plastic bag balanced on top. 'He has been dead for some time, right? Don't you think it is time to be moving on?'

People expect beautiful people to be sensitive, just like they expect beautiful cakes to be delicious, Aunty Lee thought. It was not true. 'I have moved on,' she said evenly. 'I have my shop and my business.'

'I don't understand why you need to work in a shop when you have a house this size. If you need the money, you can rent out rooms. Even better, you can convert this place into several apartments. I see you got all that land behind, nothing but grass and trees. So wasted.'

'Those are fruit trees! You should see them during mango season and *rambutan* season.'

'Women are no good at seeing business opportunities,' Jonny said complacently. 'That's why they need men.'

'I should introduce you to my partner,' Aunty Lee said. 'You two can go and talk business opportunities together!'

CHAPTER FIVE

Helen, & Aunty Lee

'So, you finally got to see Patty's *leng zai*?' was the first thing Helen Chan said to Aunty Lee. 'What did you think? That one time I saw him, he was gorgeous!'

Helen Chan was the same age as Aunty Lee. They had met in school and stayed friends over the years despite their differences. People might look at Aunty Lee and call her a typical Tai-Tai, as in a married woman of a certain age and certain class who doesn't have to work for a living. But Helen was the kind of Tai-Tai that people saw at charity fundraising dinners and in magazines like *Lady* and Singapore *Tatler*. Helen wore bouffant hair, diamond Rolexes, played mah-jong and was addicted to facials and Korean dramas. And she was a loyal friend.

Aunty Lee had phoned and told her old friend all about meeting up with Patty Kwuan-Loo's sister and husband. Helen had, of course, insisted on coming over to hear all about it in person. Since Aunty Lee did not want to talk in her own café, where Cherril was trying out yet another new serving system and two huge tubs of curry potatoes waited in the chiller, Helen had come over to collect Aunty Lee then told her driver to bring them to her favourite reflexology spa off Upper Bukit Timah Road. Such places usually discouraged talking during treatment, but at this hour there were no other clients and the staff, clearly used to Mrs Helen Chan, created a cosy corner for them with hotfoot baths and a choice of flower teas.

'I need a pedicure,' Helen observed as her feet went into the hot water.

Aunty Lee had not been for a pedicure in years. Who wanted to sit still for so long to get your toenails painted when nobody short enough to see them mattered? But as she leaned back in the luxuriously padded recliner and wriggled her toes in the fragrant water she felt the attractions of the Tai-Tai lifestyle. What if she left the running of the shop to Cherril? It was disheartening to hear that, after all her hard work, people still thought of her restaurant as a 'cake shop'.

'So, has he gone old and fat?' Helen cut into her thoughts. 'Please tell me he's bald with a big paunch. I swear I was ready to trade in the old man, given half a chance.'

'He's stupid,' Aunty Lee said crossly. 'He thinks I run a cake shop.'

'Well, your cakes are very good, *what*. Especially your pineapple tarts and your *ang ku kueh*. Nobody else gets the mix of peanuts and *mung beans* in the *ang ku kueh* filling just right. But, he's still handsome?'

'If you like the sort,' Aunty Lee said curtly.

'Hey, I'm just joking!'

The truth was, Jonny Ho looked like he could have played the lead in one of the Taiwanese or Korean soap operas ... the good but falsely maligned son who returns to avenge his foolish father and rescue his true love, who is on the verge of marrying a no-good rich playboy who will drink and gamble away her family fortune. Of course Jonny Ho would also look right playing the no-good rich playboy. Very often the evil villains in these shows were very good-looking too.

'I couldn't believe it myself when I heard about it. You know, I thought at first Patty married him out of pity, to get him out of China.'

As Helen spoke two old men greeted them in Mandarin, sat on stools at their feet and started the treatment, wrapping one foot in a warmed towel while expertly massaging the other. Though she thought of them as 'old men' compared to the young women at the reception counter, they were probably around the same age as Helen and herself, Aunty Lee thought. She wondered if, like Jonny Ho, Avon and Xuyie, and the Guangs, these old men had recently come from China to rub feet for a living.

'Shh ... ' Aunty Lee said to Helen.

'Don't worry. They don't mind. There's nobody else here, after all. Anyway, what was I saying? Oh yes. I thought Patty was just helping somebody who wanted to get a Singapore PR. Like all those men who marry girls from China and Thailand and Vietnam, and get divorced once they become permanent residents. These countries don't allow you to adopt babies from them, but you can marry them and get your own babies. Anyway, that's what I thought when I heard about Patty getting married again. Then when I saw the man I could totally understand. And he was so sweet to her, listening to her, asking if she wanted another drink. Not like the Singapore men we're used to.'

'There are a lot of very rich Chinese people coming out of China these days,' Aunty Lee said, thinking of the Guangs who had bought and extensively renovated the house next to her *kesum* leaves, 'buying houses in good estates.'

'But Jonny Ho isn't one of them. If he was, people would have been less shocked when Patty married him! Rich people can do funny things and nobody minds. Jonny Ho was one of the very very poor who clawed his way up to just very poor. Patty told me that his mother was a prostitute and pedicurist who lived in an illegal underground apartment in Beijing! She said he didn't even know who his father was, but someone sent money for him every New Year, so his mother must have known. The only money he has now is what Patty left him!'

'You were at her first wedding, right? Ken Loo was a respectable guy, but *alamak*, so boring and so ugly.'

'But I remember feeling jealous at the time. Wasn't she one of the first of our batch to get married? But we didn't really keep in touch after that.'

'Patty and Ken Loo were childhood sweethearts. They got married right after he graduated. Then the first boy was born barely six months after that. Of course, they had to go around telling people how the baby is so premature, but six pounds eight ounces so premature, meh? Maybe premature baby elephant!'

'Was that Fabian?' Aunty Lee winced slightly as her masseuse found a sore area on the outside of her left foot and worked it with gusto. Through the pain, she felt the right side of her neck loosening and relaxing. 'I remember Fabian. He was such a cute, chubby little boy.'

'No. The first boy was Roland: the one that fell off the slide and broke his neck. I heard Patty attacked the kindergarten teacher who was supposed to be watching the children. Slashed her with a pair of scissors. That's why her Fabian was so precious to Patty. No kindergarten parties, no school excursions! But that boy so precious until he don't know how to study. Cannot get into university here so they had to send him to America to study. *Wah*, there was such a fuss when they tried to get him to come back for his National Service and he refused to come back. In the end they had to find a doctor to say that he had a weak heart, cannot do NS.'

'I hear he's back now, though.'

'Oh yes. Fabian's back, and making trouble again.' Helen said. The relish in her voice *might* have come from the reflexology points in her feet. 'He ignored his old, sick mother alone for so many years, then comes back as soon as she dies, expecting her to leave him everything.'

'But she didn't? Why not?'

'Don't ask!' Helen said with a knowing laugh designed to have the opposite effect.

Aunty Lee's eyes opened wide. 'She was angry with him? He got arrested? No? He became a terrorist? Or worse – an actor? Or one of those naked dancers? No?'

'Nothing so exciting. If Fabian had done something like that it would be more understandable. But Patty's will left everything to Jonny Ho. Everything in her bank account and all her assets, including the family house that Fabian expected to inherit. Apparently he kicked up a huge fuss. My cousin plays mah-jong with a friend who is in the same Bible Study group as the wife of one of the lawyers who handled the probate, and she said Fabian went down there and accused them of helping Jonny Ho cheat his mother. He even accused his aunt of setting up Jonny Ho to marry Patty just to get her house!'

Aunty Lee could understand why Fabian would be upset. But she could also see things from Jonny Ho's side. After all, Aunty Lee was herself a second wife. And apart from substantial gifts to his first wife's children, M. L. had left everything else, including his house, to her. Thanks to her own investments, Aunty Lee had increased rather than diminished what she meant to leave to Mathilda and Mark.

'I saw the aunt … Patty's sister, Beth … also. I can't imagine her setting up anything like that.'

'She wouldn't. I think Beth was hoping to go on staying in the house after Patty died. You know she moved in with Patty after Ken died? It was driving Patty crazy. She wanted some time to herself: to get used to being on her own, to sort out Ken's things. But Beth just plonked herself in the house and said she was not going to desert her no matter what she said.'

'*Alamak.*' Having lost a husband herself, Aunty Lee knew how the pain of being alone wrestled with hating the sight of every person other than the beloved dead. And Beth didn't look as though she would be much comfort. 'That Beth is so sand-in-my-puss!'

'So *What*?'

'Sand-in-my-puss. You remember how she was in school, right? She's the same now. Only worse. Everything, also she is more proper, more Holy, more low calorie than you.'

'Sanctimonious,' Helen corrected faintly.

'That's what I said.'

'Anyway, that one was born to be an old maid. Everything must be done her way. Her way is always the "right" way.'

'You can't call Beth an old maid. She's a career woman.' Aunty Lee remembered Beth's support under Selina's childish attempts at manipulation. 'I think she's found the right line. She's got connections with some good schools, and she's starting a children's education centre. Very scientific. All about teaching children from young how to learn things and score on exams. Have you seen her recently?'

'Not since school. Remember what a pain she was back then? She out-teachered the teachers! When Patty came over to our place for mah-jong, Beth would stay with Fabian and, *alamak*, every night she would always phone two, three times: why wasn't Fabian taking the vitamins she bought for him? Where did Patty keep the assessment books she gave to Fabian?'

'Sounds like Beth was just as protective of Fabian as his mother.'

'Patty was overprotective and spoiled the boy. We all told her that and she knew it. She even laughed at herself. Beth had nothing else to do when she wasn't in school. When she was in school she bossed the students around, so when she was out of school she bossed Fabian around.'

'Just because she never joined us at parties doesn't mean she had nothing to do, *what*. She wasn't even in our year. She would have had her own friends.'

'One year older. When you are in school, one year makes a big difference, but in the real world, five years, ten years, what's the difference?'

Aunty Lee didn't pursue it. After all, she was trying to be more mature than Helen about Beth. Beth was starting the school of her dreams while Helen's Tai-Tai life revolved around gossip and foot rubs.

Aunty Lee remembered all the negative comments she had got when setting up her Peranakan café. People doing nothing with their lives always criticize those trying to do something. Of course, there had been friends who encouraged her: Patty, and Helen among them. Aunty Lee smiled to herself, remembering how, in the early days of Aunty Lee's Delights, her friends would swoop down on the shop's display counter and buy, 'ten of everything, or however many you got left', with the engine running in Helen's huge white Mercedes blocking the road outside.

'What did you do with all the *kueh* you used to buy?'

'What?'

'You used to come down and buy my *nonya* cakes from the shop, remember? I know you weren't eating them because I never saw you getting fat.'

'Oh.' Helen looked embarrassed. 'I don't remember. Maybe I just exercised a lot.'

'It was very nice of you.' Aunty Lee reached over and touched the back of Helen's hand lightly. Helen, she thought, had probably given the *kueh* to her driver or servants. Aunty Lee wanted to encourage Beth's KidStarters the way Helen had helped her.

And maybe, just a little, she wanted Selina to see how well Aunty Lee and Beth Kwuan got along. If her grandchild got into Beth's school, Grandma /Aunty Lee would be right there.

But she realized Helen was talking. 'You remember that burglary we had, right?'

'Another one?'

'No, *lah*! Now we got so much security I want to go toilet at night also got lights, got noise, got police come. So we don't even switch on. Just put up all the signs, "Alarm System Activated". Should have just bought the signs; no need to buy the alarm. *Hiyah*,' Helen sighed and hesitated.

Aunty Lee, sensing something new, perked up. 'What? Tell me!'

'I did something I didn't tell you about that time.' Helen sounded guilty.

'Those people took money. The television sets. All Peng's nice suits and belts and ties and watches. His good Italian shoes. The wedding silverware and crystals. Jewellery. Antiques. They just took the whole safe with them. All the bottles of liqueur Peng was collecting for so long. All the credit cards we didn't take with us. Electronics. That was what my son got most upset about. He said that they could very easily get info on my bank accounts and credit card accounts and information on my friends from my Facebook and email and scam them.'

'So what did you do?' Aunty Lee refused to be distracted.

'I called Patty to warn her about the identity theft thing. I was calling all my friends … '

Aunty Lee nodded. She remembered thinking that Helen had called more to vent than to warn.

'I may have said something about Chinese gangs using stolen credit cards, chequebooks Birth certificates. I think that offended her. I was so worked up I forgot that that new husband of hers was from China. After that phone call I never saw her again. Every time I phoned her to go out, she said she was too busy, she couldn't make it. Busy doing what? You say you got no time to go out, I know you are boning fish or stuffing eggplant. But Patty? Later she wouldn't even come to the phone, and she didn't even call me back. Of course, I didn't know that she was so sick.'

'Was she sick?'

'She died, *what*. Of course she was sick.'

They were both quiet for a while. Death of someone your age always brings it closer to home.

CHAPTER SIX

New Boss

Nina looked around the living room of the Jalan Kakatua house. It was large and part of what must have been a comfortable house once. The rooms were pleasantly rectangular with no awkward corners or narrow corridors. Apart from the half-completed wall insulation and the windows still waiting for their insulated glass frames, this would be an easy room to clean once the construction debris was removed. Though much of the time that depended as much on the personality of the employer as the kind of paint they put on their walls or the kind of flooring they had installed.

Nina took a deep breath. Had she been stupid to come here, just to get away from Aunty Lee's nagging? Despite Aunty Lee's bizarre demands (prawns had to be slit on their undersides even though the dark string of digestive track was nearer their backs; washing detergent was not allowed on the granite mortar used to crush garlic), Nina knew Aunty Lee was an easy boss to work for. Apart from food, Aunty Lee didn't care how something was done, as long as it got done. In fact, Nina was a great deal more particular when it came to some things: laundry, for example. Aunty Lee liked bright colours, especially on her sneakers and her batik sarongs, but as long as her clothes did not smell or make her itch, she paid very little attention to how she looked. More than once Nina had had to suggest Aunty Lee put on something dressier or more formal when special guests were expected, or strongly recommend that the 'red hot mama' tee shirt Mathilda had sent her from the UK (showing a dancing chilli pepper with two rows of protruding nipple-like seeds) might not be what Aunty Lee wanted to wear to the fish market. Nina smiled to herself. Aunty Lee had offered to give Nina the tee shirt, 'from London you know!' Nina found it easier to appreciate Aunty Lee when she was not around. These days, when Aunty Lee was around it seemed that Salim was all that she wanted to talk about!

And, of course, there was Salim. It was the exact opposite with Salim. Nina knew that when she was around Salim, or even just thinking of him, she lost all her good sense. That was why she had to keep away from him. Inspector Salim was the real reason Nina wanted to get away from Binjai Park.

Singapore law forbade foreign domestic workers from marrying Singaporeans without prior approval from the Ministry of Manpower, and Nina had never heard of permission being granted. Aunty Lee seemed to think it was just a matter of persistent applying and re-applying. Nina knew of former maids, still banned from Singapore after years of fruitless applications, with children not legally recognized by their Singaporean fathers.

Aunty Lee, for all her guts and good intentions, had no idea what it was like to be Salim, for example.

Salim Mawar was neither Chinese nor rich. Even though he refused to talk about it, Nina knew that being involved with a foreign domestic worker could put an end to Salim's career prospects. Salim knew the official line, but Nina knew the stories of women who had fallen in love with Singapore men. Thinking of Salim made Nina waver.

And there were all the other issues.

'What about religion?' Nina had said to him.

Salim had smiled and said: 'You pray to your God, I pray to my God, let them work it out.'

But Nina knew that, even if there was only one God under all the different names, it was not God but churches, mosques, politicians, and governments that would make trouble for them.

'Why are you standing here?' Beth appeared. 'Are you looking for something? Do you need the toilet?'

Employers also found it difficult getting used to a new helper, Nina knew. Having a complete stranger living in your house day and night, using the same bathrooms and fridge, made people uncomfortable at first.

Of course, after a week, some would be walking around in front of you in their underwear (or without it) and leaving the toilet door open when they went to shit. Fortunately, Miss Beth did not look as though she would be one of these. Miss Beth looked as if she would be on guard even when she was alone.

'No, Madam,' Nina said quickly. 'What would you like me to do first?' Nina would not be at the Jalan Kakatua house for long. She would do the best she could while she was there.

'So, what is it like working for the famous Aunty Lee?' Beth smiled at Nina. 'Selina says you want to get away from there because of some policeman who is after you. You should report him for bothering you, you know. I suppose Aunty Lee wants you to be nice to him?'

The implications around the way Beth said 'nice' made Nina want to throw something at her.

'Oh yes, Madam,' Nina said. She put on her best stupid expression. 'Aunty Lee wants me to be nice to everybody.'

Beth could not tell if Nina was being smart or stupid. 'Clean up what you can in here,' she said finally.

Left to herself in the strange house, Nina set to work. That was when she discovered that getting away from Aunty Lee was not enough. Her own thoughts kept returning to Salim, wondering how Aunty Lee would explain her absence and what he would do about it. She tried to throw herself into the cleaning. She could not control what Salim thought and felt. She was dangerously close to not being able to control what she herself felt.

'What are those poles doing over the windows? Are they the clothes-drying *galas* from the back?' Miss Beth sounded accusatory, but Nina had already realized this was her normal way of speaking.

'Madam said she is worried because the windows got no glass. I put the *galas* in front of the windows so that, at night, if anybody tries to come in they will make a lot of noise and we will wake up.'

Nina had hung three poles at different heights on loops of raffia across the front windows and leaned plywood sheets against the side window. They would not keep out anyone intent on coming in, but no one would be able to get into the house quietly. She had also looped the link chain she had found hanging on the front door grill through its frame and fastened the large padlock hanging from it. The kitchen door and the sliding window next to it were locked and latched, the other window left open for air. Since that window still had its (not childproof) grills, the house was as secure as it could be with a gap in the wall and no glass in the window frames. It ought to be safe enough for Singapore. Some homeowners were still nervous about housebreakers, but, as far as Nina knew, the burglars had never yet broken into a house under renovation. It stood to reason: there would be few valuables lying about.

Beth looked around. The floor was clean and for the first time in weeks no grit rasped under her feet when she came in.

'You'll have to take them down tomorrow before the workmen come back ... if they come back.' Despite Jonny's assurances, the contractor and his men had not returned that day.

'Of course, Madam.'

'It's a good idea,' Beth said, almost to herself. But Nina recognized it for the praise it was and accepted it.

Nina thought she knew Beth, but she was mistaken. She had seen women Beth's age visit Aunty Lee's Delights in packs for 'lunch with the girls' or 'tea with my buddies' or for some time alone with a book, away from domestic responsibilities. Mature voices shrieked with girlish laughter and grumble-boasted about children, husbands, and how long they had to wait for that flight out of Oslo even though they were on Business Class.

But Beth was not one of these women. As a single woman without children, even if she had the smartest outfits, the busiest mobile phone and most recently styled hair, she would always be the one they finally remembered to turn to and ask: 'How is your dog?' or 'So, are you still doing yoga?'

By nightfall, Nina had given the house a thorough general cleaning. There had been no sign of a dog, a yoga mat, or any hints as to what Beth Kwuan did with herself when she was not working.

'Tomorrow, what time are the workers coming, Madam?'

'Who knows?' Beth said, before remembering herself. 'If you take the poles down before 9 a.m. that should be fine.'

'Does Madam want me to bring tea to her room in the morning?'

'Do you bring that old woman tea in the morning?'

'Yes, Madam. Jasmine green tea. Then later, at breakfast, I make for her coffee with condensed milk.'

'All right. That sounds good. Now you better go to your room so that I can lock the door. Do you have to go to toilet first?'

When Nina did not move Beth added: 'Look, I can't let you go wandering around the house all night.'

'Madam, I don't walk around the house at night.'

'Good. Then it won't make any difference to you whether the door is locked or not.'

Her voice was so briskly matter-of-fact that Nina thought she was joking.

'It's for your own good,' Beth Kwuan told Nina. 'This way if anything goes missing, you won't be suspected because you were locked in your room.'

'But Madam, what happens if I need to go toilet? Or if there is a fire?'

Beth laughed. 'A fire! Don't be silly. Why should there be a fire? And you just make sure you go to the toilet before you go to bed. If a dog can be trained to hold it in all night, I'm sure you can!'

There wasn't anything Nina could do except let herself be locked into Julietta's old room. She could have asked to leave, of course. She didn't think Beth Kwuan could have stopped her if she phoned Aunty Lee, or if she simply unlocked the padlock, the grill, and the wooden door and walked out of the house. But where would she go – back to Aunty Lee's house in Binjai Park?

There was a small possibility Aunty Lee had set her friend up to this, just to show Nina how difficult working for somebody else could be. After all, a lot of maids got locked in by their employers. Aunty Lee probably thought that Nina had come to take her freedom for granted.

Nina decided to stay. She could stand anything for a few days. And surely once Beth got used to her she would see that Nina was not going to get up and rob her in the night. She wondered if Beth's paranoia had been triggered by Julietta's running away, or if it was the reason why Julietta had run away.

Julietta's tiny room was set into the wall at the top of the stairs. There was no window. It had clearly been designed as a small storeroom or large linen closet. A naked light bulb fixed in the ceiling showed a mattress that occupied most of the floor space. Two upright dining table chairs were stacked in a corner on top of a couple of plastic storage boxes.

Perhaps it was wise: keeping a door between strangers was a good idea after all. After Beth turned the key in the lock, Nina lifted the chairs down and wedged them against the door, the back of one chair preventing the door handle from turning. It was just a token defiance but made her feel better.

Nina was glad Aunty Lee was not there to say: 'What if there's a fire in the kitchen and you can't get out of your room to escape?' or 'What if Beth has a heart attack in the night and you can't get out to give her CPR in time?'

But then, if Aunty Lee were there she would surely have got Nina out of that storeroom and back to Binjai Park. Suddenly Nina missed her plump eccentric boss terribly. And she missed her simple, pleasant room in the Binjai Park bungalow. That was what 'home' had come to mean to Nina.

Her thoughts went again to Salim. Would Aunty Lee tell him that Nina was living and working somewhere else for a while? Or would Aunty Lee let him think Nina was successfully avoiding him?

Nina did not know what she wanted him to think. She did not want to worry him unnecessarily – that she was certain of. Her working for Beth Kwuan was illegal, and his police side would not approve. It was already difficult for him to know Nina was helping out in Aunty Lee's café, though he could see she was not being overworked.

Resolutely, Nina forced her thoughts away from Salim. She was tired and tomorrow would probably be another hard day. She closed her eyes and steadied her breathing. Even if she did not manage to sleep she could rest her body, her eyes, and her mind for the next day. And as usually happened, once she accepted this she started to drift off to sleep. The mattress had the slightly sour smell of stale sweat. Not surprising given how hot the room was – the tiny window not letting in much air. She would wash the bed sheet tomorrow, Nina thought as she drifted off to sleep, and spray sofa cleaner on the mattress. She just hoped there weren't any bugs ...

It seemed that she had barely drifted off to sleep when there was a clattering of poles from downstairs and the sound of angry voices. Or one male, angry voice and a woman's voice calming and soothing. That was Beth, Nina thought. Because the noise would surely have woken Beth, and if she did not know the man who had climbed in through the window she would be screaming now instead of talking to him. Nina lay in the dark listening. The man stopped shouting. Later, footsteps came up the stairs. As they passed her room there was a hard thump on her door. It was a thump of anger, not of someone trying to get in, which made sense because the key was in the lock and they could get in any time they wanted, though Nina could not get out.

Nina got very little sleep that night after that. She wondered what Aunty Lee was doing; wondered if Aunty Lee missed the evening cup of honey and ginger tea that Nina put by her bedside every night.

CHAPTER SEVEN

Alone Again

Of course, the real reason Aunty Lee had allowed Nina to go away for a few days was that Nina had said Aunty Lee needed her and could not be left alone in the house without her.

If not wanting to leave Aunty Lee alone was one of the reasons Nina wouldn't marry Salim, Aunty Lee was going to prove her wrong! She would show Nina that much as she appreciated her, she did not need her!

'Are you sure you'll be all right?' Cherril had asked as she dropped Aunty Lee off at the gate of her house that night. 'Do you want me to get Avon or Xuyie to come and sleep here tonight? I'm sure they won't mind.'

'Of course not!' Aunty Lee said. The thought of having the shy, clumsy Xuyie bumping into her things or Avon fingering them while talking loudly and aggressively on her mobile phone filled Aunty Lee with dread.

She went into the kitchen to put leftovers into the fridge, and switched on the electric kettle that Nina had filled that morning. Then she went, as usual, to sit in the sitting room with her glass of warm ginger tea. The furnishings were so familiar that she hardly saw them anymore. But though she often sat here, alone, in the evenings, tonight the room felt empty.

The sound of insects from the garden and traffic from a distance only made the room feel more quiet. Though Nina had barely been gone a day, it felt as though there was a thin coating of dust and silence over everything. Even the photo portrait of M. L. Lee on the low coffee table seemed distant.

'Nina will be back.' Talking to her late husband's portraits comforted Aunty Lee. A quiet man, he had seldom answered even when alive. 'I miss her. But not as much as I miss you.'

Nina always moved the photos around when she dusted or when she put Aunty Lee's evening tea on its little carpet coaster. It was her way of acknowledging both the loss and presence of M. L. Lee. M. L. would not have approved of her sending Nina away, even for a few days, Aunty Lee thought.

Aunty Lee picked up her phone and tried to call Nina. She would say she wanted her back tomorrow, even if that made it look as though she couldn't do without her. But Nina did not answer her phone.

She was probably busy, Aunty Lee thought. She would wait till tomorrow.

Apart from that, Aunty Lee was surprised not to feel more alone that first night of Nina's absence. She had half expected an echo of the misery that had enveloped her in the months following M. L.'s death. In those days even getting out of bed had seemed a pointless chore. If we are all going to die anyway, why not just lie in bed and wait for death to come?

But now, being alone in the house felt just a little like being on holiday. Because she knew it was temporary, of course. That made all the difference. Nina would stay at Beth's house overnight and maybe for another night or two and then she would be back, full of stories, and everything would return to normal.

Mark had called to remind her that they were just fifteen minutes away and that she must text them when she got up in the morning so that they would know she hadn't fallen down in the night. Aunty Lee agreed.

Cherril had offered to stop by in the morning to drive Aunty Lee the less than 50 metres between her house and the shop in the morning. Also, Helen Chan had sent her a text asking if she wanted to go over for mah-jong or join them for supper after. Aunty Lee didn't like mah-jong, but staying home because she had turned down an invitation always felt better than staying home because she had no alternative.

Mark called twice more that first night: once to tell Aunty Lee that Selina said she was welcome to spend the night in their condominium apartment though they had no spare room and would have to sleep on the sofa to let her have their bed, and a second time because Selina wanted her to check that her oven was turned off and her gate and doors locked. Selina had never quite got over her discovery that Aunty Lee often left her front door unlocked and her kitchen door open during the day. In the old *kampong* days, all the village houses left doors and windows standing open to let in air and light. Some didn't even have doors! Dogs and geese had provided all the warning systems needed.

But Singapore had changed since those days. You no longer knew the parents, grandparents and in-laws of the people living around you. Since the burglary at Helen and Kok Peng's house, and the public service warnings about break-ins in landed estates had been issued, Nina had made sure their perimeters were locked.

Aunty Lee did a walk around of the house before going to bed. She checked all the entrances (front door, back door, French windows opening onto the patio) as she walked through the house but this routine was really for her to say goodnight to all the photo portraits of M. L. There was at least one picture of him in each room.

It was time for Aunty Lee to change them, as she did regularly, but not tonight. Change may be good, but too much change all at once can make you forget who you are.

Looking at M. L.'s photographs had been painful at first, but now she found them comforting. Several photographs showed the two of them together, the much younger Rosie Lee glowing and happy. And, of course, there were some photographs of M. L. with his first wife and the young Mathilda and Mark. Aunty Lee had promised her husband she would always provide a home and be family for Mathilda if she should ever need it (M. L. had had an old Asian patriarch's distrust of the white man who married his daughter) and she kept a couple of those photographs on display ... but only in a corner of M. L.'s study.

And so to bed? It was never completely quiet in Singapore. There was always the rumble of distant traffic, a car passing nearby, dogs conversing, and when even those sounds dropped, you became aware of the wind rustling the trees and whirring of night insects. That was the difference between sound and noise. When you accepted sounds as a familiar background to your environment they stopped being 'noise'. Aunty Lee stopped by the last photograph, one of the largest, just outside her bedroom door. This one, that she had never rotated out of sight, showed M. L. in his favourite green golfing shirt. He had already been starting to fade but kept going out on the green for his nine holes thanks to golf carts, caddies, and faithful golfing buddies. Aunty Lee knew M. L. had occasionally met Ken Loo at the golf clubs, though they had not played together regularly.

There was something else about Ken Loo – no, about Patty Kwuan-Loo – on the edge of Aunty Lee's mind, tied up with the house break-ins she had been thinking about earlier. Patty's house had not been broken into, that was not it. But she had cancelled a dinner party at the last minute (or the day before, which was the same thing when you thought about the time it took to plan, shop for, and prepare to host a dinner) after hearing some friends (Helen and Peng) had had their house broken into. Aunty Lee was not sure but she thought Raja Kumar and his wife, Sumathi, had been among those disappointed. Yes, it had been Sumathi who had told her about it. This would not have been a big deal except that it was the last dinner party Patty Kwuan-Loo had planned.

After that she had retreated into social seclusion. And the next thing they knew, she was dead.

Aunty Lee remembered being just a little jealous of Patty, because she never seemed to have any fears or qualms. And what had there been to be afraid of? Looking back now, all their girlish angst about friends, boys, tests, parents and looks seemed ridiculously distant. They had all been young and beautiful and full of potential in their teens.

With sudden insight, Aunty Lee saw that, if she reached her 80s and looked back, her current self would seem equally full of youthful potential. She was still in a position to do, rather than look back wishing that she had done.

'I'm alone tonight, but I'm all right. Good night,' Aunty Lee said softly to the last portrait. It was her way of meditating out loud. Sometimes she did not know what she thought or felt until she put it in words that M. L. would have understood.

It was only when Aunty Lee was already in bed that she remembered what Jonny Ho had said about coming over to persuade her. All that the man had said about new immigrants and investments might be true, but Aunty Lee would not trust her own impressions to commit to a business deal any more than she would trust her financial advisor to choose seasonings for her sauces. However, Jonny Ho was entertaining, especially compared to the demands for money made by Mark and Selina over the years. It would be interesting to see what Darren Sim thought of him. This was a good thought to go to sleep on. There was no hurry, after all.

Aunty Lee could not help thinking about what she would wear when she met Jonny Ho again. So few men paid any attention to how you looked or what you wore, it was a pity to waste one who did. She had no idea, then, of what lay ahead.

CHAPTER EIGHT

Tuesday

Tuesday was the first day of the working week at Aunty Lee's Delights. Aunty Lee was determined that their first day without Nina would run as smoothly as any other day. She had forgotten her resolution of the night. If Nina didn't marry Salim, it would not be because Aunty Lee needed her.

Aunty Lee had walked over to the café, arriving before nine o'clock, all ready to get to work, only to find she could not get in. Nina had always unlocked the café in the morning. Aunty Lee knew she had her own set of keys somewhere but could not remember where she had last seen them. She called Avon and Xuyie upstairs but they did not have keys either. Aunty Lee had to phone Cherril to come early and let her in.

Cherril sounded sleepily alarmed when she finally answered the phone to hear Aunty Lee saying: 'It's me. No need to bother Anne. But can you come down to the shop now?'

'Aunty Lee? What happened? Why are you here so early?'

'I am always here around this time, *what*.'

'Uhm. Okay I'll be there soon.'

Early morning had become the only time she and Nina had the café kitchen to themselves. Nina would put a mug of hot soya bean milk next to the list of the day's bookings, and while Aunty

Lee went over the lists of supplies and deliveries needed and confirmed the day's specials, Nina would start the stock pots and sort the vegetables left outside the back entrance.

Today, Aunty Lee found she didn't know where the bookings ledger was kept when it wasn't put on the table in front of her. Neither did Cherril.

'What book?' Cherril looked grumpy and sleepy.

'Do you need coffee? You look half asleep!'

'I've given up coffee. Caffeine upsets the hormonal cycles.' Cherril was addicted to coffee, but she and Mycroft were trying to start a family. 'I'm not sleepy. I'm just ... ' She caught sight of herself in the large gilt-framed mirror standing in the corner of the room and yelped. 'I forgot my make-up!' In fact, she had forgotten to wash her face that morning, having dashed out in a panic when Aunty Lee called. Rushing out of the back door, Cherril almost tripped over the plastic bins of fresh vegetables wrapped in newspapers. She hurried away.

Aunty Lee hauled the vegetables in and sorted them into what would go into the fridge and the chill room and what needed to be soaked until they were ready for cooking. She could still handle the work; she didn't need Nina's help with that at all. What she missed was having somebody there to talk to and bounce ideas off. Nina might not approve of all Aunty Lee's cooking experiments, but explaining her thoughts to Nina helped Aunty Lee understand herself. She missed that.

'It's for her own good,' Aunty Lee said to the photo portrait of M. L. by the 'Today's Specials' chalk board. This photo had been taken next to one of the dwarf frangipani trees in their garden. Aunty Lee had been standing next to her husband when it was taken but she had cropped herself out of the picture. When that photo was on display Nina always brought a branch of the pink frangipani flowers for the vase next to the photo, arranging the live blossoms over those in the image. 'I miss her,' Aunty Lee said to the photo as she removed the wilted flowers.

'But it's for her own good. She has to see that I don't need her to stay with me. It is not easy to find a good man who wants to be good to you. If she marries Salim then they can face whatever happens together.' M. L., impassive in death as in life, said nothing.

Cherril, her face restored to perfection, reappeared, along with Avon and Xuyie. The girls had probably been watching out for her, Aunty Lee thought crossly. Not understanding timid people, she tried to get through to them by talking more loudly, as though they were deaf, which only made things worse.

'How did yesterday's catering go?'

'Fine. Good. The potatoes they didn't want are in the freezer,' Cherril said. 'And they ate all the basil and lemon verbena leaves garnishing the dishes but other than that they didn't eat much. A lot of food was wasted!'

'Did they pay?'

'Yes. But I wasn't sure if I should ... ' It was the first catering job Cherril had handled on her own. Aunty Lee had given herself the afternoon off after Nina's departure. After all, if Cherril was to start taking more responsibility, better she practise on a job she had brought in than on one of Aunty Lee's old friends!

'If they paid then it was a success,' Aunty Lee said firmly. 'You made a profit. That's a success.'

'Thanks.' Cherril smiled, looking pleased.

Aunty Lee knew that, despite her polished appearance, Cherril Lim-Peters was insecure about many things, especially her limited education. She gave such a good impression that Aunty Lee was always forgetting how hard Cherril had struggled to understand what Mark and Selina and Aunty Lee herself took for granted.

'Well done. Next time just serve them more leaves, less real food. You can say it is healthy and charge them more money and make them more happy!'

Aunty Lee was just congratulating herself on how well things were going in the shop, and wondering whether to phone Beth

71

to ask why Nina was not answering her mobile phone, when Jonny Ho turned up at Aunty Lee's Delights.

'Hello Rosie Lee!' The man was standing just inside the entrance.

Aunty Lee was so startled that she dropped the prawn she was carefully slitting to remove its dark string of intestine. People who knew her from her girlhood called her 'Rosie' or 'Rosalind' without her husband's surname and everybody else addressed her as 'Aunty Lee' or 'Mrs Lee'.

'Who have you annoyed now?' Cherril wondered, only half joking.

But she turned to stare at the handsome man striding across the room towards them (ignoring Avon's offer to show him to a table).

He had a huge grin on his face when he stopped in front of them and posed with his arms crossed in mock anger. 'Rosie Lee. Why you did not tell me who you are yesterday?'

He looks like a film star, Cherril thought. Avon, torn between staring and preening, obviously agreed. Shy Xuyie looked scared of him. But then everything scared Xuyie.

Jonny Ho rested a hand on the back of a chair and looked at Aunty Lee with a challenging smile. Yesterday Aunty Lee had been struck by his good looks, and she had heard Helen Chan raving about how meltingly, seductively handsome he was. Aunty Lee remembered the tingle of nervous excitement her first encounter with this man had triggered, but it didn't come today. The Taj Mahal effect she realized. Years ago, after M. L. sent her on a trip to the monument, they had agreed that if they had heard nothing of it, they would have been impressed. But thanks to a pedantic acquaintance who appointed himself their tour guide, the monument had been a let-down. (Old Vasu meant well. But nothing could have lived up to the hype he had spouted.)

That morning, Jonny Ho's flirtatious look reminded Aunty Lee of a cat that pretends to release a trapped bird, hoping it will try to escape and provide more sport before becoming a meal.

'I told you my name yesterday, *what.*' Aunty Lee peered short-sightedly at him over the top of her reading glasses. The glasses were more for cooking than reading; shelling prawns was a finicky business when you were as particular as Aunty Lee about symmetrical halves and keeping the heads (rich with roe) and tails intact.

'You told me you were Mrs Lee; do you know how many Lees there are in Singapore? Even not counting those right at the top?' He laughed again.

Aunty Lee did not.

'He works for that playschool that Silly-Nah wants to get her baby into,' Aunty Lee explained to Cherril, whose curiosity was almost steaming out of her ears. 'That Kick Star place where Nina is working for a few days. Sorry, ah, boy. I cannot remember your name.'

'Excuse me for correcting you, but I don't work for KidStarters. I own it, so you might say they all work for me. And, by the way, my name is Jonny Ho.'

Aunty Lee got the impression Jonny Ho was pausing for effect, so she allowed the pause to go on longer to greater effect.

'Do you want a table?' Cherril offered. 'Avon, Xuyie, show him to a table. And stand up straight, please.' Her curtness was not directed at Jonny Ho but at the two girls who were leaning into each other while they stared and giggled.

Jonny Ho waved one hand dismissively. 'I came to have a chat with your boss. Business talk.'

Cherril opened her mouth, probably to say something cutting, then shut it again and smiled grimly. All those articles she was always reading to Aunty Lee about 'Responding not Reacting' must have sunk in.

But Aunty Lee had not been paying enough attention and she jumped in: 'This is my partner, Cherril Peters. You got any business talk you better talk to her. I only cook.' Aunty Lee waved a slimy prawn shell dangerously near Jonny's dress shirt (dark green today, with almost black collar and cuffs). 'Careful ah, otherwise today our special instead of *Lam Mee* we got Lam Customer Shirt!'

Lam Mee literally meant to 'pour soup over noodles'. Though Jonny clearly didn't get the joke he smiled gamely, humouring her. He was certainly on his best behaviour this morning. Aunty Lee wondered what he wanted.

'You should stay and try my *Lam Mee*. Last time, when I was young, we only made it for special birthdays. *Wah*, I remember how excited we children would get and we were allowed to eat the red egg strips; that's why, even though here we are not serving it for a birthday, I said we must have the flat red egg.'

'Strips of omelette with organic food colouring,' Cherril explained quickly, seeing Jonny's doubtful look. Wherever the man came from, he had not grown up in Singapore.

'Why don't you go and sit down and talk to Jonny, Aunty Lee? Xuyie will do the prawns. I can finish up here. The stock is already ready, and the girls and I can manage from here on.'

What was there left to manage? Aunty Lee looked at the huge clay pot where the stock was simmering, rich with chicken, pork bones, pork belly, and her own personal tweak to make the soup sweet ... dried shallots, dried octopus, and dried flat fish. It might be boiling but it was certainly not 'ready'. Cherril was just trying to show Aunty Lee how well she had learned to manage in the kitchen. If she had been a minor concubine in Old China it would be time for the empress to have her poisoned or put down a well. But since they were in modern Singapore Aunty Lee knew the younger woman was only trying to prove her worth.

'I got to wash my hands first. The prawn shells, don't ... '

'Yes, I know. Don't throw. Put them back in the pot. I've watched Nina doing it a hundred times, Aunty Lee!'

Of course, she had not ... not for this particular dish anyway. Which reminded Aunty Lee this was the first time in years she had made the *Lam Mee* without Nina. In fact, in the recent few years it had been Nina who had done the bulk of the preparations for this special, with Aunty Lee providing a running litany of directions – more because it was what she had always done than because Nina actually needed help.

'So, this dish is some kind of fancy dish at your restaurant?' Jonny Ho courteously rose to pull out a chair for Aunty Lee when she joined him, drying her hands on a dishcloth.

'Not so fancy. It is basically yellow noodles in a rich stock topped with chicken, prawns, and things. It's a traditional birthday celebration dish. Last time it would only be prepared to celebrate big birthdays, like when somebody turns seventy or eighty years old. This is the dish you would serve to visitors when they come to give you red packets and *mee sua*.'

'*Mee sua*? Oh, for long life.' Jonny shook his head. 'All these old customs. By the time I was growing up there were no more things like that. So, whose birthday are you celebrating? Or do you just cook it up whenever you feel like it?'

Aunty Lee started to brush off the question, then remembered that Jonny Ho had lost his wife ... and much more recently than Aunty Lee had lost her husband. Even if he covered up his feelings, Patty's death must have left a gap in his life. Like one of her recently widowed friends said ruefully: 'Now there's suddenly nobody to get irritated with, I don't know what to do with myself!'

'My late husband's,' Aunty Lee said quietly. 'Next week he would have been seventy-nine years old. So I cook all his favourite dishes the week before: this week.'

Jonny Ho started to say something but stopped himself and nodded several times.

'You never stop missing them,' Aunty Lee said, 'but after a while you get used to it. After a while it doesn't hurt so much. At first, the worst thing for me was forgetting my husband was dead. I would see something or taste something and think: 'Oh I must show it to M. L.' and then I would remember. It took me a long time to stop doing that. And every time it happened it was like I lost him again. It hasn't been a year yet since Patty died, right? Give yourself some time to get used to your loss.'

Jonny Ho's face remained blandly polite and expressionless, but Aunty Lee assumed this was the professional mask worn by air stewardesses and other service professionals. A great deal could be going on beneath that polite demeanour. Aunty Lee had seen Cherril (who had spent years serving on Singapore's premier airline) attend with gracious professionalism to customers who she later denounced in colourful language.

'You know, you are the first person to talk to me like that? About losing my wife?' Jonny Ho shook his head. 'Everybody else is thinking I am a gold digger; that son of Patty's even accusing me of changing her will, of wanting her to die.'

'He's just upset. Fabian lost his mother after all. People are allowed to say stupid things after people die. I think there should be a one month get out of jail free card after your husband or wife dies.' Aunty Lee was joking but Jonny did not laugh. Again, Aunty Lee was glad that M. L.'s children, Mark and Mathilda (now established in London with her own family), had never given her any trouble over their father's will. That Silly wife of Mark's had tried, of course, but making trouble came naturally to Selina, and Aunty Lee did not take it personally. Especially as Selina would soon have a little Lee to distract her from what Aunty Lee might have cheated Mark out of.

'I'm sorry I didn't recognize you the other day,' Jonny surprised Aunty Lee by saying. 'You should have told me you are famous!'

Aunty Lee remembered being one of many who had speculated with great interest that Patty's new husband was *swaku* ('*swaku*' meant 'mountain tortoise', meaning an ignorant country bumpkin) who she didn't want her friends to meet.

'I would have met you long ago if Patty didn't suddenly turn into a hermit. What happened to her?' Aunty Lee asked. Now the mysterious husband was sitting at the table opposite her she thought him over rather than under sophisticated. 'We were in school together, you know. Why did she cut off contact with all of us? Was she already getting sick? Was it because of the cancer? Was it cancer?'

'My wife, Patty, was very sensitive,' Jonny Ho said.

He looked earnestly at Aunty Lee, who managed not to say Patty Kwuan-Loo was one of the least sensitive women she had ever met. Wasn't it Patty who had said to M. L. (with Aunty Lee standing right there) on hearing the news of their engagement: 'Are you sure she is still fertile? Women her age, even if they still get periods, doesn't mean their eggs are still good!'

Of course, Aunty Lee would not carry a grudge against the woman for so many years . . . still, she would not have minded a chance to say something similar to Patty on her second marriage.

Perhaps that explained Patty's sudden retreat from society? Had Patty's years of blunt talking generated a backlash once she revealed a weakness for this handsome young tour guide? But Jonny was still talking, and Aunty Lee pulled her thoughts back to the present and tried to catch up with the conversation. He had left the subject of his late wife far behind.

'So you see, what I have here is a business proposal for you.' Jonny touched his fingers together and, leaning towards her across the table, fixed her with an earnest gaze that made Aunty Lee think of real estate agents and MLM marketers.

'Huh? Sorry, what?'

A spasm of impatience flickered across Jonny Ho's handsome face. 'What I've been telling you about. For Aunty Lee's Delights to provide healthy packed meals for the children at KidStarters. We can tell people that the children are getting traditional home-cooked meals from one of Singapore's top chefs! And it would be wonderful advertising for you, because all the children's parents will want to come here and try for themselves the meals that their children are getting in school.'

'But if their children don't like my food then how? They will all run away from my restaurant! Anyway it wouldn't be home-cooked food. Nowadays I hardly ever have time to cook at home unless I am having guests. And even then I will often prepare the dishes here in the restaurant and bring home.'

'But Aunty Lee's Delights is a home-cooking restaurant.' Jonny's patient, polite veneer was back, at least on his face and voice. His index fingers were drumming impatiently on the tabletop. 'So the food can be prepared here and we can still call it home cooking.'

'I thought you might like something to drink.' Cherril put two glasses of homemade barley on the table. 'Can I get you anything else?'

Cherril had been trying to get Aunty Lee to think about expanding the business for some time, and Aunty Lee suspected she had been listening with more attention to Jonny's proposal than Aunty Lee had.

'It's a good idea to think about catering to Mark's baby's school. A lot of grandparents are babysitting these days. They can come here for children's meal packets too. Some people will do anything for their grandchildren!'

Jonny Ho looked at Cherril with new attention, clearly appreciating the grandparent angle but not yet sure if she was an ally or competitor.

'I've been trying to tell Aunty Lee that she should think about franchising,' Cherril continued, 'then we can get into the supermarkets, and we won't be limited by how many people we can seat. Here, even if you want to come and buy takeaway the parking is a headache, and it's not convenient for people without cars.'

'Good points. Your partner knows what she's talking about. I did research on you, you know … '

He must have seen the Wikipedia article that someone had put up, Aunty Lee thought. Selina had made a big fuss about the 'invasion of privacy' but Aunty Lee suspected that was only because she hadn't been mentioned. Mark and Mathilda, who did appear in the article, had been amused.

'You are not using your full potential. Right now you have a good product; you have a good name. Everybody here knows Aunty Lee's Amazing Achar and Aunty Lee's Shiok Sambal. Things like that are not going to last, you know. You must capitalize and cash out now while you can!'

Cherril nodded. She pulled out a chair and sat without being invited. Of course Cherril thought it was a good idea ... it was what she had been trying to talk Aunty Lee into since she became her business partner.

'If this works out, we can get other schools on board and make lunch boxes to sell in supermarkets.'

'But first of all we have to find you a new location. Here, no matter how good your food is, you will always be a small shop in a housing estate. You should be in District 9!'

District 9 included Orchard Road and was part of Singapore's key shopping belt which meant property rental there was the among the most expensive in Singapore. But Aunty Lee knew that price was not the same thing as value, and the value of her small shop was precisely the housing estate it was located in. Where else could she have a shop within walking distance of home? (Something that had become very important if Nina was no longer going to be around to drive her.) She looked at Cherril, who also lived in Binjai Park. But Cherril had a dreamy glow in her eyes that suggested she saw an Orchard Road location very differently ... Aunty Lee sighed. She could remember her own girlish longing for big city excitement. Now she missed life in the *kampong* days when you knew everyone in your village and everything you could need was within walking distance. And what about Cherril's mother-in-law? Anne Peters often dropped into the café and was ready to help whenever an extra pair of hands was needed. She would not be able to do that if the shop moved to Orchard Road.

Though, of course, it was entirely possible Cherril didn't mind putting a little distance between them, no matter how well they got along.

'Hey, Rosie!' Aunty Lee was as startled as if she had been slapped. Jonny Ho had reached across and rapped the table in front of her. 'Careful ah, at your age too much daydreaming – people think you got Alzheimer's!' He laughed loudly to show he was joking.

If Aunty Lee had not been so intrigued by the man, she would have found him offensive.

Cherril asked how the renovations at the school were going and when Nina would be coming back. Though Cherril had agreed they could manage very well without Nina, it could not be denied that Nina's absence was felt. Pots simmering on the stoves were no longer automatically skimmed and stirred. The dishwasher was not automatically filled and emptied, and glasses were not automatically dried and polished with glass cloths. Of course, they had staff who could be told to do all these things, but suddenly it felt as though they were giving instructions all the time.

And it was worse when deliveries arrived, because it had always been Nina who went through the orders, since she was almost as good as Aunty Lee at sussing out the quality and weight of ingredients and dry goods. And, unlike Aunty Lee, she didn't get distracted by organic coconut oil samples or the problems the deliveryman was having with his haemorrhoids.

'Renovations are coming along slowly. But we had to take some time off because your son and his wife wanted us to go and look at some renovations for their house, with the new baby coming.'

'You're handling the renovations?'

'I have contacts in all kinds of businesses so I can arrange for them very cheap, much cheaper than going to some company they don't know. If you want, I can get someone to makeover this place; give you a more up-to-date look. Plus, if you want I can arrange a new maid for you – also very cheap.'

'Then why didn't you go and arrange a maid for Beth? For your KidStarkers school?'

'Beth complained to you?' Jonny's sudden suspicion immedi-

ately interested Aunty Lee more than his salesman charm.

'Nobody complained. I want to know why didn't you go and arrange a cheap maid for her so that she doesn't have to come and steal my Nina!'

Jonny roared with laughter and actually punched Aunty Lee playfully on the arm. '*Wah!* You better not let Beth hear you say that! But you are right. You're good!'

'Well, why not? If your maid agency is so good?'

'My maid agency is the best,' Jonny said, 'plus the cheapest also. Plus, growing fastest. You should consider becoming investor and let us grow your money for you!'

'How can I?' Aunty Lee said inviting disbelief. 'My money is all invested by Cognate Finance already.' Cognate Finance was a Singapore institution. Aunty Lee's late husband had always said: 'When Cognate crashes, Singapore will crash. And if Singapore crashes no point worrying', so all their money had been invested by Cognate. They might not make the mega profits Jonny Ho described, but Aunty Lee trusted them not to lose what money she had.

Jonny took up the invitation to show (yet again) his entrepreneurial brilliance. 'I ask you, what is the biggest expense of having a maid here? The levy is $265 per month. Security bond with MOM: $5000-$7000 depending on the nationality of the helper. And say a Recommended Salary of $450 per month.'

Aunty Lee waited, not seeing the relevance.

'But if you forget about all the levy and bond and recommended nonsense, say you pay the maid $250 a month – $250 a month, that's all! And the women want to come because that is still much more than they can earn back home. So they come in by applying for tourist visas or they come in via a third country. The problem with these maids is they only want to make money; they don't know how to work. They are stupid and dirty and full of lies. But if employers need them enough they will close one eye and try to train them enough to take care of the kids and the old folks. But the bottom line is, they come here for the

money. And no matter how much money you pay them, it will not be enough, and they will come up with all kinds of tricks.'

Of course, Aunty Lee was aware that some people felt this way about their foreign domestic helpers ... but most at least pretended to see them as human beings. 'If you treat them well ... ' she started.

'Oh I know. You are one of those that likes to pamper your maid, and give her benefits like teaching her how to cook and advancing her pay so that she can send money home to her family, right? Well, I tell you, you are being conned. You think she will stop when she has got enough? No way. Next thing you know she will be asking you for more money because her father has cancer or her mother needs operation: some stupid excuse!

'But I can see you are a good trainer. So here's the deal. You take the maids and train them for me ... no security bond, no extra levy, no MOM snooping around. You pay $250 a month, big discount, right? You can save up to buy more handbags; I know you Tai-Tais like designer handbags. In return you pass them on to me for further training once they can cook, can operate washing machines, can understand basic instructions. I can even let you have two maids at a time. Good deal, right?'

Through Aunty Lee's indignation she was aware that Jonny Ho still had not answered the question of why he had not supplied Beth with a domestic helper when he had this (illegal) supply of cheap labour. Even Cherril was put off; though, only someone who knew her as well as Aunty Lee did would have noticed the tightened (still smiling) lips and narrowed eyes. But before either of them could answer him there were three interruptions: Xuyie, who was hardworking but inexperienced, wanted to know what to do with the two basins of cooked potatoes taking up space in the chiller, Avon wanted to know what to tell a caller asking whether Aunty Lee's Fish Head Curry was nut and gluten free, and a strange man rushed into the café and headed straight for Jonny Ho, shouting: 'You lousy cowardly cheater! You cannot

keep hiding from me! You're going to face me and admit what you did whether you like it or not!'

Jonny Ho stood and pushed his chair between him and the newcomer, glancing around for support. But Aunty Lee was more interested in the slightly bald, slightly chubby man who was panting as he glared at Jonny. He looked about the same age and same height but, in contrast to Jonny's careful professional outfit, the newcomer was wearing an old striped polo shirt and baggy khaki shorts ... and open-toed sandals instead of pointed Italian leather shoes. Right now his face was red with heat and rage, and sweat was beading on the shining crown of his head but Aunty Lee thought she recognized him.

'Fabby? Is that you? You are Fabian Loo, right? Little flabby Fabby?'

Taken aback, the man switched his glare over to her. 'Who are you?'

'I am your Aunty Rosie; you don't remember me? I used to come over to your house when you were so small ... I would bring you *kueh bangkit* and pineapple tarts for Chinese New Year! *Alamak*, Fabby, you look so much like your father. Ken was also only in his thirties when he started losing his hair. *Wah*, he tried everything! Western treatments, Eastern treatments, coconut oil ... until finally your mother told him to just shave his head!'

Distracted, Fabian Loo ran a hand over his balding head. 'Aunty Rosie ... yes, sure I remember you. It's been a long time. Sorry to drag you into the middle of this. But I have something to settle with this rotten cheater.' It seemed to dawn on him that Aunty Lee was sitting at Jonny's table. Cherril had moved swiftly away, and Aunty Lee would be holding her mobile phone in case she needed to summon help from the police post. 'You know this guy?'

'I just met him yesterday ... at your mother's old house. Your Aunty Beth introduced us.'

'Aunt Beth told me I would find him here. Anyway, I don't want to get you involved but, in case he's trying to pull some scam on you, you should know that he swindled me and he conned my late mother. I am going to challenge my mother's will and sue the shit out of Mr Fancy Pants Jonny Ho!'

'*Aiyoh*, Fabby. Things like that you best leave to lawyers to handle; don't chase people around yourself. Lawyers love to handle this kind of thing,' Aunty Lee put her hands on Fabian's arms and looked up at him. '*Wah*, you're all grown up and so hand-some!'

It was understandable that a Singapore boy like Fabian, brought up to be respectful to his elders whatever he might think of them, found it difficult to push her away as Aunty Lee started walking him to the exit. She very much wanted to talk to the boy, but not with Jonny Ho around. And she suspected it would not be as easy to get Jonny Ho to leave.

'Come back and talk to me another time. Or come and have dinner in my house. I want to talk to you and find out how you've been doing. Did you drive here?'

'No. Where would I get a car? That guy's taken everything, even the house that my father paid for. There's no way Mum would have left the house to him. But what's the use? Nobody here cares. They all think he's so charming, so entrepreneurial. He doesn't have anything. I thought Julietta would help me talk Mum round, but even she disappeared on me. That jerk probably paid her off. Whatever he's doing it's with my mum's money that should have come to me. Nobody gives a shit what happens to me. Aunt Beth doesn't like him, but even she says just leave it, just go back to America. Well, I'm not going to go back until I find out what's going on!'

Aunty Lee looked worriedly at the café door which she had closed behind them.

'So Fabian, you will come back and have dinner with me one day? Here, I give you my card. You call and say when you want to come, and I cook for you all your father's favourite dishes. You look so much like him you will probably like the same food.'

'I don't know. I don't feel much like eating with all this going on.' But he sounded more like a sullen schoolboy than a crazed avenger.

'There's a taxi ... *hiyah*, why doesn't it come over?' Aunty Lee waved urgently at the stationary (and slightly familiar?) taxi parked a little down the road from Jonny's flashy blue car.

'The driver's probably asleep or taking a pee break,' Fabian said. Now the fight had gone out of him he looked miserable and pathetic. 'Don't worry, Aunty Rosie. I'll walk out to the main road and get a taxi there. I'm sorry, I shouldn't have come and kicked up a fuss in your café. I was just so mad at Jonny Ho. And he's been avoiding me. He won't give me the key to the house, says they are converting it into a playschool and there's nowhere for me to stay there. That's the house I grew up in, and he's just making plans and changing things and ... look, even if he hasn't done anything wrong is that any way to behave? After all, if he married my mum he's officially my stepfather, right? Shouldn't he take some kind of responsibility for me?'

'He wouldn't let you stay in Patty's house? Who can like that!'

Fabian looked embarrassed. 'I went straight to the house when I got back. Actually, I only came back because Mum's lawyer contacted me about her new will: the one that they hadn't seen. So when I saw him I was naturally a bit upset, and this was after a travelling all the way back from the States and how many time zones worth of jet lag, and so maybe I shouted at him a bit and threw some things, and Aunt Beth was there and she got a bit scared and started crying. So Jonny made it quite clear he doesn't want me around there. Anyway I've been trying to get him to come see Mum's lawyer with me but he just ignores me.'

Fabian didn't look jet-lagged to Aunty Lee so much as a frustrated man with a grudge. Had Jonny made Julietta disappear, or had Fabian said something that made her run away? What could Flabby Fabby have done to make his own mother write him out of her will?

CHAPTER NINE

Aunty Lee Gets Involved

When Aunty Lee returned to the café she found Jonny chuffed and triumphant. Clearly he considered Fabian's ejection a triumph for himself. Cherril on the other hand was sullen ... no, not just sullen but angry ... beneath a token veneer of courtesy but Jonny was too full of himself to notice. Aunty Lee wondered what Jonny could have said or done in the short time she was outside.

To make things more complicated, Mr and Mrs Guang came in just then. They smiled and bowed to Aunty Lee, then ordered a tea each and sat.

Aunty Lee liked having people in the café because it brought good energy. And she was glad the old couple were trying to be neighbourly. Both she and Cherril tried to chat or suggest food they might try, but the Guangs seemed happy to sit quietly.

'For the free air con,' Cherril guessed.

'So, are we ready to talk arrangements?' Jonny sat, knees spread wide, and grinned at Aunty Lee with aggressive charm. Because Aunty Lee had removed Fabian (son of her old friend) rather than him (husband of that old friend) Jonny clearly thought he had her favour. He clearly did not know nobody works charm like a Peranakan Aunty. Unlike many other women who lose their charms as they grow older and wider, Peranakan Aunties become more powerful.

'What arrangements?'

'We should not waste time. Time is money, you know. I want to start helping you immediately. I also have contacts in the construction business and, just for you, I can arrange for you to get a special deal to makeover both your house and restaurant.'

'There's nothing wrong with my house, *what*.'

'But when was the last time you had a renovation?'

'I got to wait until Nina gets back,' Aunty Lee said firmly. 'Once Beth gets back her Julietta, Nina will come back here and—'

Jonny shook his head, laughing at her. 'No way Julietta is coming back. What I mean is, no way she will get back the job if she does. No fear. She had her chance and she blew it. No second chance for losers. Even if she comes back it will make no difference!'

'If she comes back we will know why she ran away. That might make all the difference,' Aunty Lee said firmly, 'and Nina is only helping Beth out until you get a replacement.'

'Your Nina may not want to come back here you know. She may want to run away from you and that policeman that is harassing her.'

Aunty Lee stared at him. She could not believe Nina had said any such thing to a stranger … it must have been that Silly-Nah. Silly must have told Beth or Jonny what she had overheard in the café when Nina said she was tired of being hounded about Salim. But it was Aunty Lee that had been doing the hounding, not Salim. Aunty Lee suddenly felt hugely irritated with Nina. This was the thanks she got for trying to get her to live happily ever after!

Jonny's mobile rang just then and he (most rudely) glanced at the number and answered in Mandarin, turning away without excusing himself.

Aunty Lee looked out of the window and saw the mysterious taxi she had seen lurking just up the road when she sent Fabian off. It was just the distraction she needed from Nina's ingratitude and Jonny's rudeness.

'I talk to you another time.' Aunty Lee grabbed her handbag and trot-shuffled out of the café.

Before the taxi driver knew what was happening, she had pulled open the door and hopped into the back seat despite the driver's loud objections.

'You are the same taxi driver that was at Jalan Kakatua yesterday, right? Outside that children's school?' Aunty Lee said breathlessly as she hurriedly arranged her handbag and herself and slammed the door.

The driver twisted around in his seat to look at her in disbelief. 'Aunty, you deaf, is it? I told you, Not For Hire, understand or not?'

'*Hiyah*! Why do they make seatbelts so tight?' Aunty Lee complained. 'And why make it so hard to stick it in underneath you? They should make them with Velcro. Just two flaps of Velcro, left and right over on top. So much easier, right?'

'Hey, Aunty, I said I'm not taking passengers.'

'Your "Hired" sign is not up. There's nobody in your car. You must drive me, otherwise I will call your company and report you for not picking up an old woman!' Aunty Lee would never have done that, of course. She disliked talking on the phone, especially to strangers, because she could not see their reactions.

'I'm waiting for somebody.'

'Then why your engine is on but your call sign is not up?'

'Why so urgent, Aunty? Got to go hospital have baby, is it?'

Looking out of the back window, Aunty Lee saw Jonny Ho, complete with plastic smile, start walking towards the taxi.

'*Alamak*,' she said.

The driver glanced in the direction of the café then suddenly the car was in gear and pulling away fast, the driver barely checking for oncoming traffic. Fortunately for him and Aunty Lee they didn't hit anything.

'Aunty? So, where are you heading?'

'Bring me to Jalan Kakatua.'

'What? Why?' The man's immediate attention and suspicion were obvious.

'My maid is working there temporarily. I want to talk to her: 221 Jalan Kakatua.'

'If your maid is working there, no way that dragon boss will let you talk to her.'

'Just drive in that direction, okay?' Aunty Lee said vaguely, turning to look out of the rear window. Jonny's fancy car could catch up with a taxi without problem but she doubted he would bother.

'Hey, I can understand you wanting to get away from that guy but I got to earn back my rental and diesel, okay. What about if I drop you around here? You can take another taxi there.'

Aunty Lee dug into her purse which (fortunately) had cash in it. 'Where you picked me up is my café. I got to go back there, just not yet. You just want to go back and follow that Jonny Ho again, right? Here … drive around for fifty dollars. Or you can park somewhere. I want to talk to you.' Nina could wait. After all, Aunty Lee knew where she was and, at the very worst, she could always send Salim to rescue her from KidStarters.

Even the back of the driver's neck looked suspicious. 'Look, I can use fifty dollars. Who cannot, right? But I don't do any funny business.'

'You weren't waiting for passengers.' As the taxi slowed down by the side of the road Aunty Lee spoke quickly to counter the possibility of being ejected. 'You were just parking there outside my shop waiting. And just now you didn't drive because I told you to, you were driving to get away from that man who followed me out; you didn't want him to see you. So you better tell me who you are or I am going back to tell him some taxi driver is following him!'

The taxi speeded up and pulled back into the flow of traffic. It belatedly occurred to Aunty Lee that hijacking and threatening a taxi driver she knew nothing about might not have been the smartest thing to do.

'What's your name?' The man did not answer. Aunty Lee pushed forward between the front seats and squinted at the identification notice displayed. 'Seetoh Ying Ping ... Mr Seetoh I want to talk to you, and I need you to pay attention so find somewhere to park.'

'Aunty, look, I don't want any trouble, *lah*. Let me just drop you off. Or I bring you back to where I pick you up, okay? And you better sit properly and put on seatbelt. Taxi drivers are fined if caught carrying unbelted passengers, and I got enough problems without *kenah* fined, okay.'

Aunty Lee started the struggle with the seatbelt again. She did not like wearing seatbelts, but she did not want to get the man into any more trouble before learning what trouble he was already in.

'Mr Seetoh, why were you following Jonny Ho?'

Horns blared as the driver's head jerked round to look at Aunty Lee, and the taxi swerved into the path of a pick-up with a (fortunately) more alert driver.

'Park first then we talk.' Aunty Lee settled back and tugged to loosen her seatbelt which had snapped against her.

'Guys like that Jonny Ho are troublemakers,' Seetoh said. 'PRCs all like that, come here to *laowah* only. Think that just because they got money they are so big shot can treat us all like shit.'

Seetoh drove them to a small parking bay along the park connector jogging route. Since the latest drive to get Singaporeans exercising, free parking could be found near most parks. Park benches could also be found and they settled on one, watching maids walking dogs and pushing prams and wheelchairs pass by. Aunty Lee could not help thinking that this would be a good place to take a grandchild walking some future day, but resolutely pulled her mind back to the present.

'But why were you following Jonny Ho?'

'I never said I follow that bastard, *what*.'

'Too late for that. Look, why not just tell me? We can exchange info.' Aunty Lee put on her best wheedling harmless family friend look. 'My friend is going to work for him. I just want to watch out for her. If you know anything about him or about his play-school, you must tell me so that I can warn her.'

Seetoh did not answer. He was younger than Aunty Lee thought, going by the back of his head, probably in his early to mid-thirties. He had a bespectacled, boyish round face with very black hair and looked as though he had been miserable and desperate for so long that he had come to accept it as his natural state. He was very properly dressed in a dark dress shirt and khaki pants that had probably been ironed when he put them on, but he looked as though that had been quite some time ago. And the man looked as worn out as his clothes. And to Aunty Lee's sharp nose, he smelled hungry.

'When was the last time you ate something?' Aunty Lee asked.

'What?'

'Drive me back to where you picked me up,' Aunty Lee said. 'You can park in front, also free. I will get you something to eat.'

'Look, first you tell me to drive away from there, then you tell me to find somewhere and park. Now you want me to drive you back ... crazy *lah*, you.'

'I had to get away from that man in my shop, but he will have left by now. And I wanted to take a good look at you, to see whether you can be trusted or not. I want to trust you, but I can't trust somebody who doesn't eat properly. If you cannot take care of your body how can you take care of anything else? You can keep my fifty dollars. How much would you earn following Jonny Ho around?'

'Julietta was my girlfriend, my fiancée,' Seetoh said. 'If she wouldn't run away with me she would never run away with

91

somebody else. That guy did something to her, and I am going to get him for it if it's the last thing I do!'

Some people fall in love regularly. For them the state of being hopelessly in love is more important than the hims or hers they are in love with. Often this is sensed by those hims and hers, so this kind of love often remains hopeless, suiting all involved. Aunty Lee fell in love with couples. She did not want to marry again – her late, beloved M. L. was still very much a part of her life – but she missed him. And the only way she knew of dealing with her loneliness was to fix up other people so she could enjoy their togetherness. Nina had refused her advice, but now Aunty Lee had found a new project,

'Oh dear. Tell me more about Julietta,' she said. 'How did you two meet?'

Aunty Lee would have dearly loved to get Nina's impression of Seetoh. No doubt Nina would distrust him on first sight. This was not really prejudice given Nina disliked and distrusted Singaporeans, Malaysians, expats, and the police on principle too. She had managed to get over her antipathy to Singaporeans and police for Aunty Lee and Salim. Or at least she seemed to have. But now Nina was gone and perhaps her biases had returned, strengthened.

But it was purely out of habit that she wanted Nina's opinion because, no matter what Nina thought of Seetoh, Aunty Lee had already decided to trust him. This inclination was strengthened into conviction when Seetoh, after declaring he was not hungry and could not possibly eat anything, took a mouthful, then another, then finished the platter of stir fried *beehoon* (a double serving for most people) without seeming to notice. The man's worry over Julietta had been enough to put him off his food but his body appreciated the nutrition in Aunty Lee's simple good food. That was enough for Aunty Lee.

However, it might not be enough for anybody else looking for the missing foreign domestic worker, so Aunty Lee took him through his story, digging into all the tangles and unravelling loose threads till she traced them back to their source.

Seetoh had been seeing Julietta for over a year.

'Only, after eight months I found out she was married! She has two daughters, you know.'

'Still married?' Aunty Lee worried that she might unleash another round of despairing self-recrimination but Seetoh only shook his head at Aunty Lee's naïveté.

'Divorced. Or she would be divorced if she wasn't so Catholic. But the guy is not in the picture anymore. Would any real husband make his wife choose between letting her children starve and leaving them to go hundreds of miles away to earn enough money to keep them in school? Because no matter how shitty the work here is, Julietta refused to even consider leaving. Because she wanted her children to stay in school. Tell me, do you believe a woman like that would just leave her children behind and run off with some guy? No way.'

Aunty Lee read the message beneath the indignation. 'You asked her to run away with you and she refused?' And the indignation deflated. 'So now what you really can't understand is, if Julietta wouldn't run away with you, why would she go off with somebody else.'

'She wouldn't.'

Aunty Lee heard a man trying to convince himself.

'You must try my *otak*,' she said.

There were few bad situations that could not be improved by a really good charcoal grilled fish cake.

Seetoh admitted he had been outside KidStarters the previous day and had followed Jonny to Aunty Lee's Delights.

'If you were following him, you must have seen what happened the day Fabian went to the house? The day that Julietta disappeared?'

'Nah, *lah*. I only started watching him after that. Look, you don't have to tell me she is no angel. Yes, she got taken in by that guy at first. That guy is a lousy bully. He took photos of her, you know. Sexy photos. When she tried to break up with him, he said she would show them to Miss Beth and Mrs Patty. And later he forced her to have sex with him again before he would delete the photos … and she believed him. But even though he let her delete her photos from his phone, he must have made copies, because he threatened to show them to her children. And she was not the only one. He had photos of other women on his phone!'

Aunty Lee could not help wondering what Seetoh's first reaction had been. Now he was after Jonny Ho for seducing Julietta. But what if he had been angry with Julietta when she told him what happened? Had he been angry enough to do something to her?

'Don't worry. Where there's life there's hope,' Aunty Lee said, stressing 'life'.

'More like where there's money, there's hope,' Seetoh said with Singaporean pragmatism. 'I got no money, so no hope.'

'Look, I am going to find out where your Julietta went,' Aunty Lee sounded more confident than she felt, 'then you two can work it out between yourselves.'

'All I want is to know what he did with her.'

That could mean many things, Aunty Lee thought. 'You cannot force a woman to stay with you if she doesn't want to. Can you drop me off at the police post? I show you where; it's on the way out.'

Seetoh looked alarmed.

Aunty Lee thought taxi drivers assumed women only went to police stations to make complaints … about taxi drivers, among other things. 'I got a friend working there,' she explained. 'I can go and see him, and then somebody there will drive me back home.'

Meanwhile, Nina was listening to Jonny Ho telling Beth about his visit to Aunty Lee's Delights. She didn't have to eavesdrop. She might have been a cat or dog or piece of wood for all the attention they paid to her.

From the way Jonny told it, he had Aunty Lee's admiration and full support.

'Did she say when she wants me to go back?' Nina finally asked.

'She doesn't want you back,' Beth said. 'You must have talked back to her or something. She was paying you far above market rate. I told her she can train a new girl to do what you are doing for much less.'

Aunty Lee had done it for Salim, Nina thought. If Aunty Lee didn't want her back in Binjai Park it was because, like Nina, she wanted to spare Salim from accidentally bumping into her.

'If Aunty Lee doesn't want me to work for her, I will go back to Philippines,' Nina said.

'No,' Jonny Ho said. 'You are working for us now. It's about time you started doing something to earn all the money that old woman has been throwing at you.' He looked at Nina, who was wishing she had not spoken up. 'I have some very important things for you to do.'

CHAPTER TEN

Salim and Housebreaking

Inspector Salim Mawar did not know how else he could have put his case to Nina. He felt he had let her down by asking her to marry him. But before that he had felt he was letting them both down by not asking.

Why hadn't he offered to leave Singapore with her? He had a law degree; he would manage to support them somehow, at least after he had served out his bond or paid it back. Interracial marriage had never been a big issue in Singapore. Inter-religious marriage could be a bit touchier but, unless the families involved wanted an excuse to make trouble, most people found a way around it … or went to live in Australia or Canada.

Salim did not really want to leave Singapore. He knew from his time abroad that he would be able to fit in almost anywhere. But there was no other place in the world to which he felt an equal commitment. He had a stake in the survival of the tiny struggling island city. Someday he hoped to pass this on to his sons and daughters. And he longed to share this love and commitment with the woman he loved.

It would have been easier for Salim if he could have thrown himself into his work, but there were no pressing cases at the moment. This was nothing new for Singapore, of course. And even more so at the Bukit Tinggi Police Post. The only high priority case was the still unsolved string of residential break-ins including some under their jurisdiction.

The rash of burglaries had started roughly three years before. Then, after a break, four more break-ins over three weeks. The newspapers had talked about a gang of burglars flying into Singapore, and social experts had frightened the populace further by talking about the rise of 'organized crime'.

Going through all the reports, Salim suspected that at least two of the 'robberies' had been invented by homeowners jumping at the chance to get something back on their insurance policies. But he also knew it was possible that not all the break-ins had been reported. Some people preferred to suffer their loss in silence if they had things in their homes that should not have been there. All that added to the confusion, of course. But the biggest problem of all was that there was still so little to go on. All the houses targeted were free-standing bungalows, and there had been no witnesses. It would have been a lot easier to find someone who had seen something in a Housing Development Board flat, or even one of the private condominiums with security guards, and gardeners, and maids walking dogs and babies in the grounds.

It was either remarkably bad luck for the police, or good planning on the part of the burglars. Each time, the burglars had managed to strike when no one was home. Salim was certain they had some way of getting information on the homeowners, but so far no links had come up.

He looked at the notes on his computer again. It was more complicated than just waiting for any children to go to school and any adults to go to work. Houses like these had gardeners coming in on different days, full-time and part-time house-cleaners from Amahs On Wheels, and live-in maids who were in and out of the house doing the shopping or accompanying children from school and after school activities ...

The housebreaking burglars had largely faded from the newspapers and public attention but the police … and therefore Salim … knew cases were still coming up regularly. Once every two or three months, scattered in different housing estates all across the island without any apparent reason, so not enough people had put them together to make it news.

There were comments online, of course; the exaggerations and speculations growing wilder in the ether as they always did. Was it an employment agency behind it, sending out maids to spy out potential houses to break into? Were the police in on it or had they been bribed into silence? One person even accused the Buddhist sisters and the Catholic nuns living in the Canossian Convent because the modest habits they wore could conceal the tools to get them in and the loot they carried out. Salim glanced over these forums occasionally, just in case something useful showed up. That was how desperate they were for leads. But still there were no witnesses. At least, because of the criminals' good luck or good planning no one had been hurt.

He pushed his seat back. Part of him wanted to go over to the café, but there was no point.

Aunty Lee told him that Nina was away; she had gone away to help a friend. She would be gone for a week, possibly a little longer. Aunty Lee knew as well as he did that this was illegal, and also that he would not say anything. Salim should have resented the old woman for putting him in such a difficult position but he was grateful for the information. Even if Nina did not want to see or talk to him, Salim liked to know where she was, wanted to be certain she was all right. Which was why he had made Aunty Lee tell him who her friend was and where she lived.

He had looked closely at Beth Kwuan and her proposed child education centre. There was little on Beth, but her KidStarters shared an address with one of the houses broken into in the original rash of burglaries. The house break-in had been reported by a Mr and Mrs Jonny Ho. A little more time online informed him that the late Mrs Jonny Ho née Patricia Kwuan had been Beth

Kwuan's sister. And Jonny Ho, the bereaved husband, was Beth's partner in the child education business. Some families were close, Salim supposed, though he could not imagine his mother going into business with any of his late father's brothers. And it probably made sense to try to turn a house into a paying business. He turned back to the original report. The Hos had been out to dinner with their maid when the break-in occurred. They had returned a little after 11 p.m. to find the back door had been removed from its hinges and said the thieves had taken cash, the small house safe containing all Mrs Ho's jewellery, and all the smartphones, laptops, and electronic tablets in the house. This followed the pattern of all the other burglaries except for one small detail … the Hos had only reported the break-in two weeks after it happened, after reading about a similar case in the newspapers.

'We thought there was no point reporting it right away,' Mr Jonny Ho had said in his statement. 'The burglars were clearly gone, and we were tired and wanted to get some sleep. We know the police work hard, and there was no reason to disturb them at night. Who likes to be disturbed at night, right? And then the next day we thought it was not so serious after all. What's the point? We're not going to get anything back.' Though not directly relevant this statement had clearly struck the transcriber enough to make a note of it.

Most people whose homes had been burglarized phoned the police right away, in alarm, indignation, and anger. However little faith they had in the police getting their things back they felt invaded and violated, and calling the police meant that they had handed their problem over to someone whose responsibility it was to protect them.

Curiously enough, Salim had read somewhere that the more the victims of a crime might rant and rail at the police officers who responded to a call for help (like a child raging at a parent who let it get hurt) the more likely they were to respond positively when asked their opinion of police first responders in later months. You had to trust the police to some degree before you dared to let your guard down in front of them. Then what did that say about the Hos who had come home to find they had been robbed and decided to wait a week and more before reporting the break-in?

But then, how the Hos reacted could have nothing to do with who had robbed them ... and all that had nothing to do with Nina. Nina, who was the only reason why Salim had looked up the old case, had never even met the late Mrs Patty Ho. It was the late Mrs Ho's sister, Beth Kwuan, who Nina was working for.

And despite Aunty Lee trying to blame it on her friend's temporary renovation difficulties, Salim was certain Aunty Lee had arranged this with her friend because Nina wanted to get further away from him.

Well at least Nina was still in Singapore. Inspector Salim was glad of that. He would stay away, of course, given Nina had made clear she did not want to see him around. But he was glad she was still in Singapore.

The night before, Nina would have welcomed the sight of Salim Mawar. Or of anyone other than the furious Jonny Ho hunched over on her bed. Nina was standing in the corner, holding a hairbrush in one hand and a wooden stool in the other.

'Don't try to sell me your shit. To get the kind of money that old woman is paying you, you must have been screwing her husband, right?'

Jonny wasn't even trying to keep quiet after the yell he let out when Nina woke to find him on top of her on her narrow bed and jammed her knee into his crotch.

'What's happening?' Beth demanded sharply from the doorway.

'She flirted with me and told me to come to her room after you were asleep,' Jonny Ho invented glibly. He winced as he stood up. 'She complained that you locked her in. I came to see what she had in mind, that's all.'

'He tried to rape me!' Nina cried. She thought it was obvious.

Beth eyed her with distaste. For a moment Nina hoped she was going to order her out of the house immediately.

'You are disgusting,' Beth said. 'No wonder Rosie doesn't want you back. I thought it was only because you cost so much. I suppose you threatened to tell people you were sleeping with her husband. Well, that's not going to work here.'

But Nina noticed that from then on Beth took the key with her after locking Nina in at night. And whenever Jonny was in the house, Beth kept suspicious eyes on either him or Nina. Her little comments were even more cruel but at least her jealousy kept Nina safe from Jonny Ho.

CHAPTER ELEVEN

Researching Recipes

'Nina is still busy. What do you need this time?'

Aunty Lee had picked up the phone to call Nina's mobile as automatically as she turned to her helper several times a day. And when Nina's mobile did not answer, Aunty Lee called the landline at the Jalan Kakatua house.

'I think her phone is out of battery. It doesn't ring,' Aunty Lee told Beth.

'Rosie, you know that Selina is worried that you are too much under Nina's influence?'

Aunty Lee cackled in laughter. 'That Selina worries about everything! Did she tell you not to let Nina talk to me? Don't worry! Put her on the phone!'

'Selina is not the one who's worried.' Beth's voice was low and confidential over the phone. 'Look, I don't know if you know this, Nina feels that you are controlling her life too much.'

'Where got?' Aunty Lee prided herself on how much she trusted Nina. 'Let me talk to her!' She would clear this up in an instant.

'She says you are always checking up on her ... I didn't want to believe her, but you've been phoning her non-stop since she got here.'

'Not non-stop, *what*. Only a few times.' In fact Aunty Lee had not actually managed to talk to Nina since she moved to Jalan Kakatua. 'I only want to make sure that she is all right.'

'Nina is all right. Don't you believe me? While she is staying with me, I will take care of her.' With a little laugh Beth managed to imply she would make sure Nina was not bothered by old women with too much time on their hands, without quite saying it, so Aunty Lee could not protest.

'Look, Rosie,' Beth's voice dropped lower still, as though she was afraid Nina might be listening in, 'you've been good to Nina, and she doesn't want to hurt your feelings. But she feels that you are trying to her control her and make her do things she doesn't want to.'

A month ago, Aunty Lee would have laughed at this. But now Aunty Lee remembered her arguments with Nina over the past two weeks. Her arguments *at* Nina, rather, given Nina had never argued back beyond saying that she did not want to see Salim again and she did not want to talk about it. After Aunty Lee had made an appointment for Salim and Nina to talk to a relationship counsellor (which they had both refused), Nina had not talked to her for two whole days.

'Why do you want to talk to her?' Beth wanted to know when Aunty Lee phoned.

'I just want to make sure she is all right.'

'She's fine! Don't you trust me? Rosie, don't let her fool you. That Nina of yours is too smart; the smart ones are always troublemakers. You got to watch them every minute. But the stupid ones are so stupid you sometimes just want to knock their skulls together!'

Aunty Lee was sure that Nina would come round. After all, it was her future that Aunty Lee was concerned about. But perhaps it was best to leave her alone for a while. Unfortunately, she seemed to be getting along with Beth Kwuan and unlikely to ask to be sent back to Binjai Park.

* * *

103

Life and work went on in Aunty Lee's Delights. Without Nina around, Aunty Lee depended more on Cherril, Avon, and Xuyie and, though there were mistakes and omissions, they learned faster in two weeks than they had in the previous six months. Much busier by day and more tired by night, the days sped past for Aunty Lee.

She made new friends too. The Guangs had come by to try Aunty Lee's *laksa* and loved it. They said they came from Sichuan and it reminded them of their own hot and sour soup.

'Your *assam laksa* is good. Put pig blood, taste better!' Mr Guang earnestly advised. He was a retired professor, and Mrs Guang was an artist and calligrapher.

Aunty Lee obliged, presenting them a version of 'hot sour *laksa* soup' concocted by adding lily buds and wood ear fungus to the rice noodles in a stock flavoured with pork blood; Mr Guang had started climbing into the drain by his house to harvest bunches of *kesum* leaves for her.

'Cut on top now, more grow,' he explained when he brought them over to the shop.

Cherril liked the old couple too, though she did not understand how Aunty Lee had this effect on some people. They seemed to fall a little in love with her once she fed them.

'We do t'ai chi in the garden in the morning. Very gentle. Very good for old people. You come and learn Yang style t'ai chi, 108 forms.' Mrs Guang had invited Aunty Lee to join them. 'Then you can collect weeds to cook after. Collect in the early morning is good, better, best!'

'You come and learn to do push hands!' Mr Guang had said. 'Self-defence!'

Perhaps, Aunty Lee thought, and perhaps she might even learn some Mandarin herself from the Guangs.

Mr Guang had been in the shop one day when Jonny Ho dropped in to pick up a takeaway.

'Samples,' he said to Avon and Xuyie, not offering to pay for his food. Jonny spoke to them in rapid Mandarin, saying something that made Avon giggle and pout flirtatiously and Xuyie look worried.

'What did he say?' Aunty Lee had asked Mr Guang.

'Bad language.'

'You mean swear words?'

It had taken a moment for Mr Guang to translate question and answer in his head, then he said: 'No. The man does not speak good Standard Mandarin. It is like your Singlish here. And a good man does not say such things to young girls, about finding love and money while they are young and beautiful.'

To Aunty Lee's surprise, Cherril snorted.

'What?'

'Nothing.'

With all this going on, Aunty Lee barely had time to worry about Nina. She had decided not to phone Beth's house again until she heard from Nina. According to Selina there was still no sign of Julietta, and Beth was finding Nina very helpful. Of course Nina was very helpful, Aunty Lee thought crossly, that was why she wanted her back as soon as possible! And if Julietta didn't come back, was Nina going to stay at Beth's place indefinitely? Aunty Lee was working so hard to quash her dislike of Beth that she didn't even allow herself to indulge in her normal delicious gossipy speculations about the woman. Beth was a mission school girl, like herself and Patty and Helen. Therefore, Beth could be trusted.

Selina seemed to think that once the renovations were completed, and KidStarters launched, things would settle into a routine and Beth would return Nina … if Nina wanted to come.

'She seems very happy there! You better not say anything to that policeman always snooping around her. Don't make more trouble for yourself!' she said, as though forgetting she was the one who had threatened to expose Nina's illegal hours at the café. Selina didn't think it necessary to mention she had not seen Nina herself.

All this would be resolved once Julietta reappeared. Aunty Lee decided she had to find Julietta. It was not that she could not do without Nina ... she had already succeeded in proving that. She wanted her friend and companion back. And she also missed Salim, who had stopped dropping in at the café.

It was so frustrating, given Salim could have helped her find out if Julietta had left the island but she wasn't allowed to tell him the woman was missing. And she was sure Nina could have helped her trace Julietta by now, but Nina wasn't around to talk to other helpers and their contacts. Beth might appreciate Nina as a good worker, but Aunty Lee was sure Nina's special talents were wasted on her.

And there was something else Aunty Lee wanted to look into. If Mark and Selina were investing money in KidStarters, Aunty Lee felt duty-bound to find out more about it. She had only vague memories of Elizabeth Kwuan as a dull, officious school prefect not much different from the dull, officious woman she had grown into. In the old days it seemed Beth Kwuan had always been following her sister and Patty's friends around, looking for the chance to report misbehaviour to parents or school authorities. Now it seemed she was doing the same to Patty's young husband. Aunty Lee felt sorry for Jonny Ho.

Ordinarily, Aunty Lee would simply have asked Nina to go online and get hold of as much information on Elizabeth Kwuan and Jonny Ho as she could. Since Nina was out of reach, she was reduced to calling old schoolmates who would have known Beth in school.

Beth didn't seem to have stayed in touch with any of the women she had been in school with. This surprised Aunty Lee, who thought Beth's schooldays would have remained the high point of her life.

'Beth was always willing to help organize reunions and meetups,' one old friend told Aunty Lee. 'But she always had to run things and boss people around. Most of us just wanted to meet up for drinks and have fun. After she tried to set up a subscription for cultural discussions most of us just stopped going.'

The people Aunty Lee spoke to at Beth's church and the schools where she had taught said much the same thing: 'She volunteered on a lot of committees and things. But she could be difficult if things weren't done her way. And she was always claiming that people had personal vendettas against her.'

'Did they?'

'I doubt it. They just didn't like doing things with her.'

Hearing all this made Aunty Lee feel guilty. She and her friends had avoided Beth Kwuan in much the same way in school and after school.

Patty Kwuan had also liked having things done her way. The difference was that Patty had been beautiful, confident, and charming. Aunty Lee felt sorry for Beth. What silly shallow little girls they had been!

'Maybe if we had been nicer to Beth in the old days, she might be more easy-going now,' Aunty Lee told Helen Chan.

'No way,' Helen Chan said. 'Beth was already a fussy old woman when we were in school!'

Helen said she had called Beth as soon as she heard about Patty's death.

'I asked about helping with the funeral service. It's been a long time but I thought we could all do something. You know, for old times' sake. But Beth said it was for family only because that's how Patty wanted it.'

'The funeral was over by the time I heard about it,' Aunty Lee said, thinking about the fine line between privacy and secrecy. 'Maybe her husband wasn't up to dealing with all her friends. I know M. L. used to run away when we all got together.' Her late husband had said – affectionately – that Aunty Lee and her girlfriends cackled together like geese. 'How did he seem that time when you met him at your house? Most of the girls were there, right?'

'The beautiful Jonny? He was the only husband there that night but he didn't seem to have any problem dealing with the old girls at my place. We were talking about retirement plans. The commune, you know?'

'Still?' Over the years it had ranged from a row of terraced houses near Gleneagles Hospital, a gated community in Johore, and beachfront villas in Thailand. 'Why was he the only hubby there?'

'It was a girls' night out. Patty just brought him to introduce him all round. I think he was supposed to come back and pick her up later, but he ended up staying. It was just fun, you know. Jonny Ho was way too young to be thinking about such things, at least not with us old fogeys, but he was saying how we ought to get people to come in and give us massage therapy … it was Patty who didn't seem to want him to talk about it. I thought it was a bit funny, but Peng said it probably reminded her of their age difference.'

'Beth Kwuan didn't join you, did she?' Aunty Lee asked, since Beth did not seem to have kept in touch with the girls from her own year in school.

'No, *lah*! Why should she?'

'Why not? She was staying with Patty and Jonny Ho at the time, right. Why didn't you invite her with them?'

'That one walks into a room and everybody inside gets depressed.'

Till now, Aunty Lee had shared Helen's view of Beth Kwuan – and worse. But now Aunty Lee was afraid that some of her resentment came from jealousy. Nina had agreed to work for Beth. Now Nina didn't want to talk to her, probably because she didn't want to hear more Salim. That was so unfair, Aunty Lee thought. But it was Nina who was being unfair. Aunty Lee struggled not to make it another reason for not liking Beth Kwuan. Beth Kwuan was like cold banana fritters, Aunty Lee thought. They might look just as crispy as when they were freshly lifted out of hot oil, but the damp stains on the paper underneath them warned you off. Beth Kwuan was like that paper, always there in the background absorbing and revealing people's weaknesses … no, stop. Aunty Lee resolutely pulled her thoughts back. The trouble was, it was so easy to think bad things about Beth.

'Anyway, Patty was kicking her out,' Helen said with relish.

'What?' Aunty Lee had missed the first part of the story.

'Well, Beth only moved in with Patty after Ken died because she didn't want Patty to be alone in the house. Fabian never even offered to come back to Singapore. Patty thought it was just temporary but, even though she had a live-in helper, Beth wouldn't leave. She said Patty needed her to manage the helper. You know, I always wondered if Patty got married again so fast so that Beth would leave. But it didn't work. Finally, she told Beth that Fabian was coming back to meet Jonny and she needed his room back. Actually I think Fabian just wanted to make sure Jonny didn't get all his mum's money! It was Fabian's room Beth was staying in. Luckily Beth hadn't managed to sell or rent out her own flat yet. But then Patty got sick and died before Beth moved out.'

'And Beth is still at the house,' Aunty Lee said. Patty would never have let her beautiful home be turned into an early education centre. She reminded herself that Patty was dead and noisy children running around couldn't hurt her.

She had to get Fabian's side of the story, Aunty Lee decided. Helen's mention of money had made her wonder about the financial side of things. She knew her investment bank had also handled the late Patty Kwuan-Loo's investments. And looking into money might distract her from sending nasty thoughts in Beth's direction till Nina returned to her senses and to Binjai Park.

Mr Darren Sim, the investment manager at Cognate Finance who Aunty Lee had inherited from her late husband, told her he could not discuss anyone else's accounts. Aunty Lee was prepared for this. After all, she would not want him discussing her investments with any of her nosy friends.

'I know, *lah*. I don't care about how much money she got. But I am interested in an investment that Patty's sister told me about. Her sister is starting this early education school. She said that Patty also invested. I want to know whether that is true or not.' For authenticity she repeated what Jonny Ho had told her about his investments on Patty's behalf. 'If my friend put money there, then it should be safe for me also.'

The banker's alarm came loud and down the line: 'Wait – Mrs Lee – No, please don't. I strongly advise you not to make any investments without letting me look them over first.'

'Patty's husband said that if I go through you and the bank you all will charge me so much processing fees – profit all disappear.'

'Mrs Lee, it's not about profits, it's about risk – risk to your capital.'

'Exactly.' Aunty Lee was pleased. She was fond of the young man who was delivering the precise script she expected. 'That's why I ask you to check for me how risky is this guy.'

A brief silence followed. Mr Sim was clearly debating the risk of this flighty old lady putting all her money into some doubtful get-rich-quick con.

'I know Patricia Kwuan-Loo's personal banker. I'll talk to her and see what she says.'

Soon after, Aunty Lee got a call from the agent's assistant saying that, while they couldn't disclose details of Patty's investments, there was nothing to worry about there. It was not much information, but so much more than Aunty Lee had expected that she worried a little about trusting her money to Darren Sim.

CHAPTER TWELVE

Cognate

Using the excuse of a missing granite mortar to break her resolution not to call, Aunty Lee finally managed to get Beth Kwuan to answer her landline. Beth told her Nina was fine but could not talk on the phone.

'I will give her your message. I don't believe in letting helpers use the phone. You only create bad habits and make more trouble for yourself. Mobile phones even worse. They can sneak away and make calls without you knowing! That is how they go and find boyfriends and get pregnant, and next thing you know you *kenah* forfeit your bond plus your medical deposit also! I'm only trying to watch out for you. It's your money involved here. A lot of money, okay!'

The compulsory medical and personal accident insurance for domestic helpers was a sore point for many employers so Aunty Lee could understand Beth's caution. But she had long ago stopped thinking of Nina as a pregnancy or flight risk.

'Nina already has a mobile phone. I'm just worried why it's not working. I tried to phone her but no answer.'

'I'm keeping her phone locked up while she is working here. It's you I'm watching out for you, you know, Rosie. You are too trusting!'

For once Aunty Lee was at a loss. She could decide what was best for Nina when Nina was under her own roof, but she could not tell Beth what to do. And taking away a phone could not be considered maid abuse, could it? Beth, like Aunty Lee, had grown up in an era before mobile phones. Aunty Lee could remember her parents going to use the ten-cent phone in the grocer's shop when they wanted to talk to relatives up in Malaysia.

'I need to talk to Nina. I want to ask her something.'

'What do you want to ask her?'

'Just where she stored something. My big mortar – the *batu lesung*. I need to use it and I can't find it.'

That was true. In fact, not being able to ask Nina where something was was one of the things Aunty Lee missed most. It was not that Nina knew where everything was, or that Aunty Lee expected her to solve every problem. But somehow the act of asking aloud and then responding to Nina's calm questions: 'When did you last use it?' 'What do you want to cook with 50 kg of unshelled ground nuts even if they are on sale cheap?' helped Aunty Lee solve her own problems. It was not the same asking Cherril things. Cherril seemed to think Aunty Lee wanted her to come up with solutions, whereas Aunty Lee only needed to discuss her problems out loud.

She could have talked to M. L.'s photo portraits, of course. But Aunty Lee usually only told good things to her dead husband's photos. That way she could believe that his warm eyes and serene smile were on her and happy for her. She would not go to those precious photos with her everyday problems and frustrations, and that was why she missed Nina so much.

'What?'

'My big granite mortar and pestle. The one I use to pound peanuts to make *kueh*. I want to know where she keeps it.'

'Nina is busy right now,' Beth said after a pause. 'I will ask her and phone you back.'

Aunty Lee decided Nina had told Beth to tell her that because she didn't want to talk to her. Was Nina trying to show Beth what an ideal employee she was? For years Nina had tried to convince Aunty Lee that the phone didn't have to be answered every time it rang … if it was anything important, people would leave a message. But Aunty Lee, who had never learned to retrieve phone messages without Nina's help, could not continue with anything, even something as time crucial as deep frying, with a phone ringing in the vicinity. And she would not allow Nina to turn off the ringer, just in case it was Mathilda phoning from England with an emergency. Was Nina trying to show her that once away from Binjai Park she had stopped answering phones?

'No need,' Aunty Lee said. The impulse to hear Nina's voice had passed. Cherril would pulverize the peanuts in the multipurpose blender as she did everything else. Aunty Lee was feeling cross with herself for going back on her decision not to phone Nina till Nina called her.

'How is the renovation work going? Still no sign of Julietta? Don't you think it's time that you reported her to the agency for running away?'

Beth interrupted with: 'Wait, Jonny wants to talk to you.'

There was a silence on the phone as Aunty Lee wondered whether she had gone too far. She wasn't worried about Nina but she did not understand why Nina should be refusing to talk to her. Also, what Beth had said about taking away Nina's phone had sunk in. It was true that Aunty Lee had lived most of her youth without a phone and survived, but Nina had used her smartphone to source ingredients, check suppliers, double-check goods prices, and look up locations and people for Aunty Lee. It was almost an extension of her.

'Rosie, I have been wanting to talk to you. There is someone who wants to meet you. I will come and pick you up from your house in thirty minutes' time,' Jonny Ho said.

'I'm not at the house! I'm at my shop!' Aunty Lee said quickly.

'I will come and pick you up from your shop in thirty minutes' time.'

'Maybe he wants to kidnap you and hold you for ransom,' Cherril said when Aunty Lee told her who she was going out with. 'Thanks a lot for running away that day he came. I thought he was going to stick around until you agreed to let him take over this place, but as soon as he saw you weren't coming back he just turned and left. Didn't even offer to pay for the drink.'

Aunty Lee remembered how interested Cherril had been in Jonny Ho's plans. 'What did Jonny Ho do to make you angry with him? I know there must be something, because at first you two were so happy talking about this plan, that plan, but now when you hear his name you put on your frozen face.'

'It's nothing. He asked me about my surname: whether I was married to an Indian man or English man.'

'Why … ?' Aunty was stopped by the expression on her partner's face.

'Why did he ask? Or why did I find it offensive?'

'Both. More the second one because I think the reason he asked is because he wanted to know. If I don't know Mycroft's family I also would ask you, *what.*'

Fortunately, this made Cherril laugh. Her face relaxed. 'You're different. Oh I don't know. Maybe I overreacted. I suppose because some people seem to think it's a step up to have a Caucasian husband and a step down to have an Indian one, and I could tell Jonny Ho is one of those. I just pretended not to hear him. I think he saw I minded because he tried to make it better by telling me that he was surprised because I was very pretty and should have no problem finding a Chinese husband. Of course that made it worse. Then later he said I was lucky to have such fair skin; unless my husband was very dark we could still have cute babies.'

'*Alamak!*'

'That's what he told me. "I can help you, you know. You don't have to stay with the black-skin husband. Even if you don't like me, I have many Chinese friends, I can find you a good man".'

Aunty Lee snorted. 'Maybe he wants to make cute babies with you. You should have offered to sell him skin-whitening products.'

'He probably manufactures the stuff. Can you believe how many businesses he's involved in? What does he want to see you about, anyway?'

It was Thursday afternoon after the lunch rush. The part-time helpers had gone off till it was time to make and pack the dinner takeaway orders. Cherril could cope with any teatime guests on her own. Arranging for people to order takeaway dinners online and by phone had been one of Cherril's better ideas. It saved a lot of time because people were forced to decide on what they wanted ahead of time instead of asking questions about every ingredient in every dish till something sparked their appetite. Since the café was close to several large housing estates and condominiums, they could still close their doors at 8 p.m. on most days. This allowed most people to collect 'home cooked' dinners on their way home; it wouldn't have been possible if they served dinners on the premises. Nina and Mark had set up the automated phone order system, and there were several promising buzzes that Aunty Lee forced herself not to leap up to process.

Cherril had finally sat down to her own lunch and would go through the orders after. Aunty Lee was seldom hungry after a morning of sampling and taste testing sauces and dishes but Cherril had made herself a peanut butter sandwich, 'just for a change,' she had said when she saw Aunty Lee looking at it. Aunty Lee understood perfectly. Sometimes you needed something just a little different and disconcerting to remind you not to take for granted the things that you had chosen to keep close to you in daily life.

That was what Aunty Lee thought of Jonny Ho.

Jonny Ho was very interesting indeed, even apart from his soap opera-star good looks. Aunty Lee thought she could see a little of what Patty had found so attractive in the man. His English was far too proper to have been picked up naturally, at least in Singapore, but at least he could be easily understood. Maybe he could get a job as a MediaCorp actor if his many businesses didn't work out. MediaCorp was Singapore's main commercial media company, turning out plots that reminded Aunty Lee of Jonny Ho's more flamboyant ideas. It was his dynamic energy that was his most attractive point. Even if you did not like what people were doing, the mere fact of their doing something while others stood by drew your attention to them.

The blare of a car horn sounded just then.

'I suppose I'm going to find out,' Aunty Lee said. 'I'm just going to the toilet first. Go and tell him I'm coming so that he doesn't blare his horn anymore. Don't let me forget my handbag. Tell him I'll be out in a minute!'

Stationing herself by the entrance with Aunty Lee's large handbag, Cherril saw Jonny Ho's blue Subaru idling on the feeder road in front the café. He touched his horn again on seeing her instead of Aunty Lee, and she decided to let him wait. The loud horn went perfectly with the loud person driving the loud car.

Cherril knew Nina would not have approved of someone summoning Aunty Lee out of the café with a car horn, even less would she have approved of Aunty Lee responding. Suddenly Cherril missed Nina very much. Nina would have told Jonny Ho off with no second thoughts. But she knew … or suspected … it was precisely because of Nina that Aunty Lee was leading Jonny Ho on. Surely she could not seriously consider working with the man!

'*Wah*, had to pack your suitcase, is it?' Jonny said when Aunty Lee approached the car, having taken her handbag from Cherril.

She could tell he meant it as a joke. The man was out to charm

116

her, which he did by throwing out flirtatious insults in the manner of adolescent boys. Some men never grew up beyond that stage. He was nervous and that gave his words an accusing edge: 'Come out for car ride also take so long. Get in, quick. We got to get going.'

'Where are we going?'

'Wait and you'll see. Do you like my car?' He revved the engine and they took off in the direction of Dunearn Road.

'Your car is designed for skinny young people with good knees, not people like me. Are we going to meet with Nina? I want to see Nina. Can you turn around and stop by my house first, to get some things for Nina?'

'Who is Nina? Oh … no, not today. Beth is still very busy and working very hard and she needs Nina to help her. Anyway Beth will get her whatever she needs.' His face darkened when Nina's name came up, so Aunty Lee pursued the matter.

'I want to pass some things to Nina. She does not have very many of her clothes with her. And she must have finished her vitamins by now. I want to pass her a new tube. Do you take Vitamin C? It is very good for you, you know. And psyllium husk also. Since we started taking psyllium husk, no more problem in the bathroom!'

But Jonny Ho continued heading towards Dunearn Road and the city rather than turning back into Binjai Park where Aunty Lee's house was.

He was an impatient driver, changing lanes left and right to get out from behind slower cars and keeping up a running commentary on how stupid the other drivers were. He kept his engine revving even when they were stopped at a red light, and the car sounded like a powerful beast dying to be unleashed. The powerful beast was frustrated along the length of Orchard Road, where there were junctions and pedestrian crossings every few hundred metres. Indeed, the whole of Singapore offered few opportunities to exercise such a car. You could beat all the other cars by taking off as soon as the light changed in your favour, but they would catch up with you at the next light.

'Do you drive up to Malaysia?' Aunty Lee wondered whether Jonny Ho was one of the daredevils that went expressway racing.

'What for? I am sounding out some business deals there, but flying is faster.'

He had business deals everywhere, and ideas for more. Jonny Ho's gusto for new ideas and projects reminded Aunty Lee of her stepson, Mark, who was also always in search of something to devote himself to. The problem with Mark was that throughout his schooldays he had always been in the top class of a top school without ever being a top student. He had been an average runner and average swimmer without ever making the school team in any sport. As a result, he had been labelled 'creative' and 'artistic' and come to think of himself as an innovator and entrepreneur. But his interest seldom went beyond coming up with ideas and talking about them. He had never learned to work hard at anything, dropping out of every challenge once the real work began.

Fortunately, or not, his wife, Selina, saw herself as sensible, practical, and organized. She had been very impressed by how well she organized and disciplined other girls during her time as Head Prefect, and so far the rest of her life had not measured up to that glowing start. Selina might have made a good CEO or army sergeant or hospital administrator, but her time in school had also conditioned her to believe that in order to be fulfilled she needed to be married to a successful man. Without her Mark Lee might have been an artistic dilettante respected for his gourmet tastes and musical talents. Thanks to his wife he was an impulsive entrepreneur who had lost a substantial amount of money over the years, because Selina, unfortunately, was not much better at managing money than her husband.

There was something about Beth Kwuan that reminded Aunty Lee of Selina. But what? Selina was married and having a baby; Beth had never married and didn't seem likely to. Selina invested all her energy into making something of her husband; Beth was following her dreams and setting up her own school. The two women couldn't have been more different, other than both having been school prefects ... and they had both kept the habit of telling other people to follow the rules they knew better than anyone else.

Jonny Ho drove them to Ngee Ann City off Orchard Boulevard. As he started up the winding ramp to the car park, Aunty Lee suddenly remembered why she had avoided that mall for so long: the ginseng chicken at the Crystal Jade restaurant. That ginseng chicken was the bane of her cooking existence. Despite many attempts she had never managed to get her chicken as simultaneously tender and flavourful as theirs.

A new thought struck her now. 'Do you think I should rear my own chickens? If we rear the chickens and feed ginseng to them then the taste will be inside the chicken meat.'

'You want chickens? I can source chickens for you,' Jonny Ho told her without slowing down. 'I can find you the best chicken meat at the best price. But before we talk business we got to trust each other, right? That's why we are here today.'

Aunty Lee did not see how a trip to Ngee Ann City could inspire trust, but Jonny Ho led her to the office lifts in the Podium Block and pressed the button for the seventeenth floor.

'What are we doing here?' Aunty Lee looked around the plush lobby. The whole floor was occupied by a branch of Cognate Finance, and the lifts opened onto a lobby with mirrors and antique-looking tables with pots of orchids boasting massive sprays of blooms.

'Real,,' Aunty Lee confirmed after a test pinch and sniff. These days imitation orchids were looking so authentic only the 'green culture' fanatics and the very wealthy bothered to cultivate the real thing. Cognate Finance definitely catered to the very wealthy. Aunty Lee knew Cognate took care of her investments but she had never been to this branch. It was much nicer than the Raffles Place branch, she thought. That office was surrounded by office blocks and other banks, but here you had shopping centres and restaurants.

'Afterwards I want to go down to the basement food hall and see what is new there. I heard there is a sticky rice place and the Thai seafood stall has moved in also.'

Jonny Ho wasn't listening. He seemed to be looking around for someone. He took Aunty Lee's arm and guided her through the entrance doors when they slid open and now he stood, still holding her arm, in what might have been a posh airport business lounge. There were several conversational clusters (comfortably upholstered chairs around low coffee tables) and a discreet desk against the far wall. Aunty Lee was surprised but did not mind. It was nice that this young man was concerned about her falling down or wandering off, whatever he thought of her mental state.

'We're going to talk to a banker about Patty's investments. I think you will find it quite interesting.'

Aunty Lee didn't tell him Patty's personal banker had already turned down her inquiry. She only hoped the banker wouldn't mention it in the presence of Patty's husband.

'Can I help you?' A tall dark woman in a grey skirt suit paused on her way past them.

'No problem. We are waiting for somebody,' Jonny said brusquely.

'Well, have a good day.' The woman smiled, nodded to Aunty Lee, and left.

Jonny Ho's polite deference disappeared even before the doors slid shut after the woman. "'Have a good day', 'Have a good day,'" he mocked with an exaggerated Indian accent. 'Trying to sound so important. Who do you think you are talking to ... Finally!

What took you so long? We were standing here looking stupid, answering stupid questions!'

'I'm so sorry, Jonny. My boss was on the phone and got held up, then she had some things for me to do ... ' The girl looked and sounded flustered but she looked sweet and smiled at Aunty Lee.

Aunty Lee smiled back and studied her curiously. The young woman was plump and dressed in a soft, pale blue, long-sleeved knitwear blouse over a bright pink floral skirt. The colours suited her and matched the blue highlights on her eyelids and blue stones in her earrings. Aunty Lee saw that, despite her hurry, she had found time to freshen her lipstick ... which, like the pink shimmer on her nails, matched the flowers on her skirt. Unless she was this perfectly coordinated every day (which was, of course, possible) this girl had dressed up specially to impress someone. And Aunty Lee knew who that someone was. She looked up at Jonny Ho expecting embarrassed awareness. But Jonny was looking around the room. For all the attention he paid her, the girl might have been a piece of furniture. But Aunty Lee knew he must have cultivated her at some point. A woman's interest in a man needs some encouragement before she displays it.

'Why don't we talk inside your office?' Jonny Ho started to walk in the direction the girl had come from. His hand was still holding Aunty Lee's forearm from below and she walked along with him, slightly faster than she would have on her own. She didn't get a chance to look at the paintings on the walls or into the rooms they were passing along the corridor. Many of these seemed to be empty conference rooms. He might have been supporting a frail grandmother protectively, Aunty Lee thought, or a girlfriend possessively.

'Of course. We can talk in my office.' The woman edged past them and hurried on ahead, right to the end of the corridor. She had chunky legs and didn't seem very steady on the high heels she was wearing.

Aunty Lee could not remember much of the Raffles Place branch of Cognate so she looked around with interest. She remembered the feeling of being surrounded by luxury that encouraged you to take it for granted. That was present here too. The thick carpeting of the room the girl now led them into, for instance. It was neither dark nor light nor thick enough to draw your attention to it but Aunty Lee knew that if she had been alone in this room she would have been tempted to take off her shoes so she could sink her toes through the thick soft pile.

It was a large corner room. Windows on two walls met at a right angle and gave the impression the desk at their apex was suspended over the city.

'Please have a seat ... both of you.' The girl seated herself behind the desk and opened a file in front of her. 'Jonny ... Mr Ho ... it's good to see you again. What can I do for you today?'

'I told you, you call me Jonny.' Jonny's confident assurance returned as he settled into his chair and stretched out his long legs. 'We are all friends here together, right? Miss Wong, I want to introduce you to Mrs M. L. Lee. Mrs Lee and I are thinking of going into a business partnership together. But in such cases you cannot be too careful, right? So since we are both clients of your banking services I thought the best thing we can do is come here and get you to check us out for each other.'

'Hello, Mrs Lee, I am Miss Wong. And if I may say so that's very wise of you,' the girl said. 'Let me just show you both what we have.'

'You haven't been working here long, right?' Aunty Lee said conversationally, looking around the office. The name plaque on the desk read Ms Wilhelmina Wong. The girl did not, Aunty Lee thought, look like a 'Wilhelmina'.

'Why do you say that?' Miss Wong said with a little laugh.

'The decoration here doesn't suit you. You wear such pretty bright colours but your office decor all so dark and sophisticated.'

What Aunty Lee really meant was that the elegant, minimalist office decor (three sprigs of dark red orchids in a curved tube of black glass) seemed designed by an older, more assured woman who probably did Pilates and asked for *Hokkien Mee* without fried lard cubes … if indeed she ever ate fried *Hokkien Mee*. The plump, sweet Miss Wong behind the desk looked as though she would order her *Hokkien Mee* with extra pork and would be more at home in Aunty Lee's own cheerful, cluttered kitchen.

'Also, the name on your desk says "Ms Wong" but you call yourself "Miss Wong". Why ah?'

'I use both,' Miss Wong said, again prefacing it with a little laugh. It was a buying time laugh, Aunty Lee thought. Someone must have told her to laugh every time she felt inclined to say 'Uhm' or 'Er'.

'When dealing with the younger, more Westernized clients, I use "Ms". But when dealing with the older, more respectable clients such as yourself I use "Miss". It's all about making the clients feel at ease.'

'The office decor here is all professionally done,' Jonny Ho explained. 'Everything here is standardized. That's how it's done in big companies.' He turned back to the girl. 'Go ahead.'

Miss Wong went ahead. To Aunty Lee's surprise she began with a list of Aunty Lee's own investments. Aunty Lee had never paid much attention to the trading of her investments. As M. L. had always said, it was no use celebrating paper gains or crying over paper losses. He had not invested to make money and was content as long as he preserved his capital and made more than he would have got from a fixed deposit account.

Darren persisted in sending Aunty Lee printouts of all transactions made on her behalf, but she trusted him and seldom bothered to read them. Since these were single-sided printouts on beautiful thick paper (such a waste of the trees cut down to produce them) Aunty Lee used them as rough paper for shopping reminders, instructions, and recipe corrections. As far as she could tell, what Miss Wong was reading sounded fairly accurate.

'That's quite impressive,' Jonny Ho said. 'I can tell you are very conservative in your investments, which is not a bad thing if you don't know much about investing. You don't know it, but keeping your money in safe investments is a myth. There is no such thing as a safe investment. And there is no such thing as preserving your capital. The cost of living is always going up, true or not? Especially in a place like Singapore? Therefore, if you keep your capital the same, your money is actually decreasing. The only way you can stay safe from inflation in old age is to make sure that your capital is growing faster than inflation. And for that it is no use sticking with the safe old investments because by the time people around here decide something is safe that means that it is already dead! Going downhill! But you listen to Miss Wong tell you about my investments here first. Fair's fair, right? I find out about your investments, you find out about mine. Then after that, when we understand each other and trust each other, I will explain to you how you can increase your value to match mine.'

Aunty Lee nodded agreeably enough. Since her goal was to find out more about Jonny Ho all this suited her perfectly, and her only concern was not to look too interested as Miss Wong started reading. Aunty Lee knew she would not remember all the figures but later she would get Nina to source them for her somehow … a fresh pang of loss struck her as she remembered Nina was occupied doing legal things elsewhere. Well, Aunty Lee would give her another week to come to her senses. Nina might be stubborn but nobody could be as stubborn as Aunty Lee when she had a point to prove!

'So what do you think?'

Caught up in her own thoughts, Aunty Lee had not realized Miss Wong had finished reading. Both she and Jonny were looking at Aunty Lee expectantly.

'Sorry,' Aunty Lee said vaguely, 'old lady like me, so many numbers, my head cannot compute.'

Old lady or not, she saw clearly that they both looked relieved.

'I believe you knew Mrs Patricia Kwuan-Loo,' Miss Wong said.

Drat these bankers, Aunty Lee thought, wondering if she was going to bring up her phone inquiry. She looked guiltily at Jonny Ho, who only smiled at her.

'Your investment portfolios are very similar,' Miss Wong said, speaking more slowly. 'With some minor differences, of course. Now that Mr Ho has taken over your friend … his wife's … investments they have grown considerably, but that is because he is more actively involved with growing his own portfolio.'

'In such a short time?' Aunty Lee could not help asking.

'The professionals can only take you so far,' Jonny said. 'For them it is just a job, just a nine-to-five responsibility. But for me, my investments are important to me 24/7. Like my family. For example, if you are a teacher then once the children leave school they are no longer your responsibility anymore. But if you are a mother? Ah, then whether your children are at home or in school you are thinking about them, worrying about them, responsible for them non-stop 24/7 even, true or not?'

Aunty Lee nodded, because it was clearly what was expected of her. His use of the phrase '24/7' had made her think of the 7-Eleven convenience stores that were so named because they had once been open from 7 a.m. to 11 p.m. but were now open twenty-four hours a day. Didn't their name suggest they were less than they actually were?

'Sometimes opportunities come up that can be guaranteed to pay off. But you have to keep an eye on them. The so-called professionals working in a place like this cannot be bothered to do that for you because it means they have to work overtime and, if they do it, they are doing it for their own selves, not for you and me.'

Aunty Lee looked at the professional sitting across the desk from them but Miss Wong did not seem offended. She smiled encouragingly at Aunty Lee, who returned her attention to Jonny.

'So when such guaranteed opportunities come up, I withdraw

my investments from here and take advantage of the opportunities to invest. And then, at the right time, I sell out and take my profits and give them back to these people here to look after for me until the next opportunity comes along. That's the only way to do it if you want your capital to grow faster than inflation. That's why my numbers on the books here are higher than your numbers. But the reason I brought you here to show you I can be trusted is because I am about to invest my funds in a guaranteed opportunity, and I am offering you the chance to join me. Don't worry, I will take care of everything. And everything that you invest in, rest assured that I am investing in double, so you know that I will be paying two hundred per cent attention on the perfect moment to sell out. All you have to worry about is what you are going to do with all the bonus profits that I hand to you. Look, here are the forms. All you have to do is to write down your name for me.'

Aunty Lee was almost tempted, out of curiosity rather than greed, to go along just to see what his next step would be. But thanks to safeguards set up by the late M. L. Lee, she could not make any major transfers without her lawyer and doctor present to confirm she was not acting under duress. Dear M. L., Aunty Lee thought fondly, he had always believed in taking precautions so that they wouldn't be needed. Though in this case, she suspected he had been more concerned about what his son … or rather his son's wife … might try to pressure his widow into doing.

At such times it was easy for Aunty Lee to slip into her vague, pre-Alzheimer's Aunty persona and make a fuss to change the subject. These young people thought that anyone over fifty was senile anyway.

'I don't want to sit down for anymore,' Aunty Lee said loudly, rising to her feet. 'I need to drink some hot water! And I need my pills! Where are my pills?'

'Look, just sign these forms and you can go.' Jonny Ho gestured to Miss Wong, who passed a sheaf of papers across the table. 'Just put your signature here, Rosie.'

The cheek of the young punk, calling her 'Rosie'! Aunty Lee raised her volume and her confusion: 'Where's Nina? I want Nina to come and take me home!'

But Miss Wong only said: 'You must excuse me, I have a meeting coming up.'

'Go ahead,' Jonny Ho said without looking round.

'My meeting is here,' Miss Wong said firmly. 'I'm afraid this is all the time I have for you today. Please continue your discussion elsewhere. Jonny, you better take your forms … '

'Come on.' Jonny Ho again attached his hand to Aunty Lee's arm to help her rise out of her chair. 'Let's go.'

'Since we're here can we walk through the Food Village in the Takashimaya basement?' Aunty Lee recovered as soon as they were out of the door. 'And I want to go to the back door of the Crystal Jade restaurant. Sometimes the staff go outside to smoke. I can ask them about their chicken!'

CHAPTER THIRTEEN

Kopitiam

Aunty Lee did not get to see the Takashimaya food basement after all. Once the meeting was over, Jonny Ho seemed as eager to get out of Ngee Ann City as he had been to get into it earlier. They ended up in a *kopitiam* off Sunset Drive.

'We have to talk,' Jonny Ho said. 'But not in your café. Neutral territory, okay?'

On leaving the Ngee Ann City car park, Jonny had suggested any number of well-reviewed restaurants, or restaurants where he had contacts who could get them a good table without a reservation, but Aunty Lee, sulky over how close she had come to the secrets of ginseng chicken, not to mention checking out how long the queues were for Korean beef, kimchi soup, *Bakerzin* and Japanese cuisine at the Ngee Ann City food court, kept saying 'no, no, drive on,' till they left Orchard Road and its good restaurants behind them.

Holland Road was less fraught but Aunty Lee vetoed Holland Village as well, eventually telling Jonny to turn in at Sunset Drive.

'Ah, I know there is a live seafood restaurant here,' Jonny said, 'but I don't know about the quality … '

'I don't want to go to the seafood restaurant,' Aunty Lee said firmly. 'If you want to talk, I need to think. For me to think properly I need more people around, more people eating and minding their own business.'

They ended up in the *kopitiam*. It was a large space with a high ceiling and open on all sides to the car park and industrial buildings in the area. Despite three rows of ceiling fans it was hot and humid, the sound of rain drumming on the metal roof competing with the buzz of conversation, people shouting orders to stall holders, who, on their part, were calling out invitations. There were also two large television sets suspended from the ceiling: one turned to an English news channel and the other a Chinese soap opera or drama. Though Aunty Lee had not deliberately chosen a place where Jonny would feel uncomfortable, this *kopitiam* worked very well. She suspected this was not because he was unfamiliar with such places but because he was all too familiar.

But she had chosen this place because the food and the location were just what she needed right then. The good-natured shouts, the 'stall for rent' signs, the mélange of stalls selling Indian Muslim food, chilli crabs, roasted chickens, ducks and pork ribs side by side with the Xin De An Medical and Minimart on one side and, beyond it, the back of the Veterinary Clinic (now restored) where the terrible fire had taken place not so long ago … all these things were part of the Singapore that Aunty Lee felt most at home in.

The gold Buddha statue in the small shrine set high into the wall (higher than the television sets) looked down benignly on all. Because of the rain the tables were more crowded than usual. The older folks who normally sat on benches outside their apartment blocks or on the stone seats in the public courtyards had all been driven indoors by the weather. Now nursing glasses of tea or coffee or bottles of beer, they unhappily tapped packets of forbidden cigarettes. Smoking was forbidden not only in the food centre but within the vicinity of the food centre.

Jonny shook his head, snorted at the signs, making Aunty Lee wonder if he was a smoker. She had never seen him with a cigarette, but then his breath always smelled of mouthwash or mint gum, which made Aunty Lee think he was hiding either bad habits or bad breath.

'So, you like this place? What's good here?' Jonny was still trying to be nice. He still thought he could win her over.

'I want to try something I haven't tried before. Maybe that Thai stall. It's new.'

Aunty Lee had her own system for trying new stalls. She examined the photographs on display, dishes being carried away by previous customers, ingredients on display, and finally engaged the cook in conversation; what did he or she recommend? How long had they been cooking? Where did they source their ingredients? Though, if it was a crowded time of day, the questions could wait till after the food was sampled.

But Jonny's impatience got in the way of the comforting ritual.

'No point eating here. You want to eat Thai food, I can recommend a genuine Thai restaurant run by genuine Thai people. The only stall here worth trying is that seafood one. I'll see what they have. You stay here. If the drinks guy comes round order me a coffee.'

Well, Aunty Lee was certainly learning more about Jonny Ho. He wasn't so much interested in new food experiences as making sure he patronized the right places. It was as though he was playing life like an online game and only spending energy on activities that would bring him bonus points. And that being seen in the wrong places or in the wrong company would lose him points. What, then, was he doing with her, she wondered?

He ordered crab noodles. Aunty Lee thought this was meant to impress her, because on looking through the lunch menu at Aunty Lee's Delights on his last visit Jonny had said: 'No pepper crab? Pepper crab is supposed to be Singapore's top dish. How can you call yourself a Singaporean restaurant if you don't sell pepper crab!' That just showed he didn't know much about Singapore cafés and was not good at making jokes, but still, it stung a little.

Still, Aunty Lee had to admit the hot noodles with tender crab in coconut gravy was delicious. The crabs were fresh ... fished out of the live tank in front of the stall. Jonny Ho had not only chosen their crabs himself but insisted on watching them slaughtered and shelled so that no substitutions could be made. As he told Aunty Lee: 'That's where they look to making their money you know. If you don't watch and make sure they kill the crab you are paying for, they will just give you old crab out of their freezer and, once you are gone, plop the live crab back into the tank!'

'People will taste the difference!' Aunty Lee wasn't sure if she was defending the honesty of hawkers or taste buds of diners.

'Put in enough tasty sauce, nobody can tell what is underneath. That one of the things I want to talk to you about. You are in the food business. The first thing you got to remember about that is that it is a business! You are in it to make money, to show profit, otherwise why are you doing it? If you love cooking so much, why not just cooking at home for your family, for your friends?'

This was something Aunty Lee had tried to tell Mark on his previous (failed) ventures. In the course of his attempt to set up a fine wine adjunct to her café, Aunty Lee had often wished that Mark had a sharper business sense. If only he had been a bit more cautious and not so particular about maintaining a higher standard than any of their customers could appreciate ... in short, if only Mark had been a bit more like Jonny Ho ... he might have made a success of it. But then Mark also got tired of things quickly. He was more interested in the grand idea, the big launch and the write up in the Life! section of the *Straits Times* than in the daily grind and monthly accounting. Jonny Ho seemed to have started as many projects as Mark, but Jonny's projects seemed to be surviving.

'How do you keep up with so many projects?' Aunty Lee asked, interrupting what seemed to be turning into a business pitch. The crab noodles were good. She had detected a trace of salted egg yolk in the sauce which gave her an idea for a sauce for pork ribs and she was feeling happy again. 'You are doing construction, that children's school, now you are interested in the food business. How do you manage it all?'

Jonny Ho looked taken aback for a moment, then beamed as though Aunty Lee had asked the very question he was waiting for. 'I don't. I leave the managing in the hands of the experts ... people like you. I handle the business side of it for you. I watch the bottom line. I make sure that you are paying the lowest price and charging the highest price so that you can concentrate on making customers happy. Perfect partnership, right?'

She had been wrong, Aunty Lee thought. It was not Mark but Selina who was the aspiring Jonny Ho. Selina, who believed that anybody could be a success if only you organized them better. But where Jonny Ho was going around tirelessly trying to create business connections, Selina had only worked on Mark so far. It was impossible to say whether she would have succeeded with someone else, or whether Mark, left to his own devices, would have stuck with his ventures long enough to reach success if his wife hadn't been constantly reminding him that he was failing on the bottom line. It might be interesting, Aunty Lee thought, to see how Jonny Ho managed one of his perfect partnership businesses.

'So what do you say? You take me on as a business manager, and I turn your business around in eighteen months or you're free to fire me.'

'I think I want to see a trial run first.'

'That's what the eighteen months is for. A year and a half. You pay me salary, that's all. Then afterwards we can talk percentages. You like the Food Village in the Takashimaya basement so much? I can guarantee you your own stall there within two years, if you put yourself in my hands!'

'The trial run can be the children's playschool. You and Beth are partners there, right? And my daughter-in-law is investing money in it. I want to see how that turns out first. Say, wait five years and then see how.'

Aunty Lee saw an angry, petulant look flash across Jonny Ho's face before he dismissed it. This was clearly off script for him. 'Children's schools are different. I'm leaving that entirely to Beth. If it doesn't work that is her fault, not mine. After all, how often do people have children, right? Compared to how often they have dinner. Frankly it is much easier to get fast turnaround in the food business. You just need a good name and an okay product. That's why I'm so keen on turning your café into a franchise. You already got the product that people like, but no branding at all! Can I speak to you honestly? The childcare education business is new to me. But there is clearly a need for it in Singapore. All we did is send out the survey and already so many parents are interested. But Beth is also new to this line. I tell you, if she wasn't my wife's sister I wouldn't be in partnership with her. And results won't come as fast as with the catering business. Better that you say, we work together on your café business as the trial. Then if you are happy with the results, you can invest in KidStarters. That way you can get rich first, and the childcare centre will be ready in time for your grandchildren. Good, right? What do you say?'

'I'm so full,' Aunty Lee said. 'I ate too much. I can't think. Can we *tarpow* the rest for me to bring back?' She waved, and a server from the stall was happy to accept her approval and take away the leftovers to pack for Aunty Lee to take home.

'That's exactly why you need somebody like me to think for you!' Jonny Ho persisted as soon as the server was gone.

'I need to burp,' said Aunty Lee. 'When there's too much hot air it is very difficult to make decisions.'

For a while they talked about other things ... digestive medications for example. Jonny Ho didn't approve of commercial medications. 'I don't trust those Western doctors; all of them are only trying to line their own pockets. You know they are all sponsored by drug companies to recommend their own drugs?'

'I make my own ginger tea.' Aunty Lee did not hold much with Western doctors either. She had liked the late Dr Ken Loo but most of the doctors she had seen recently all seemed so young and so obsessed with height to weight ratios and BMIs. They all seemed to think Aunty Lee was shorter than she ought to be for her weight, but there was nothing she could do about it so she avoided going to doctors as far as she could.

'But there's always Traditional Chinese Medicine,' Jonny Ho said.

Aunty Lee wondered whether Jonny Ho's connections extended to suppliers of TCM products. It wouldn't be surprising … he seemed to have so many contacts in Mainland China.

Jonny Ho reached over the table and put a hand over Aunty Lee's. 'Chinese should use Chinese products,' he said. 'There are so many things I can introduce to you. I can see that you are open to new experiences.' Was he flirting with her? Aunty Lee felt something stir inside her. No, not desire. It was more like the feeling at the start of a roller-coaster ride where you both can't wait for it to start and want to get off while you still can.

'I use traditional Singapore medicine,' Aunty Lee said firmly, removing her hand to scratch her nose. 'If got stomach ache from eating too much the best thing is *daun kesum*.'

'That's a brand name?'

'*Kesum* is a plant. You can find it growing along drains and in the forest reserves around the ponds. Very good for making *assam laksa* and treating dandruff also. You can pick off the leaves and use and the plant will grow back. But you got to be careful. These days some people see you pick one leaf off the ground also must go and call police!' But she spoke without rancour. The Guangs had become friends, making Aunty Lee even more fond of the minty weed.

But Jonny Ho was not listening. Aunty Lee's mention of the police coincided with the image on the large television screen of policemen milling around a construction site. Someone had found a dead body.

CHAPTER FOURTEEN

Add Water and Stir

It was raining again. The workers complained automatically, but without really meaning it. Memories of the last two months of haze blown over from the Indonesian forest fires were still strong, and the large gentle drops of warm rain were welcome.

Work at the construction site had not been halted even when the haze was at its worst. The government had ordered schools closed and non-essential outdoor work stopped when the Pollutant Standards Index rose above 300 into the 'Hazardous' range, but this was a private company and the contract workers knew better than to protest. They could be fired as easily as they had been hired, and there were too many other men who would be happy to take over their jobs. They would work through any conditions as long as they were paid but they had to stop when the monsoon winds brought the lashing, blinding rains. It was dangerous to work when they could not see three feet in front of them, dangerous for the machinery, which was far more valuable to the company than the men operating it.

There was little shelter at the worksite but they stayed there, smoking and waiting till the rains slowed or the pickup truck came to bring them back to their quarters. They were only in Singapore to earn money and there was no point getting angry at the weather or the mud. They even laughed when part of the reinforced tank sagged and ripped, releasing a flood of muddy water. But they stopped, shocked, when they saw ... and smelled ... the bundle of cloth that clogged the drainage from the foundation pit, one thin blackened arm trailing in the water that continued to seep out around it.

The police came to collect the body. The area was cordoned off and work halted indefinitely as the men were questioned. They all said they had no idea who the woman was or how her body had got there. One thing was clear; if the rains had not interrupted the work and the concrete had been poured on schedule, the body would never have been discovered. They had been disposing of various odds and ends ... mostly metal but also any rubbish they accumulated ... into the foundation dump. It was standard practice and anyway it made no difference to the concrete foundation.

'Sir?'

Inspector Salim Mawar looked up to see Staff Sergeant Panchal standing in the open doorway to his office.

'Yes?'

'That body that was found in the construction site this morning? It is a female, aged between thirty and thirty-five. Possibly a female foreign domestic worker.'

It took Salim a moment to pull his thoughts back from the nightmare that immediately flashed into his mind ... Nina dead with glazed unseeing eyes in a pool of mud in the construction site ... that was why she had not been answering any of his phone calls ... There had been photos with the report but he had not paid much attention to them. What they showed of the decomposing body would not help identification. And Yio Chu Kang was far out of his jurisdiction. But now his fingers moved to his computer keyboard to call up the recent reports. Of course it could not be Nina. Nina was safe in the house of Aunty Lee's friend. She was safe because he was staying away from her, as she had asked him to.

Inna lillah hi wa inna ilaihi rajioon

To Him we belong and to Him shall we return

Without realizing it, Salim's lips formed the words of the *dua*, familiar from childhood: 'Inna lillah hi wa inna ilaihi rajioon,' he murmured automatically. Almost as though his prayer was visible, Panchal kept her eyes officiously on the printout she was holding. 'Life of my heart and the light of my breast, and a departure for my sorrow and a release for my anxiety ... '

Salim's police and legal training surfaced through the panic. There had not been time for a post-mortem. How had a preliminary scan determined the deceased had been a foreign domestic worker? Race, possibly. These days too many Singaporeans had a tendency to assume any Pinoy or Indonesian woman was a foreign domestic worker.

'Were there documents with her? ID?'

'Nothing yet. This is all we've got.' Glad her boss had taken the news so well, Panchal put the paperwork on his desk and left the room without pointing out that the information would be on his computer. She had picked up some tact since joining the Bukit Tinggi Neighbourhood Police Post.

Inspector Salim Mawar stared at the printout without touching it. It was over three weeks since he had last seen Nina Balignasay, three weeks since he had last asked her (again) to think about marrying him. He had been diffident, as he always was, because he did not want to push her into anything. And because he believed it more important to do things right than to do them fast. But there had been nothing diffident or slow about Nina's response this time. Not only had she told him she was not going to marry him (which was something she always said), this time she had gone as far as to say she did not want to see him again.

'You don't mean that.'

138

'I do mean it. There's no point,'

Nina was afraid that being involved with a foreign domestic worker would jeopardize his career. As far as Salim was concerned, there could be no greater proof that Nina loved him. Not in the way Western romances portrayed love, but in the way of wanting what was best for him more than she wanted to be with him. Now his treacherous mind looked for ways to blame itself; if only he had not asked her again (couldn't he take a hint?) to marry him, Nina might not have left the safety of Aunty Lee's house and shop. There would have been no possibility of her ending up dead in a construction site!

Inspector Salim Mawar was only too aware of the restrictions governing relations with foreign domestic workers in Singapore. Indeed, he had got to know Nina Balignasay because of a complaint that she was violating her domestic work contract by working in a shop. Though he already knew the shop and Aunty Lee, he had dutifully followed up on that report, and Aunty Lee, agreeing that proper procedures must be followed, had invited him to check through Nina's work documents. It turned out the complaint had come from Aunty Lee's daughter-in-law.

'I had to inform the authorities because I was unwittingly involved,' Mrs Selina Lee had said.

He smiled to himself, remembering how furious Nina had been ... furious at Aunty Lee as well as at him. As it had turned out, they were only two very small fish among the many that Aunty Lee had been frying. In some ways Salim had more in common with Aunty Lee than he would ever have with Nina.

Nina had grown up in a small village in the Philippines where she had learned to distrust authority in any form, especially the government and including the police, and she had brought that distrust with her to Singapore. Salim, on the other hand, had grown up in Singapore where one of the few things people had in common was a conviction that the government was over strict and heavy-handed but well-intentioned. And that policemen and taxi drivers could be trusted. Salim's father had been a taxi driver. He had been so proud, telling all his passengers that his son was studying law at the National University of Singapore on a police scholarship. Mr Mawar would have been even more proud that a Singapore Police Force Overseas Scholarship next sent his son to Cambridge University to get his masters of philosophy in criminology and law. Unfortunately, he had not lived to see Salim graduate. A drunk driver in a Nissan GT-R sports car was estimated to have been travelling at over 140 kilometres an hour on the Seletar Link when it hit the old taxi from behind, sending it off the expressway. Salim had booked himself on a flight back to Singapore as soon as he heard the news, but Mr Mawar's heart stopped for the third and final time when his son was still somewhere over Afghanistan. Salim had considered dropping out of the course to stay home with his mother. But his mother insisted that he go back to England: 'Your father was so proud of you.'

Inspector Salim knew that some thought he was being groomed to be one of the token Malays in a largely Chinese administration. So far no one had said anything officially to him, and he was happy in his present job. So happy, in fact, that he had turned down several positions that had been unofficially suggested (no senior post was officially offered until acceptance was confirmed) to remain at the Bukit Tinggi Neighbourhood Police Post where he had first come to work as a Senior Staff Sergeant. Salim's rapid promotion to Inspector was also seen by some as a sign that the people upstairs had their eye on him and his future. Times were changing in Singapore.

Even the conservative majority was changing. Formerly they had blamed Malays, Indians, and homosexuals for everything that went wrong in Singapore. But recent massive immigration from the People's Republic of China had brought new tensions and scapegoats. Since the new immigrants were ethnic Chinese, it became necessary to show how Singaporean they were. And apart from the more vicious Christian leaders, most embraced their Singaporean identity. That meant they were more favourably disposed to accept someone like Salim, who was a true-born and bred Singaporean.

Salim still felt like an outsider at times. But more and more this was because of his education and position in the force than because of his race. And that was not necessarily a bad thing. After all, creating the person you were meant to be day by day was all about making choices that defined you as an individual. It was only on statistic reports that people could be lumped together in masses and their actions predicted.

'I worry about you, you know,' Salim's mother had said to him after the last big case had been wrapped up. His name had been mentioned in the newspaper report, and the neighbours had come round to congratulate his mother and flatter him … and introduce him to their daughters and nieces and cousins. All of them seemed to be very pleasant girls who would fit right into his family and their circle. The problem was, Salim's thoughts kept returning to a young woman who would not fit in with his family at all, and who was not being at all pleasant to him at the moment.

'You should find a wife to look after you now. I will not be here to look after you forever. And you need children to look after you when you grow old. I hope your children will be as good to you as you are to me.'

Salim had not told his mother that he had already met the woman who he wanted to marry. And that she had turned him down.

But he would not push Nina to change her mind. Like every other survivor of the Singaporean school system, Salim knew how to keep his mouth shut and work towards producing quantifiable results. He had not given up. He would try again when he had something more concrete to offer her.

Salim had not been over to Aunty Lee's Delights since Nina's departure, but Aunty Lee had come by to drop off 'extra' food for the night shift at the station. She had not come into Salim's office, only stopped in the main office to chat with SS Panchal about the recent housebreaking episodes.

Salim knew Aunty Lee had tried to change Nina's mind on his behalf. And since there was nothing patient or subtle about Aunty Lee once she got her mind set on something, it seemed likely Nina had gone away to get some respite from Aunty Lee. It was not just him she had run away from.

Salim had not been able to resist texting Nina. He had taken her silence as an answer. But what if something terrible had happened to her? He tried Nina's mobile phone again, calling this time instead of texting. Nina still did not answer.

Perhaps she recognized his caller ID and did not want to talk to him. Or perhaps she could not.

CHAPTER FIFTEEN

Beth Gets News

In the *kopitiam*, Aunty Lee stared at the television screen. It was a news brief. Though the sound was off a young woman reporter in a yellow rain jacket over a white shirt caught the attention of the diners as she mouthed her report to the camera against a backdrop of policemen who were standing around a dead body. There was a lot of yellow police tape and clusters of workmen and uniformed policemen standing around. '*Dead Body discovered in construction site near the Yio Chu Kang flyover*' said the 'Latest Updates' panel at the bottom of the screen. Aunty Lee was not the only one staring at the screen in thrilled horror. Neither was she the only one calling for the sound to be put on. That didn't happen, but no matter. All over the *kopitiam* people were calling up news updates and rumours on their mobile devices and sharing them in a variety of dialects.

'That expressway sure to be haunted after this,' the old cleaner remarked, eyes on the screen as she cleared their table. 'Maybe already haunted, that's why that woman died. Some of these expressways ah, they build through the old cemeteries, the spirits don't like it.'

At once Aunty Lee thought of Nina – was that why she had not been answering her phone? It was the most impossible of coincidences, of course, but Aunty Lee was used to impossible things happening to her. She fumbled for her mobile phone.

'Come on,' Jonny Ho said. 'Let's go.'

He strode off in the direction of the multi-storey car park. There was no supporting arm for Aunty Lee this time. In fact, she almost had to trot to keep up with him, and he was already revving up the engine as she half crawled, half climbed into the passenger seat. The fancy car was so low it was like sitting down in a child's toy car.

They had just turned left onto Clementi Road when Jonny's phone rang. He had ignored several calls during their meeting at Cognate, but he glanced at the screen and answered this one.

'You should use your hands-free kit. Police see, you sure *kenah* fined,' Aunty Lee told him, hoping to listen in, but he ignored her.

Even without the advantage of a speakerphone Aunty Lee could hear a shrill, excited woman's voice and she wondered if it was the Miss Wong they had seen earlier. Though she couldn't be sure, she thought she heard the words 'police' and 'body'.

'Shut up,' Jonny said. 'Bring her phone with you.'

Completely abandoning her vague flutterings, Aunty Lee looked expectantly at Jonny when he clicked off the connection. 'Did somebody tell you whose body was found?'

'Look, something came up at work.' Jonny was tense, his mind clearly on something other than Aunty Lee. 'I have to go. I'm dropping you here. You can take a taxi home.'

He barely glanced into his rear-view mirror before cutting across two lanes of cars. Angry horns blared but without impact and, before she knew it, Aunty Lee found herself ejected onto the grass verge by the side of the road. It took her a few moments to get herself sorted out. Her knees especially did not like getting out of sporty low car seats any more than they had liked getting into them. And above all, Aunty Lee was taken aback. Of course she could get home on her own. This was Singapore, after all, where taxi drivers were known as much for their good hearts as for their bad tempers. But she couldn't remember the last time she was so unceremoniously dumped. She could see a bus stop less than fifty metres away but it had been a long time since Aunty Lee had taken a bus without Nina.

She tried to phone Nina again. This time Nina's mobile phone went directly to voicemail without ringing. A cold dread came upon Aunty Lee. Suppose Nina wasn't safely at KidStarters working hard and ignoring phone calls … ?

But no. That was too ridiculous. Nina wasn't missing, she was with Beth at Jalan Kakatua. If it was a maid's body that had been found it was more likely to be the missing Julietta than Nina. Could the phone call have been from Beth? If Beth had seen the news, she might think so.

A blue comfort cab slowed down invitingly, and Aunty Lee hopped in and directed the driver to the Bukit Tinggi Police Post.

'Aunty, if somebody robbed you and stole your purse there are other police stations closer than that.'

'Nobody robbed me. I just got to go to that station to talk to somebody. Quick, quick go *lah*! What are you waiting for?'

Reassured, the driver signalled and pulled out into traffic. Of course, he would not have refused a passenger whose purse had just been stolen, but it was always good to know he was going to be paid for this trip. He even turned on the radio for her.

'Did you hear about the dead body they found? They say it is Filipina maid, got pregnant and then her boyfriend killed her.'

'What boyfriend?' Aunty Lee asked, thinking of Salim. 'Who said she was pregnant?'

'Whatever boyfriend. If no boyfriend how to get pregnant?' The driver cackled like a small boy at his own joke.

Aunty Lee wanted to smack him on the back of his head but reminded herself he was a driver. The fines for assaulting taxi drivers had recently been increased.

If Nina had been there she would have told Aunty Lee not to

allow herself to imagine so many crazy things, but then, if Nina had been there, Aunty Lee would have been relishing these crazy imaginings, not worrying herself sick over them. If only Nina was all right, Aunty Lee swore that never again would she make her helper do anything for her own good.

Beth stared at the tiny screen propped up on top of the mess of papers on her work desk. Since Patty's death, she had cancelled newspaper delivery to the house. It more was ecological – and cheaper – to keep up with the news on her iPad.

Actually, the iPad had also been Patty's. Another great waste. Patty had only used it to play Candy Crush and talk to her son on Skype. Every time Beth put on one of Patty's old dresses (clothes were another unnecessary indulgence Patty had spent too much on) or watched something educational on Patty's iPad, Beth felt the triumph of knowing that she had not wasted a cent on these things and was putting them to far better use than her sister would have.

But today all her glow of virtue was discombobulated by the news that a woman's body had been found in a construction site. If the concrete had been poured on schedule her body would never have been discovered, the reporter announced. But, because of flooding caused by the recent rainy weather, work had stopped temporarily, and when the workmen returned to work this morning they found a body in the mud.

Beth stared, feeling dizzy. The screen speed scrolled several pages down under the pressure of her damp fingers (damn that touch screen!) and she held her breath till she laboriously fingered her way back to the original news report. But there was nothing more than her first glance had told her: an unidentified woman's body had been flushed out by floods in a construction site. The workers were being questioned. The woman's identity was being sought.

Could it be Julietta's body they had found?

Beth did not want to think of Julietta as dead. She had found Julietta annoying and rude and careless with the housework. But then Beth found most people annoying and careless. And she knew it had been mostly Patty's fault for not keeping a stricter eye on her helper. Given time, Beth was sure she could have trained Julietta properly. And in time even Julietta would have had to admit that she learned more working for Miss Beth than Madam Patty.

Since Julietta's disappearance, Beth had almost convinced herself that the maid had run off with a boyfriend. When Beth confiscated Julietta's phone she had found text messages that suggested she was seeing a local man, so this wasn't too far-fetched. Well, if it was really Julietta's body that had been found, it must have been that man she was seeing. Surely it would be obvious to anyone that Julietta must have run off with a man: a man who had killed her and put her body in that construction site. Or even if the man had not intended to murder her, perhaps Julietta had met him at the construction site for an assignation and she had had a fatal accident (weren't there always reports of fatal worksite accidents?) and the man had not dared to report it. Perhaps she should tell the police about Julietta's phone? But then the police might ask her why she had not reported Julietta missing ...

'Madam, are you all right?' It was Nina, the maid that Selina Lee had planted in her house, no doubt to spy on her. As though Selina's daily 'Good Morning' and 'This is the Day the Lord has made' text messages weren't irritating enough.

Beth wished she had never met Selina Lee. But Jonny said Selina and Mark Lee were worth knowing because they were part of the younger married set who had money and would soon have children. He didn't seem to think much of Beth's friends, though she knew most of the people Patty had been friends with.

'Of course I'm all right. Why are you standing around looking at me? Didn't I tell you to wipe up the rain that came in?'

147

'Finish already, Madam.'

'How can you finish already? It's still raining! The water is still coming in!'

It was still raining, but it was not thundering down with the same force it had an hour ago, and the sheets of blue tarpaulin that Nina had tacked over the empty window frames kept the rain out.

Nina had weighted down the edges with some of the metal strips left by the workers and the remainder was neatly stacked against one wall. The rags and buckets they had left had also been cleaned and stacked. The floor was dry, and as far as Beth could see, shone with cleanliness. She could not see anything in the room to find fault with, except for the incomplete windows and she could not blame Nina for that. Suddenly, she found herself crying. Why couldn't it always be like that? Why hadn't Julietta kept the house clean and herself quiet?

'Sit down, Madam,' Nina said firmly, 'I will bring you some hot tea.'

'I don't like tea,' Beth said faintly.

But Nina had already gone. And when she returned with a cup of hot ginger tea (no caffeine, no tannin, sweetened with honey instead of sugar) Beth allowed herself to be persuaded to sit down and put her feet up. She drank the hot, warming tea and felt herself relaxing and dissolving. It was very good and sweet and just what she needed, though she usually tried to avoid sugar in her drinks. That had always been her biggest weakness. She could only relax when someone told her to, and when she relaxed she let her guard down.

'Madam, you want something to eat?' Nina asked. 'I can fix something for you?'

Beth pulled herself together with an effort. 'Don't pretend to be concerned. You just want the chance to steal food.'

Nina got one piece of bread for breakfast and a packet of instant noodles for lunch and dinner, same as Julietta had got.

Julietta had always tried to steal leftovers so Beth assumed Nina would too.

'Go and clean the toilets.'

'Madam, I cleaned the toilets already.'

'Go and clean them again. And don't talk back to me!'

CHAPTER SIXTEEN

Questions

'We have an ID, Sir.'

'That was quick.' Inspector Salim managed not to say 'for once'.

'One of the maid agencies has identified her, Sir. Her name is Mirasol Santos. They said they were quite worried about her, because some of her family members called them to say that she did not contact them at home for a while. The agency owner said he also tried to call but got no answer. He tried to call her employer but also no answer, so he assumed the family went on holiday and took the maid with them and that's why she did not respond to her family's calls.'

'Have you managed to contact her employer? They didn't report her missing?'

'No. The employer didn't report. We are trying to call them now. So far no answer. You want somebody to go round to the house?'

'Whereabouts?'

'Bukit Timah NPP.'

'What is the maid's name again?' Salim looked down at the file. He had already skimmed through it but the woman's name had not stuck.

'Miss Mirasol J. Santos. But the agent says she went by the name Julietta.'

Aunty Lee was being excluded. She had made it to the Bukit Tinggi Police Post before the questioning started, but she was most definitely being excluded from what was going on. It didn't help that she didn't have Nina to keep her informed of the latest news reports. When she told SS Panchal to tell Inspector Salim that the dead woman may have been a foreign domestic helper employed by her friend, the officer had nodded and whispered: 'He already knows. Her employers are being brought in for questioning.'

It was all about outsiders and insiders, Aunty Lee thought. Right from school days when coming from the right school made so much difference to who you knew and what groups you belonged to: which school, which nationality, which race ... the sad thing was when the bond within a group had less to do with what they had in common than who they could exclude.

Jonny, Beth and, to Aunty Lee's surprise, Fabian, had all been brought in to give their statements. Aunty Lee thought of Seetoh, the taxi driver, who had seemed so in love with Julietta. Ought she tell Salim about Seetoh? It didn't seem possible that Seetoh could have done anything to hurt Julietta. But she remembered Seetoh's almost insane obsession with Jonny Ho and wondered. She would try to talk him into going to the police himself, she decided.

And there was something else that Aunty Lee wanted to talk to Salim about. This had nothing to do with the dead woman, so it was probably not a good time. But with Jonny Ho already at the police post it was too good an opportunity to miss.

Station Superintendent Mark Sheridan looked doubtfully at the plump lady who wanted him to pass a note to Inspector Salim. He was relatively new to the posting and, despite the title on his desk, one of the most junior officers apart from the uniformed station receptionist.

'The Inspector is very busy, Madam. Are you sure that I can't help you?' Most of the problems brought to the station since he arrived had been to do with misplaced keys, purses, and dogs, though last week there had been a python scare that had been quite exciting. 'What is it about?'

'Several things. Well, first I heard that you found my friend's missing maid dead, right?'

'I cannot say, Madam. All information … '

'Well, just in case you did find my friend's maid, Julietta, dead in a construction site like it says on the news, will you tell Salim to make sure to check if Julietta's work permit, phone, and passport were found with her. And if not, were they left at her workplace?'

'I'm sure Inspector Salim knows what to do, Madam.' Sheridan scribbled a reminder on his notepad just in case.

'Oh, I'm sure he does. And the other thing is, I believe the husband of another friend of mine is here, a Mr Jonny Ho.'

'I cannot say, Madam.'

But Aunty Lee saw the heavyset young man's eyes dart to a line on the log in front of him and was satisfied.

'Anyway, another friend and I were talking about those house break-ins that have been going on.'

'We are doing what we can, Madam. We have increased bicycle patrols in all the affected estates and—'

'Rosie Lee! What are you doing here? Are you being questioned also? What are you questioning her for?'

Aunty Lee looked around. She was the only woman in the vicinity apart from SS Panchal, who had come out of the 'restricted' area escorting Jonny Ho. And Jonny Ho seemed to be talking to her. It was as though he had forgotten all about how he had dumped her unceremoniously on the side of the road before rushing off. But Aunty Lee had not forgotten.

'The lady is not being questioned,' SS Sheridan said. 'She was just leaving.'

'Good to hear. We can escape, then. Come on, Rosie. I will take you home.'

'I'm not ready to go home yet. I want to wait and talk to Inspector Salim first. And I want to see Fabian.'

'Fabian will be stuck here for a long time. Maybe forever, ha-ha! And Inspector Salim is probably going to be here even longer. And even when he comes out he's not going to have time for you. Come on, I want to finish our discussion. We can have a meeting in the car. And I will make sure that Inspector Salim makes time to talk to you later, okay? Fabian also. But I should warn you that Fabian may not be going home for some time. I had to tell them the truth about him. Beth also. We didn't want to say anything earlier, but you can only keep quiet about things for so long, right?'

Aunty Lee sensed tension and alarm under Jonny Ho's bright charming chatter. Was it from being at the police station or was it from seeing Aunty Lee there? Did he think she had chased after him to complain about being abandoned?

'Sorry our date got interrupted! Come on, let me make it up to you!'

'What did the police question you about? Do they know yet what happened to Julietta?'

Jonny looked surprised, then grinned. 'Scared that I am a killer, is it? Don't worry, I make killer deals that's all. Anyway I told them the same thing as Beth told them. We were together all day that day at the house. Big headache with the renovations. Crazy regulations say supposed to have sound insulated walls … do they expect us to tear down the walls to put sound insulation then build back again? Might as well tear down the whole house and build from scratch! Anyway you cannot keep kids indoors all day, right? Kids will run around outside, so what's the point in insulating the wall? Anyway we were discussing the rules and the renovations and the costs … business stuff. That's why we didn't even notice that Julietta went out. We saw her talking to that Fabian outside. If you want to suspect somebody of being a killer that's the guy I would recommend, that Fabian. The guy is a psycho. We had to tell the police that.'

Aunty Lee hesitated, pulled in different directions. There was so much more she wanted to learn from Jonny, especially what more he could tell her about Fabian. And there was no telling how much longer the wait would be to see Salim. Aunty Lee had nothing against waiting as long as you knew progress was being made, like queuing before sales or waiting for a state funeral cortege. You knew that as long as you kept waiting the doors would eventually open or the coffin would eventually pass. But in this case, she had caught a glimpse of Inspector Salim when she first arrived. She knew he had seen her because she had waved and called and he had given her the nod that a waiter gives to quieten an impatient customer; I see you, but your order is in the hands of the kitchen/the gods.

Aunty Lee had no idea when or even if Salim would talk to her. Recently he had avoided all her attempts to advise him on how best to talk Nina round. And if Aunty Lee wanted to find out what Beth and Jonny Ho had told the police and what the police had told Beth and Jonny, surely it would be much easier to get the information from Jonny than from the police!

But what about Fabian? There was still no sign of him. Station Superintendent Sheridan called Jonny Ho over to sign out, and Aunty Lee hurried to SS Panchal and passed her a flyer with the address and phone number of Aunty Lee's Delights. 'Give this to Fabian Loo. Tell him to come back to my shop and I will cook something good for him. I used to know his parents, and I was in school with his Mum. Tell him I will make for him the stewed ginger root chicken that his mother used to like so much.'

It was not just about finding out what Fabian might have said to Julietta the day she disappeared. Aunty Lee had first seen Fabian

Loo when he was a plump little boy, and she felt some responsibility for the plump unhappy young man that he had become. Even if he was a killer, at least she could give him a last meal before he got put in prison.

SS Panchal looked at Aunty Lee, then at the card. Aunty Lee saw Jonny Ho heading in her direction.

'Just give Fabian the card. I knew his mother. Really I did.' Aunty Lee said. 'Tell him to phone me and I will try to help him. And I will cook some good food for him. For free, as a guest, not as a customer.'

'Let's get going, Rosie. I'll drive you back to your house. I'm not going to leave you here alone.'

'What about Beth? Are they keeping her here?'

'They are taking her to identify Julietta.'

'Aren't you going with her?'

'One ID is enough.'

Jonny Ho settled Aunty Lee into his flashy car again. He was obviously in a hurry to get out of the police presence but, as before, there was something about him that made her think of a little boy trying to impress. Aunty Lee found that quite touching. She decided to be impressed, to make him happy. Very often it was only when people no longer needed to make a good impression that they relaxed and let you see what they were really like. So Aunty Lee tried to say all the nice things she could think of. Unfortunately, she had to repeat the things she had said on her first two car rides because there was only so much you could say about the inside of a car: '*Wah*, your seats are so comfortable' and 'the cup holders are big enough to hold the Starbucks Wendy cup' but Jonny didn't seem to mind, in fact he seemed genuinely pleased. Aunty Lee knew he was listening, because on her first ride in his car Jonny Ho had asked her: 'What is a Wendy cup?'

'Wendy Cup is the Starbucks biggest cup. The middle size they call the Grand Prix cup, and the smallest one they call Tall. Like people are always telling the smallest children, "*Wah* you so tall now".'

That time he had looked suspicious, as though suspecting she was making fun of him in some way. But when she repeated the cup compliment this time he just smiled, looking pleased. Aunty Lee thought she had confirmed his suspicion that she was just an old woman who repeated herself.

'It may interest you to know,' Jonny said, 'I am complaining to the people in charge. The big boys, you may call them. I know all those people. I have worked with them. They know me and they trust me. Brother–Brother.'

'What did you complain about?'

'I told them their precious Inspector Salim physically abused me.' He said it like the punchline of a joke, roaring with laughter as he pulled into traffic.

If there was a joke, Aunty Lee didn't get it. 'Inspector Salim? Why, what happened?'

'We were alone in the room. My word against his. I have a degree and a business. And I have powerful connections. He is wearing a uniform chasing people from parking in handicap lots. Who do you think they will believe?' Jonny grinned. He looked very young and very confident and struck her as someone posing for a photograph as financial advisor or dentist … those whitened teeth.

'Besides, he has no business being here, did you know that? This isn't even his police station. He doesn't even have an office here. He had to kick the dirty-blood cop off his desk to use his phone. I told the guy he should also file a complaint!'

'"Dirty-blood cop?"'

Jonny said something in Mandarin that Aunty Lee did not understand, then: 'You know, the same meaning as "prostitute's son" in English.' Jonny and Aunty Lee had clearly learned their English from different sources.

'You mean the *grago* policeman? Station Superintendent Sheridan?'

'Grago', a Singlish term to describe Eurasians, came from the name of the shrimps mixed into *belacan*, or shrimp paste, to give it its flavour. Given Aunty Lee's passion for *sambal belacan*, she could never see why some people objected to it. She wouldn't have minded being named after something that was so necessary and tasted so good.

'Sheridan, that's it. The big guy that talked to me while Inspector Big Shot Salim was on the phone. Sheridan is the one that took down my complaint for me. He told me he will make sure it goes through. Things like that you got to submit directly to the top, and you got to submit multiple copies at the same time. Otherwise they will close one eye here, pretend didn't see; you scratch my back, I fill your pocket. I explained to him very clearly what to do. That's the way these things work, I told him. Most policemen are not very bright. That's why they are policeman, right? But if you are good to the smarter ones, they will remember you. It is important to remember that. It can be very useful.'

There were many things in Jonny's statement that Aunty Lee would have liked to discuss in greater detail. Mark Sheridan was a large young man with a broad face, carrying a bit more weight than you would expect to see on an active officer. What made Jonny think him smarter than someone like Inspector Salim? But first things first.

'What did Inspector Salim do to you?'

'I didn't specify. Didn't have time to specify. But I will come up with something, don't worry.' Jonny grinned. 'I said that my old aunty has got a weak heart, and I got to drive you home before you get a heart attack at the police station because the family is sure to sue the police.'

'I'm sure they know that I'm not your aunt. And I have got nothing wrong with my heart.'

'Don't worry about it. Once you are over a certain age every-body has got something wrong somewhere. You just got to know the right doctors to go to. They are always testifying in court, very experienced at it. The problem with policemen is they need to be told exactly what to do. You got to keep a strict eye on them. Once they get a little power it goes to their heads and they think they are emperors like that. That's why here you don't allow Malays and Indians in senior positions in the army, right? They should not be allowed them in the police also. Think about it. The police cover more areas than the army; they have access to so many more places. Far more dangerous, right?'

Aunty Lee thought that might be the reason Cherril seemed to hate Jonny Ho so much. He made disparaging remarks about other races without being aware how offensive he was.

'Beth is also going to report that Malay cop. Such things are always more effective if you get more than one person to complain. Otherwise they don't take you seriously, try to cover it up. But once you get more than one complaint they will think "no smoke without fire". You know what, you should really make a complaint too. People like that, if you don't keep them in their place they start thinking they are big shots. How about it? Beth can write the letter for you; all you have to do is sign it. Then the next time the police turn down your licence application or try to fine you for some rubbish you can accuse them of harassing you because your previous complaint is on record. Best to set up such things in advance. Chances are, they will close one eye and let you off. They are scared you will go and post online and make them look bad. So how about it? And now you've had time to think things over, are you going to let me take your business to the next level?'

Aunty Lee barely heard his questions. She was still processing what he had said earlier, 'Why would Beth complain? Salim didn't even interview Beth, *what*. I saw Sergeant Panchal talking to her.'

Of course Aunty Lee complained as much as and usually more loudly than everyone else; it was one of her greatest social pleasures. But her complaints were delivered as feedback, not meant to get anyone into trouble and certainly not gain an advantage.

'Is Beth complaining about Salim because you asked her to? I thought you two didn't get along. And why didn't you wait to drive back with her?'

'She's going back to the house. I have work to do. We have a business relationship. We're partners in the childcare-school business so we work together to do what's best for the business. If they know we are not scared to complain about them they won't give us so much trouble. Beth's complaint is reporting that Malay cop for stalking and harassing a foreign domestic worker.'

'Julietta?' Aunty Lee asked blankly. 'Inspector Salim was harassing Julietta? The woman who got killed? I cannot believe that. Where would he have the time? He has barely got time to see Nina. And Nina treats him so badly. Why would he go and stalk this Julietta?' She thought of Ying, lurking in his taxi. Could Seetoh have been mistaken for a policeman?

'What? No! He's been stalking your maid, Nina! Since she went to work for Beth, this policeman has been stalking and harassing her. We have her mobile phone with all Inspector Big Shot's luring messages and texts for evidence.'

'No!' Aunty Lee protested. 'They are friends!' She wanted to say that they were more than friends, that she ought to be more than friends and that was what had driven the wedge between them, even before her own clumsy efforts had driven Nina out of her house.

'You will get into trouble too, Rosie, if it comes out that you knew your maid is carrying on with a policeman and didn't stop her. All kinds of things might come out.'

CHAPTER SEVENTEEN

Fabian

Nina sat on the mattress in the storage room. It felt like she had been there for hours, but Nina could not tell how much time had passed because there was no clock in the storeroom and Beth still had her mobile phone.

Nina had stretched and tried to massage her own feet but now she was just sitting. Nina had taken a reflexology course, but most of the reflexology centres in Singapore malls hired only Chinese speakers from China or Malaysia. M. L. Lee had said Nina was better at massaging his feet than any of the old men charging sixty dollars an hour and had insisted on paying her that on top of her monthly salary. He said it was a discount for him, since he didn't have to pay parking charges as he would have had to at a mall. Nina missed the old man, who had been kind to her. And Nina knew that it was because Aunty Lee missed her husband that she tried to matchmake Nina and Salim, as though she was vicariously trying to regain that love and companionship.

Nina put Aunty Lee firmly out of her mind. She was here to take care of Beth's house in Julietta's absence. And if, as she suspected, Julietta had just been found, it would only be a matter of time before Nina was back with Aunty Lee in Binjai Park. Nina remembered the look on Beth's face before she locked her into her room in the middle of the day without explanation. Perhaps it was not Julietta they had found, but Julietta's body.

Nina decided to look through Julietta's things. She had always been too tired by the time Beth locked her in at night. If something had happened to Julietta, her things would have to be sorted through. It was wrong to go through someone's things without permission but it was also wrong that Nina had been locked up with those things. The small cabinet had two drawers that looked as though someone had rummaged roughly through then pushed them shut. She pulled one of them out so that she could look through it without having to bend sideways over the stack of chairs. That was when she saw the small cloth bag hanging by a loop off a nail on the back of the drawer. There was a phone inside it … but the battery was flat, and there was no sign of a charger.

By sticking strictly to vague, fluttery platitudes and pleading a desperate need for the toilet, Aunty Lee got Jonny Ho to drop her back at the café without committing herself to either a business partnership, signing a letter of complaint, or getting dumped by the roadside. He was not in top badgering form and clearly had other things on his mind. Aunty Lee was more certain than ever that his motive had been to get her away from the police post. She only wished she knew why!

Her phone had buzzed along the way. Aunty Lee let it ring. If, as Aunty Lee hoped, Nina had got over her stubbornness and was ready to return home she did not want to talk to her in front of Jonny Ho.

But the call was not from Nina.

'This is Fabian Loo.'

'Fabian? Where are you now? Did they arrest you?'

'They let me go. But they made it very clear that I'm under suspicion and told me not to leave Singapore. They're probably watching my every step.' Fabian sounded peevish and whiney.

'That's good, right? Then nobody can rob you. And if you

161

get lost you can ask the police following you where you are. It is like having your own bodyguards, except you don't have to pay them.'

'They're not going to protect me from being arrested for something I didn't do. Anyway it's obvious they think that I killed that stupid maid. Why would I want to do something like that? Even Aunt Beth thinks so. Just now at the police station I asked her what I was going to do. I was upset, in a panic. I mean, I've been away for so long and I don't know anybody here anymore. All I wanted to know was whether she had a lawyer who could help me. But Aunt Beth just brushed me off. She said we shouldn't talk because it would look like we were trying to match our statements, and make them suspicious. That's when I knew for sure that Aunt Beth thinks I killed Julietta. She wouldn't even look at me. I suppose she thinks I'm a killer and a criminal.'

Fabian was a moaner, Aunty Lee thought. People like that could drone on about their real or imagined problems forever. At least being suspected of murder probably counted as a real problem.

'Where are you staying while you're in Singapore?'

'I've got a room at the Orchard YMCA. But I don't know what they will say if they know I'm suspected of murder. I'm sure they already think it's strange that I'm staying there alone when my family has a house in Singapore. My mother always said she was going to leave the house to me.'

Aunty Lee very much doubted the staff at the YMCA International House would be concerned about anything other than Fabian's credit card. Of course that might change if he was really arrested for murdering Julietta. Then again, if he was arrested, that would take care of his accommodations. She tried to remind herself that he might be a killer, but it was difficult.

'Why don't you go and stay in your parents' old house then?

They haven't started the school yet. I'm sure your Aunt Beth won't mind you staying in your old room.'

If Fabian was staying at the Jalan Kakatua house, he could sign for supplies and keep an eye on the workers and Nina could return to Binjai Park.

'It's my parents' house. But I can't stay there even if I am welcome, and I know that I'm not. Aunty Beth says it's because of all the renovation work going on there but if there's room for her and That Man I don't see why there isn't any room for me. It isn't as though I take up so much space. In the old days when my parents were still around, my dad's relatives would come down from Ipoh to stay with us. My uncle and aunty and three cousins: they would all just pack in somehow. But now there's no room for me in my own house. When my mum was alive she said I would always be welcome to come back. Not that I would stay there when That Man was there.'

'Come over to my shop,' Aunty Lee urged again. 'You came before, *what*. If you are still at the police station then my shop is very nearby. Tell the police to bring you here.' She suspected that if the police were not charging Fabian, they would not be sorry to get him off their hands.

Fabian looked definitely worse for wear when he arrived. If she hadn't known he had only been brought in that morning, Aunty Lee would have thought the Singapore police tortured people with sleep deprivation.

'Come, come and sit down. Did the police tell you why they kept you for so long?'

'They didn't have to tell me … obviously they think I killed Julietta. What a joke, right?' Fabian's laugh was unconvincing.

'The police are questioning everybody who knew Julietta.'

'Well, they kept me the longest. They didn't even start talking to me until they finished talking to Aunty Beth and That Man.

163

I was starting to think they had forgotten all about me. Julietta worked for my parents for years, you know. Why would I do anything to her? Of course, I resented her for not trying to talk some sense into Mum and for not warning me about what was going on. And I kept her secrets for her too. Did you know that she has two children back home in the Philippines? Did you know she had a boyfriend here too?'

Aunty Lee thought it best not to mention she had met Seetoh. 'How do you know?'

'Mum knew. She always knew everything that was going on, even if she didn't say. About Julietta. About That Man's China thug friends. But they don't believe me. Aunt Beth and That Man told them they saw me talking to Julietta before she disappeared, so, of course, they think I must have killed her!'

'But you did see Julietta the day she disappeared?'

'How was I to know when she disappeared?' Fabian's voice rose.

Aunty Lee remembered the scene he had created on his first visit and moved a water glass slightly further away. Fabian noticed. His shoulders slumped again.

The door chimes rattled, and Helen Chan hurried in, crying at the sight of the plump balding man: 'Fabby, you poor boy! How are you? Rosie, why didn't you call me sooner?'

Aunty Lee, who had called Helen to talk about something else altogether before hearing from Fabian, left her to talk to their old friend's son while she went into the kitchen to get drinks. 'Let me feed him first then we talk,' she warned Helen.

'Your friend's car is in front of the fire hydrant.' Cherril was uncomfortable with Aunty Lee's old school friends.

'She's a senior citizen.' Aunty Lee pulled open the door to the chill room.

'I may have got a bit emotional and aggressive,' Fabian was saying when Aunty Lee returned with bowls of hot curry-flavoured potato and leek soup, and cool honey lemon water for Helen. 'But it's not fair, don't you agree?'

'It's not fair at all!' Helen cooed. 'Oh, you poor boy! Here, have some of this nice soup.'

'What's in it? I have a very sensitive stomach. Anything funny makes me throw up.'

'Don't be scared. Nothing funny in my soup!'

Fabian obviously enjoyed the babying. Fabian reminded Aunty Lee of Jonny Ho. The two men looked completely different, of course. Fabian was bald, paunchy, and peevishly pouting, while Jonny was beautiful and muscular and always smiling to show his white teeth. But they were both completely self-centred.

As Aunty Lee had guessed. Fabian had gone to the Jalan Kakatua house to confront Beth.

'I could not believe that she was just going to stand by and let that man cheat me of everything. She just kept saying that married couples leaving everything to each other is automatic. I would accept that if the couple has been married for twenty years and made their fortune together. But in this case, you're talking about everything that my mum and my dad owned together going to this outsider!'

'Aunty Beth totally let me down. She said I should talk to That Man even though she knows very well what I think of him. Anyway I wasn't going to hang around and talk to him. Julietta followed me out, and I stopped to talk to her. I suppose Aunty Beth or the neighbours saw us talking, that's why they kept asking me where I took her. As if we went somewhere together. They seem to think I was the last person to see her alive, but that's ridiculous.'

'What did Julietta want to talk to you about?'

'Julietta has a son and daughter in the Philippines. My mum had always said that she would leave them something to pay their fees if they made it into university. She asked me if I remembered that. I said, of course. And I would have done the same but now

I don't have the money to do it. She wanted me to text her so we could meet to talk when nobody else was at the house. Can you believe my mother would … '

'There was nothing for Julietta in your mother's last will?'

'No. And she wouldn't have forgotten it. And Julietta was still working for her; Mum would have seen her every day. You see why I say there's grounds to contest the will? If she was of unsound mind or if she was under undue influence when the will was made, it can be declared invalid.'

'Was your mother of unsound mind?' That would explain Patty's abrupt withdrawal from the social scene, Aunty Lee thought. 'Was she doing or saying anything funny?'

'I don't know. I wasn't here. That's why I needed Aunty Beth and Julietta to say something. It's obvious that something was wrong with her … just look at the will! I thought they would be on my side because this supposed will doesn't leave anything to them either.'

'Not even to your aunt?'

'No. But then Mum always said she had spent most of her life supporting Aunty Beth so she wouldn't have left her any money. I thought she would leave her something sentimental like her old CDs or something. Mum said for her birthdays and Christmas Aunty Beth always gave her the CDs she wanted to listen to herself. I should have known something was wrong when Julietta never messaged me.'

'Beth must have taken her phone away. She took Nina's phone away.'

'Julietta had a phone,' Fabian said. 'She gave me her number. Her boyfriend gave her the phone. She said she knew how to get out of the house without Aunty Beth knowing.'

Xuyie put a platter of seafood fried rice with a side of mutton curry on the table in front of Fabian with a shy smile. Avon, who Aunty Lee remembered had flirted shamelessly when Jonny Ho was there, didn't bother to appear.

'Thank you,' Aunty Lee said, but Fabian, turning his attention to the food, did not bother.

It was possible that Patty had changed her mind, of course. It wasn't inconceivable that a woman in love with her new husband might decide to leave everything she had to him instead of to the son who spent so little time in the country that he couldn't even say whether she was of sound mind.

'I think he's trying to frame me,' Fabian said. 'Once he saw I wasn't going to give up and go away. Nobody is going to believe anything I say about my mum's will if they're all busy accusing me of killing Julietta. I don't know any lawyers here. Even if I did I don't have any money to pay them. I can't even afford to go back to New York. Mummy always paid for my tickets when I came back. And even if I get back to New York, what am I going to live on? That Man is controlling Mum's account, and he's stopped my allowance!'

'I thought you were working with computers,' Aunty Lee tried to remember who had told her this but could not. 'That you had started your own company, and you're working with companies like Apple and IBM.'

'I am. But these things take time,' Fabian said shortly. Now he reminded Aunty Lee of Mark and all his failed ventures. What was it with this generation?

Aunty Lee thought Fabian was the one who didn't understand what was going on. He had been taken care of all his life. Now he probably expected his Aunt Beth to come to her senses and bail him out. That was likely his parents' fault, Aunty Lee thought with all the superiority of a childless woman; Patty and Ken had been the sort of parents who shielded their precious boy from all responsibility. Now they were gone and he had never learned to be responsible for himself.

'And the police were asking all kinds of crazy questions. Like why would I know how to use a nail gun, right?'

'They asked you about a nail gun?'

'I know. Crazy, right? They asked if I had done any DIY work, had I used a nail gun recently. I got so upset I just couldn't take anymore. I started crying, and they gave up and said I could go.'

Aunty Lee desperately wanted to know more about the nail gun. But she had to deal with Fabian, and she wanted to talk to Helen. Fabian's misery and hopeless situation had not affected his appetite, Aunty Lee was glad to see. This made her think that Fabian was not finding things were as hopeless as he said. Surely men who believe themselves about to be arrested for murder don't say: 'Why not, I don't mind,' to a second helping of deep fried prawn nuggets? Even if they didn't notice the shy girl offering them.

Aunty Lee did feel sorry for Fabian. Just because you could not solve all the big problems in the universe was no reason not to tackle the small ones that cropped up underfoot. You could listen to an unhappy person talk and feed one hungry murder suspect.

'So, Rosie, the more I think about what you said, the more I think you may be right!' Helen could not keep it in any longer. 'Patty was always so loyal. Or rather, she would never admit that she made a mistake. If Patty thought that her precious Jonny Ho told someone that our house was going to be empty while Peng and I were away, she would never tell me but she would never let him near any of her friends again. And that's exactly what happened, right?'

Aunty Lee glared at Helen. 'I told you not to say anything in front of people.'

'Fabian isn't people, *what*! He's not going to tell them!'

'You think my mum was afraid That Man's friends were robbing her friends?'

Fabian wasn't as slow as he appeared, Aunty Lee thought.

'That would totally explain why Patty stopped all her friends altogether! I knew it wasn't just the cancer!' Helen crowed.

'It was just an idea,' Aunty Lee said, signalling for a fresh basket of crunchy *keropok* for Fabian. 'We have no way to prove it. And even after Patty died the house break-ins are still happening.'

'But not as many! And since then, nobody else that we know. Before that they broke into my house, into Siew and Jean's place, into Ying's mother's house … why didn't I see it earlier?'

Fabian helped himself to a savoury prawn cracker … and then another. 'But it's no use talking to the police. They don't want to listen to anything that might mean more work for them. Like I told them I probably knew why Julietta was killed.'

'Why?'

'Because she knew that my mother was murdered by Jonny Ho.'

'Be careful of Fabian Loo,' said Inspector Salim when Aunty Lee finally managed to get him on the phone. 'He was seen with Julietta the day she disappeared. He was on bad terms with his mother for years, so he shouldn't be surprised that she wrote him out of her will. And he has been harassing and threatening his aunt and stepfather.'

'I suppose you got that from Jonny Ho?'

'From several sources.' Salim lowered his voice. 'Neighbours saw Fabian shouting at Julietta outside the house. I shouldn't be telling you this, but I want you to be careful.'

Aunty Lee dismissed the report of neighbours. Hadn't she herself been reported as a burglar by neighbours? 'Did you see the note I left you? About the break-ins?'

'I'll get round to that when this is sorted out.' New murders took priority over old burglaries. 'Nina's okay?'

'She's okay.' Aunty Lee said firmly. Salim had more than enough to worry about. He didn't have to know that Aunty Lee intended to get Nina back to Binjai Park as soon as possible.

'And Fabian told you Julietta was murdered because she had proof that his mother was murdered?'

'Patricia Kwuan-Loo was not murdered. She had colon cancer

169

with secondaries in the pancreas. We have gone through the hospital records and talked to her doctors, believe me.'

'I suppose they warned you to watch out for me,' Fabian said miserably when Aunty Lee got off the phone. 'I know they suspected me. Now you suspect me too.'

'I don't let other people tell me who to suspect. I only want to make sure that you are all right. From what I remember of Patty, she would not have left you with nothing. She would not have left Julietta with nothing. She probably expected Jonny to set up some kind of trust for you. You should talk to him.'

'I shouldn't have to crawl to that bugger to get what's mine.'

'At least talk things over with your Aunt Beth, because family shouldn't fight. Maybe she will try to get Jonny to do the right thing. Shouting at him and threatening him won't do any good. Actually,' Aunty Lee looked at Helen, who was plainly dying to confront Jonny Ho herself, 'I have an idea.'

CHAPTER EIGHTEEN

Salim Suspended

Aunty Lee did not think much of it when there was no word from Inspector Salim. In fact, she barely noticed that no one from the Bukit Tinggi Neighbourhood Police Post stopped by Aunty Lee's Delights for lunch or snacks.

Despite Aunty Lee's confidence in her plan, she wanted to mention it to Salim before putting it into action. More than anything, she needed to discuss it with somebody, because she only knew exactly what she had to do when she was telling somebody. Normally she would talk to Nina, but, in Nina's absence, Aunty Lee turned to the person she knew must be missing Nina as much as herself.

Also, Aunty Lee felt a little guilty towards Salim. Without her interference, he might have worked things out between him and Nina in time.

But not in my lifetime, Aunty Lee thought crossly, given how over slow and over patient the man was. This guilt resulted in the *pandan chiffon cake* and a waxed brown paper packet of *ondeh ondeh* that she brought with her to the neighbourhood police post.

'For all of you,' Aunty Lee announced, putting the gifts on Mark Sheridan's desk. 'The cake can be put in the fridge but the *ondeh*

ondeh better eat now.' Aunty Lee opened and flourished the packet of glutinous rice balls. They were plump with *gula melaka* (liquid palm sugar) and fragrantly coated with freshly shredded coconut. 'No artificial colouring. Even the *pandan* is from my own plants, don't worry.' *Pandan* or *screw pine leaves* were another staple that Aunty Lee could never have enough of. Thanks to Nina there were several healthy plants in the garden of the Binjai Park bungalow as well as two pots outside the back door of the café. Aunty Lee was also in the habit of pinching and sniff testing every *pandan* plant she encountered, which had led to minor neighbourly altercations in the past. 'I know Inspector Salim likes my *ondeh ondeh*. Call him and tell him to come out and eat.'

'Inspector Salim is not here,' a stiff-lipped Staff Sergeant Panchal told her.

'When will he be back?'

'Sorry, I cannot say, Madam.'

Aunty Lee had had her differences with the young woman officer before. Being female, Indian and a police sergeant, Panchal had got where she was by hard work, and she had tried to hold others to the same strictest standards she imposed on herself. Aunty Lee believed in adapting standards to people and situations. Still, Panchal had unwound sufficiently to accept that Aunty Lee meant no harm.

'*Aiyoh*. I walked all the way here to bring just for him because I know he likes,' Aunty Lee said pleadingly. The walk had taken her less than fifteen minutes, and that included stopping to chat with a neighbour walking a dog, another neighbour polishing her car, and a third working on the vertical garden he was constructing on the outer perimeter of his home. 'Nah, I better leave them here for you all. Better eat first, don't waste.'

The young policewoman unbent sufficiently to ask: 'Should I call somebody to come and bring you back?'

'No *lah*, what for? My place so nearby.' Aunty Lee didn't elaborate that with Nina gone there was no one she could call except Cherril, and she didn't want Cherril to know she was meddling. Again.

'I'll come and help you flag down a taxi,' Panchal said. 'Sheridan, I'm taking a break. Take over the phones for me.'

There was something in Panchal's manner that brooked no argument. Aunty Lee allowed herself to be ushered out of the station and onto the sidewalk. Once outside Panchal steered her towards a small children's play area some twenty metres away. The bench between the sandpit and curvy slide was empty, and they settled on it.

'Inspector Salim is on suspension from active duty. Please don't tell anybody I told you.'

When Panchal was first assigned to the Bukit Tinggi Neighbourhood Police Post, Aunty Lee had thought rapid advancement was the only thing on her mind. Panchal had reported her colleagues for violations of the rules, including eating while on duty and carrying personal mobile phones on station premises. At one time she had even reported Salim, her superior officer, for coming into work late without calling in, even though he had been on duty till 3 a.m. and everyone at the station and HQ knew about the case he had just wrapped up. Panchal had been upset … after all, what were rules for if they could be set aside at any time? Now she was looking upset for a different reason.

'What happened?'

'There were some complaints about him. Some civilians reported that he mistreated them while they were in the station.'

Aunty Lee remembered overhearing Jonny telling Beth to complain. She had thought it was macho pride and had not thought Beth would take him seriously. She had not given the man enough credit; he had made Beth follow through. And the police force had been taken in? Any idiot should have been able to see through such a ridiculous complaint!

'Rubbish! I know who made the complaints. He made them up. Anybody who knows Salim should know that's not true!' Aunty Lee glared at SS Panchal.

Panchal looked worried, but not for herself. There was hope for the girl yet, Aunty Lee thought. She resolved to make some of her special cakes for SS Panchal, whose pleasantly padded figure suggested a definite fondness for sweet things, but not right now. Right now she had more important things to take care of.

'Don't worry. I won't say that you are the one who told me.'

Aunty Lee speed walked home in record time. She had a phone call to make, in private. Cherril saw her boss padding swiftly and grimly past the café and wasn't surprised when her wave went unanswered. Aunty Lee might be a great one for noticing details other people missed, but like a dog on the scent of a rat or a loan shark after a debtor, nothing distracted her from her purpose once she found it.

Right then Cherril would have been only too happy to be distracted. She had been pleased at the good response to her catered home party meals. As she had guessed, people who put effort into doing up their homes appreciated the opportunity to show them off to friends, while enjoying the party with them rather than worrying about the catering. The problem was so many of them seemed to enjoy worrying about the menu. Some of her clients phoned daily, wanting to discuss new ideas they had got. Aunty Lee would have told them they would love whatever she cooked and get away with it, even if she didn't decide what to prepare until she visited the market on the morning of the party. But even though Cherril prepared detailed menus based on her clients' food allergies, food preferences, and the best seasonal produce her clients still called her for daily discussions. One hostess had even passed the number to her invited guests and told Cherril to go through her favourite foods quiz with them so that the meal would suit everyone. The phone rang again now, even as Cherril wondered whether something had upset Aunty Lee – if she should go after her.

'Phone for you, Madam Cherry,' one of the part-timers interrupted her thoughts of escape. Cherril was starting to hate telephones.

Pacing up and down the porch behind in her bungalow because she was generating too much energy to sit still, Aunty Lee was not enjoying her phone call either. 'What do you mean you cannot do anything? I'm telling you that this guy boasted he's going to make a false report about your Inspector! A false report! And you say you got to believe him? You say you cannot do anything except believe this liar? If you cannot do anything then who can? Who should I be talking to?'

No one complains with as much skill and energy as a Peranakan Aunty, and Aunty Lee was the essence of Peranakan Aunties personified.

'I did not say we believe the complaint. I said we have to investigate the complaint. We investigate all complaints made against our officers,' Commissioner Raja said. He did not tell his old friend he had been expecting her call. 'We have to follow the law or change the law. That is what having the law is all about. Not just following it when it suits you.'

'Just like that? Without even asking what happened? That means any time I get angry with my policeman I can phone and say he harassed me and you will sack him? How can I like that!'

'There is no "like that". There are procedures. For ranks below Inspector they are charged immediately, and what happens to them depends on whether they plead guilty or claim a hearing. For those of Inspector rank and above, like Salim, there is internal investigation first. Salim is waiting for his internal investigation to be scheduled, and he opted to take unpaid leave until the investigation is over.'

'I still think it is stupid and unfair.'

Aunty Lee called Mark next. She did not talk to Selina on the phone if she could help it, because Selina tended to shout over the phone and Aunty Lee (who shouted herself) found it painful.

'I need to get Nina back. Tell Silly-Nah to tell her business partner that. Since Beth's maid is dead she can make the agency send her another maid.'

'It's not that simple.' Mark sounded tired. 'Now there's an investigation going on into the agency too. I don't know what's happening. Apparently there was something wrong with Julietta's papers, and there aren't any more maids. Jonny was in the process of buying out the company. Selina says to tell you to just let Nina stay with Beth for now, or she will be in trouble with the police for working two places. She'll come back when the investigation dies down. It's only to stop you and Nina from getting into trouble. You should know it's illegal for Nina to work in your shop.'

Aunty Lee would have slammed down the phone if she could. Just pressing a tiny 'Off' button didn't give the same satisfaction. For a moment she considered throwing her mobile phone against the wall, just to release some of the pressure inside her. But that would probably spoil the phone. That made her think of Nina, who didn't have her phone with her, and Julietta, who had had a phone Beth didn't know about. Had Julietta's phone been found with her body? Aunty Lee forced herself to calm down and think what was the best thing to do. She had to get Nina away from the Jalan Kakatua house as soon as possible. Something about that place was starting to make Aunty Lee very uncomfortable. She sensed the presence of unpleasantness like a kitchen with cockroaches in the pantry and rats in the drains. She would get Nina safely away from there. And she would get Nina to tell the police that Salim had not been harassing her, even if it meant Nina losing her Singapore work permit.

It took a bit more time but Aunty Lee finally managed to track down Salim's home number.

'Salim! Why aren't you answering your mobile phone? I was

worried about you! What happened to you? Are you sick? Do you need some healing soup?'

'Hello, Aunty Lee.' Salim didn't want to talk to anyone, but the old lady's delight at finally getting to speak to him was touching, and he couldn't help smiling. 'How are you?'

'*Aiyoh*, I don't know what is happening around here anymore. You want me to write letters to the newspapers and say that we don't feel safe because the stupid police force suspends good policemen anyhow?'

'Please don't. This is my first holiday in a long time.'

'If you are so free then come and eat lunch at my shop? Bring your mother to come and eat! I want to see what she thinks of my *sayur lodeh*!'

It would be a memorable encounter, Salim thought. His mother was as proud of her *sayur lodeh* – vegetables in a coconut based curry – as Aunty Lee was of hers. At a previous meeting the two had almost got into a fight over whether sweetcorn kernels, baby corn or cross sections of corn cob were preferable or even permissible. Yet both old ladies recalled the encounter fondly.

'Sometime, maybe, but not now.' He knew Aunty Lee meant well, but he didn't want to meet up with anyone in the Bukit Tinggi jurisdiction just yet. Whatever anyone tried to say, being suspended was a disgrace. 'How is Nina?'

'I don't know.'

Silence. Then: 'I understand. Nina doesn't want you to talk about her to me.'

'You don't understand anything! I can't talk to Nina. That's why I need you to do a favour for me. Right now you are not working so you got nothing to do, right?'

That was not strictly true. Salim's mother was almost as good as Aunty Lee at making the most of good quality ingredients and people. In his few days off he had already dismantled and cleaned behind the washer-dryer and above the ceiling fans, and now she was talking about a friend and neighbour who could really use the same help ... especially as she only had three daughters and no sons to help her ... three beautiful and smart daughters.

'What do you want me to do?'

The rolling of a *poh piah* at the dining table seems simple. But that is only because of all the work that has already gone into preparing the individual ingredients for each diner to select for each spring roll. Aunty Lee started to put together her ingredients. But where to start?

Aunty Lee knew there was no point trying to phone Nina. Nina's mobile phone was being held by the police as evidence against Salim. With some trepidation she called Ying. If Seetoh hadn't killed Julietta, he would be feeling terrible. And if he had?

'Julietta had another mobile phone, didn't she? Other than the one that Beth took away from her?'

'What difference does it make now?'

'No difference at all. But if she didn't have a phone, she couldn't get in touch with you, right?'

'I got her another phone. But that was because she needed to be able to talk to her children. And she was worried that in an emergency they would not be able to reach her. When I came to see her she would charge it in my taxi.'

'Do you know where she kept it?'

'Maybe whoever killed her took it.'

'If not?'

'If not then it will still be in the house. She hid it somewhere in her room, where Miss Beth wouldn't find it.'

CHAPTER NINETEEN

Beth and Nephew

Beth was surprised when Aunty Lee, Helen Chan, and Fabian turned up at the Jalan Kakatua house in Helen's pale blue Jaguar. Fabian was accompanied by a rolling suitcase and matching cabin bag. Both pieces of luggage bore Singapore Airlines Business Class labels that suggested he had not been left as short on funds as he claimed.

'Jonny is not here,' Beth said. But Aunty Lee could tell from the worried way she glanced at the stairs behind her that she was lying; Jonny was somewhere in the house. It looked like poor Beth, who had spent years trying to expose Patty for lying, was now lying for Patty's husband. Aunty Lee, who didn't approve of lying for anyone other than herself, felt a twinge of genuine pity for Beth.

Beth stepped out and pulled the door shut behind her. 'It's been a stressful time, and I am very busy. Sorry to be rude, but what do you want?'

'Aunty Helen is going away with her husband and doesn't want to leave me alone in the house,' Fabian announced with sing-song truculence. 'And Aunty Rosie doesn't want me alone in the house with her. So I am coming back to stay here.'

'Helen's still upset after that burglary,' Aunty Lee leaned in confidentially. 'So hard to move on. But I told her that if her husband can buy new electronics she can jolly well buy new jewellery, right? And her husband got this motion sensor burglar alarm that videos everything so she doesn't even want to go downstairs without putting on her make-up.'

Helen gave Aunty Lee a sour look. 'Anyway, we don't want to leave Fabian alone in the house. It's not that we don't trust him. But the stupid security system is so complicated, and if you don't remember the code in time the police car comes and scolds you for wasting their time.'

Aunty Lee was impressed by Helen's elaboration. Beth seized on her mention of the police.

'The police told Fabian to stay at your house. If he moves out, they will put him back in prison!'

'I told the police I was coming here to stay in my old room, and they said okay.'

That was not strictly true, but would be true once Aunty Lee got back to Salim.

'And I am bringing Nina home with me now,' Aunty Lee said firmly. 'So you will have space for him.'

'You are being unreasonable,' Beth said flatly. 'We had an agreement. You can't just march in here at any time of day and demand your servant back. Remember her work permit complication? Does Selina know you're here?'

'This is not Selina's business.' In fact, Aunty Lee had not seen or heard from Selina since the news that Julietta's body had been found. Was she backing away for once? 'Nina is working for me, not for Selina. Nina!' Aunty Lee called out, shouting over Beth's protests. She thought she heard a muffled response, but couldn't make out the words. At least Nina didn't sound hurt or upset!

'I told you Nina is busy. This is my house, and you are making a nuisance of yourself.' Beth stepped backwards and stood with her back against the door, decisively blocking Aunty Lee, who had tried to step around her. 'Why are you desperate to have her back in your house? Rosie, this is not healthy you know. You should talk to a therapist.'

'I need her to come back and sort out my computer. She has to put up next week's lunchtime specials. I don't like getting outside people to do my website because I heard those IT young-sters are always trying to put up cartoons of naked politicians doing funny things.'

Any normal person, Aunty Lee was sure, would have asked *which* politicians and *what* things. Beth zoomed in on the website.

'No computers. That's another thing I must warn you about. You should never let them go online. That's how they connect and pass on secrets to each other!'

'Secrets? You mean like my recipes? Nina would never tell anybody else my recipes! Has she been cooking for you here? If she cooked my recipes for you then she must come back and cook your recipes for me!'

There was a pause. Aunty Lee wondered whether she had gone too far. But apparently Beth put no limits on the stupidity of her late sister's friends.

'You should just get a recipe book. Anyway, I will tell Nina you want her to go back. But I warn you, she may not want to. I don't think she wants to be around that policeman who is stalking her. These foreigners are always scared of the police. Nina is better off here, and you are better off not getting involved. You will both thank me later.'

'You let me see her I can say thank you to you now.'

'Not now,' Beth said. 'This is the middle of her work day.'

Beth must still miss the strict schedules of her schooldays, Aunty Lee thought.

'Then when?'

'When she finishes. That girl is so slow and so clumsy. I'm sure it's on purpose. Your fault, for giving her too much freedom. She's clever. You can never trust these clever ones; they are the most lazy. They are always watching you to see what they can get away with.'

Aunty Lee could not deny Nina's cleverness. She remembered how quickly Nina got things done once she realized that Aunty Lee was more interested in getting things done than keeping her helper fully occupied ... as Aunty Lee suspected Beth of being.

'Tell you what,' Helen said. 'I'm not in any hurry. Rosie, why don't you call Mycroft and tell him to pick you up from here for your meeting with Cognate? I will wait here and settle Fabian in. Then I will drive Nina home when she's finished whatever.'

The mention of a Cognate meeting upset Beth. She opened the door and started backing in. 'I've had enough of your nonsense!' She clearly intended to close it after her.

Fabian, moving surprisingly quickly, stuck his foot in the door. 'I have to stay here. I've already given this address to the police station.' Though a little breathless he sounded petulantly bored as usual. 'I have to be here when they come to check.'

Beth Kwuan looked indecisive. 'I must talk to Jonny first.'

This was the opening Aunty Lee had been waiting for. 'Do you have to ask Jonny Ho permission to let Fabian stay in his own mother's house? Beth ... has that man been threatening you? Are you scared of him?'

'Of course not! That is so ridiculous! So absurd! You are mad. Please leave at once. Get out of my house, all of you!'

'I want to see Nina first.' Aunty Lee knew that she sounded querulous and unreasonable. 'If I don't see her, I'm not leaving.' She might be embarrassing Helen and Fabian but she didn't care. In fact, neither of them was backing down, and they seemed as interested in seeing Nina as she was.

Beth shrugged ungraciously. She tried to push the door shut, but a piece of Fabian's luggage had joined his foot and the door stayed open. Beth sighed exaggeratedly and said: 'Wait here.'

They watched her go up the stairs with slow, forceful steps, then heard her bang on the door, then say loudly: 'somebody wants to talk to you,' as she unlocked it.

Aunty Lee could not hear what Beth was muttering to Nina

as she walked her Nina down the stairs. But she was so glad to finally see Nina again that she didn't care.

Nina was all right. That was all that mattered, Aunty Lee thought, hurrying to her. She immediately forgot all the dread dark thoughts that had been swarming inside her head. Of course Nina could look after herself!

'Oh Nina! I missed you so much! You must come back. I won't nag you anymore.'

Nina looked years older and much more tired compared to the last time Aunty Lee had seen her. The whites of her eyes were yellow, her cheeks hollow, and face lined with new wrinkles. Dehydrated, Aunty Lee thought, looks like she has not been eating or sleeping enough.

'I cannot go back to your house until I finish my work here, Madam,' Nina said mechanically. Clearly these were words Beth had told her to say, and just as clearly Beth didn't like the way she had said them because she pinched the flesh on Nina's arm and twisted it.

Aunty Lee was struck by how automatic it was. And how it barely seemed to register with Nina. She batted Beth's hand away. 'Nina, you must come back with me right away!' Aunty Lee said. 'I need you!' She felt tears welling up in her eyes.

Nina stepped forward and put her arms around Aunty Lee, murmuring comforting words to her.

Beth watched suspiciously, muttering: 'Nonsense,' and 'No self-respect' to no one in particular.

Helen looked confused but not uncomfortable. She didn't know what was going on, but was quite willing to wait and watch.

And Fabian sighed with exaggerated satisfaction: 'This is better than reality TV.'

'I must stay here and finish my work first,' Nina said, stepping back.

Beth's thin lips straightened in triumph.

'After I finish I will come back to your house,' Nina continued.

'I will try to come tonight. Please can you tell my friend that I lost my phone? That is very important.'

'Not tonight, tonight is too soon … ' Beth started to say.

'I'll wait for you,' Helen said brightly. 'Go and finish whatever you have to do … I'll even help. Then I can drive you back to Binjai Park with your things.'

'Don't be ridiculous,' Beth said coldly.

'Oh, don't be silly, Beth. I'm not completely useless, you know! If there's a lot of work to be done, you can use an extra pair of hands. Show me what Nina is working on in that room you locked her in and I will help. Rosie, you go off first. I know you have a meeting later, right?'

Aunty Lee left quietly. She knew that Helen would not leave without Nina. Helen, behind her perfectly made-up face, was totally set on solving the burglaries. It was personal for her, since her house had been the first broken into.

Only when she was safely away from the house did Aunty Lee look at the phone Nina had slipped out of her own pocket and into her purse when she hugged her. It was encased in a disposable latex glove, much like one of the gloves Aunty Lee distributed to customers who ordered chilli crab or black pepper crab and wanted to savour the juiciest claw tips without getting their fingernails dirty. It did not look like Nina's phone. Aunty Lee tapped the 'Power On' button through the glove but the phone was dead. She did not know whose phone it was, or why Nina wanted her to pass it to Salim. Hopefully Salim would be able to make sense of it. And then she would go for her meeting.

Of course, it might be a complete waste of time. But there would be no harm done. It is always better to find out you are on the wrong track than continue along it happily and pointlessly.

CHAPTER TWENTY

Miss Wong

A puzzled but agreeable Mycroft had arranged the meeting for Aunty Lee. Mycroft Peters was happy to indulge the sweet old aunty who his mother was so fond of, and who his wife so enjoyed working with. Even if Cherril didn't earn much at the café, she came home happy and to Mycroft that was worth a great deal more than money.

'Miss Wong will be happy to meet with you,' he told her as she got into his car. That was not strictly accurate. Wilhelmina Wong had protested her schedule and her busyness and the point-lessness of her meeting with a woman who was not her client. But Aunty Lee's account with Cognate was a large one and when Darren Sim (junior to her, but coming up fast) added his request to Mycroft's, Miss Wong decided there were different kinds of busyness and made the appointment.

Back at Ngee Ann City, they headed back up to the Cognate offices via the Tower A lift lobby. Darren Sim met them in the lobby area, coming forward even as Mycroft pushed open the tinted glass doors. At Aunty Lee's request, Mycroft had not given any reason for the meeting request, and Darren looked appre-hensive.

'Is everything all right?' Darren addressed Aunty Lee but looked nervously at Mycroft, who was looking his most lawyerly that morning.

Aunty Lee was more used to seeing Mycroft Peters in grungy shirts and shorts when he came to meet Cherril at the shop, and she had to admit he cleaned up quite impressively.

'You'll have to ask Mrs Lee.'

'Where is Miss Wong? Miss Willy-something Wong? You arranged for us to meet her, right?' Aunty Lee tucked a hand into Darren's arm as though he was a grandchild, even as she put him in charge of directions. 'Take me to see her now, can you?'

'I'll show you to Miss Wong's office. You didn't say what this meeting is about ... anyway I prepared all your files in case you wanted to take a look at any of your portfolios? I can explain anything that you are concerned about ... '

'Are you concerned? Then what for I get concerned? You are taking care of everything, right? Now, let's go to Miss Wong's office.'

They arrived at the same office that Aunty Lee had visited with Jonny Ho. However, a different woman was sitting behind the broad, polished desk. She rose to greet them as Darren showed them in: a tall woman in a grey-green dress and dark green jacket, slightly older and quite a bit more solid than the previous 'Miss Wong' Aunty Lee had met. She smiled warmly ... a Chinese–Indian mix like Mycroft Peters, Aunty Lee thought, or Eurasian–Indian mix. She was darker than Mycroft, but with a muscular grace that suggested her colouring came from outdoor activities as well as genetics. She was certainly not the plump, awkward Chinese girl Aunty Lee had spoken to on her previous visit, yet she was vaguely familiar. And despite her un-Chinese looks she suited the name on the engraved desk plate far better.

'Pleased to meet you, Mrs Lee. I'm Wilhelmina Wong. You were here last week, weren't you? I saw you coming out of the lift ... I thought I recognized you. Aunty Lee's Amazing Achar right? I'm addicted to the stuff! Please come and take a seat. Hello, Mycroft. What can I do for you today?' She did not greet or acknowledge Darren, who might have been part of the furniture. From Darren's obsequious manner it was clear that he was worried about remaining part of the company furniture. But if a valued client had found some problem, however unjustified, with his management he knew the company would do what it could to appease her ... and he might be out of a job.

'I also thought I saw you last week,' Aunty Lee told Wilhelmina Wong. She kept her hold on Darren's arm until he deposited her carefully on a seat. 'Thank you, Darren. But not inside this office here where I was introduced to you. Only, it wasn't you. I think I did see you outside the lift last week but I didn't know who you were. You said "Hello" to me, right? And then I came here, to this same office, and I talked to Miss Willy-Mini-something Wong; only, it wasn't you. That's why I wanted to come back and check.'

Wilhelmina Wong studied Aunty Lee (looking for possible signs of dementia ... the woman seemed harmless) then darted over Mycroft (impassive and non-committal) and finally Darren. She raised an eyebrow at Darren, finally deigning to acknowledge him.

'There must be some mistake,' Darren said. His relief at learning he was not the focus of Aunty Lee's visit was clear. 'Your accounts aren't being handled out of this branch. That's why I was so surprised you wanted to meet here. Of course, I can transfer everything over to this branch, but I thought that for your convenience you would prefer ... '

Miss Wilhelmina Wong cut him off with the slightest shake of her head. This example of her authority impressed Aunty Lee. Darren immediately switched tracks, which also impressed Aunty Lee.

'You said you came to this office last week, Mrs Lee?'

'Yes! I came to this office, and I thought I talked to Miss Willy-something Wong who is the big boss here. She knew all about the investments you made for me also. She talked about the McDonald's Corporation and New York Stock Exchange and I don't know what not, but I remember that name because of the French fries.'

'French fries?'

'Yes! When Darren told me about McDonald Corporation, I said "McDonald like in French fries?" and he said 'yes'. I told him that if he likes French fries one day he should come and I will make my French fries for him. I fry them in lard. The taste is so good, once you taste my French fries you will never eat the McDonald's ones again!'

Darren glanced at the files he was still holding. 'You did have some notes with the McDonald's Corporation but I believe we let them go several months ago. After handling fees and the Goods and Services tax you made a good profit.'

Aunty Lee waived that off as irrelevant. 'I told you: all that stuff I leave to you. But that is why I remember you told me about buying McDonald's. So I knew that that other Miss Wong knew about my stuff.'

'Your equities,' Wilhelmina Wong corrected almost absent-mindedly. 'There is no other Miss Wong here that I know of. Certainly not at this level in this office. Nobody here should know about your portfolio aside from you and your relationship manager.' She nodded towards Darren.

'I keep her updated,' Darren said to Wilhelmina Wong. 'I made sure I sent her all the documentation … ' Again he was waved aside.

'You said someone spoke to you here, in this office, as Miss Wong, that day when I saw you,' Wilhelmina said to Aunty Lee. 'Given it clearly wasn't me, can you tell me what the meeting was about? Were you asked to sign anything? To hand over anything?'

'No *lah*, I am not so stupid as that. I never sign anything unless I show these two young men first.' There was a release of tension in the atmosphere at that as both 'young men' and Miss Wong relaxed slightly on hearing this. 'That Miss Wong wanted me to sign. She said that, nowadays with all the computer fraud and online fraud, you can't trust anything you get on the computer or printed out, so the only recommendation you can trust is one you get in person from Cognate. That's why I had to come here and in person. But I didn't sign because that is the first time I saw her. Then today I come back to Cognate and you are also Miss Willy-Mini-Wong, but you are a different woman. So how can I trust you?'

'I assure you I am Wilhelmina Wong,' Wilhelmina Wong said. She tapped the name plate on the desk. She certainly seemed more comfortable in this office than the other 'Miss Wong' Aunty Lee had met. The cool minimalist dark wood decor in the office matched her calm, authoritative manner and the deceptively simple elegance of her silky green dress and perfectly fitted jacket. 'If you'll wait here for a moment I'll see if I can locate the person you are looking for. Darren … with me.'

Mycroft released a huge breath once the door closed behind them. 'Why didn't you tell me? You can't just let strangers bring you places without telling anybody. You're lucky they just tried to con you. If this was anywhere other than Singapore, you might have been kidnapped and held for ransom!'

'If this was anywhere other than Singapore, I wouldn't have got into his car.' Aunty Lee was unrepentant. Her eyes were shining, and she was excited. Things were finally coming together! 'Anyway, I put chilli oil in a perfume spray bottle and when I was inside his car I kept my hand on it. If he did anything … Sssss.' Aunty Lee whipped out the little perfume bottle. 'I didn't clean out all the perfume so, even if he can't see, he will smell nice.'

The young woman whom Aunty Lee had met on her previous visit was re-introduced as Eva Tan, one of Miss Wong's legal assistants. Eva might have been about the same age as her boss, but they had little else in common. Eva's attempts to look good … the glossy pink lipstick, the thick concealer … were far more obvious and far less effective than anything Wilhelmina might have done. Aunty Lee recognized the 'Miss Wong' of her previous visit at once when she was brought back into the office, and Eva's initial attempts to laugh it off as 'just a joke' were rapidly crushed.

'It's not a joke,' Mycroft spoke up. 'You are probably going to lose your job here and, after you are reported, you will probably be disbarred by the Law Society and lose your licence to practice law in Singapore. Do you think that's funny?'

'No harm was done,' Eva said, looking scared but defensive. 'All we did was talk. It was all a joke. Anyway no harm was done.'

'I phoned up to ask about Patty's account here. I was put through to Miss Wong's office, but you must have taken the message and told Jonny Ho instead of Miss Wong, right?'

Miss Wong was stony-faced and not giving away anything in front of outsiders but her look did not bode well for Eva's future career within the company. Eva probably knew this and thought she had nothing to lose. Aunty Lee thought the young woman had the air of an amateur actor taking on a role practised many times in her mind. And she wasn't playing the role of the exposed criminal, but the heroine who knows she is in a temporary setback, but that everything will come out all right in the end. Any attempt to force her to admit she and Jonny Ho had deliberately tried to deceive Aunty Lee would only be met by further declarations that it had all been 'just a joke'. Eva Tan had probably already said it to herself so many times that she believed it.

'No harm done,' Aunty Lee said quickly. 'It was just a joke.' The others looked at her in surprise and varying degrees of suspicion. Eva herself looked the most surprised.

'You are the girl in those photos he took, right?'

Eva stared. 'I don't know what you're talking about. What photos?' Now she looked worried. But it was too late. Aunty Lee knew she was right.

Aunty Lee knew many wannabe cooks like Jonny Ho. Their

focus was always on themselves, and they thought their strength was in their recipes which they changed as little as they could. They were lazy-minded people who served the same dishes over and over again to different people because they assumed that something that worked once would work forever.

'Jonny Ho took photos of you, didn't he?' Aunty Lee turned to include Darren and Miss Wong in her explanation. 'That man has been going around taking photos of naked women. She is not the only one he took advantage of.' Unlike those cooks who put their faith in secret recipes and techniques, Aunty Lee adapted her dishes to the people she served them to. Everything she did was adapted to the people she was serving and how she wanted to make them feel. Most of the time this was generic, of course … back in the café it was generally safe to bet that her customers were hungry people who wanted familiar food that took a bit more effort and energy than they were willing to invest at home. But even there she adapted, experimented, influenced their choices by offering tasting portions of dishes she knew they would fall in love with … and falling in love was something that had happened here too, she suspected.

'No, he didn't!' Eva spoke automatically but she was staring at Aunty Lee in a shocked way that showed she thought the old woman had seen the photographs. Aunty Lee's guess about the photos had been verified.

'That had nothing to do with anything here!' Eva looked at Miss Wong. 'Those were private pictures. I don't know how Mrs Lee got hold of them but they have nothing to do with her.'

'You do know this Jonny Ho?' Miss Wong asked. There was sympathy in her voice. 'He made you impersonate me in my office?' Darren and Mycroft looked confused and embarrassed, but this woman had immediately picked up what Aunty Lee was trying to do and joined her. Aunty Lee was impressed. She made a mental note to bring Miss Wong some curry puffs along with a giant jar of *achar*.

'I know him. We're friends. Actually, we are more than friends. We are going to get married once we work things out properly.'

'Financially?' Miss Wong still sounded understanding, though she was leading Eva into incriminating herself further.

'Yes … not just financially. We needed to work out the money side of things, yes. But also we wanted to do it properly. Those pictures she saw … ' Eva jerked her head in Aunty Lee's direction without meeting her eyes, 'it's not like she makes them sound. They are artistic pictures. Jonny is very artistic, and photography is one of his passions.'

An involuntary laugh came out of Darren.

Eva glared at him. 'People like you will never understand.'

No, Aunty Lee thought, Darren would probably never understand someone like Jonny Ho. But though he might never rise to the heights scaled by Jonny Ho's reckless self-confidence, Darren would likely never crash as disastrously as Jonny was going to. It was saddest for the Eva Tans of the world, who might have spent their lives comfortably discontent with Darrens if they hadn't been swept up in someone's warped vision of himself. Even if Jonny Ho made it to the top, the Eva Tans he made use of on the way up would be jettisoned once he got there.

Miss Wong must have tapped a call button at some point, because there was a discreet knock on the door and a young woman looked in inquiringly,

'Take Miss Tan to clear out her personal items from her desk. Eva, give Christy your key cards.'

Eva looked shocked and started crying. 'You don't understand. Once Jonny got the capital he needed, he would have made Mrs Lee rich too. It would have been for her own good! Jonny could guarantee her money back plus guarantee her profits … '

'No such thing as guaranteed profits,' Darren said automatically.

'You only think so because they got you totally brainwashed to slave for them,' Eva snapped tearfully. 'You are all so stupid.

Mrs Lee, you know that Jonny only did it to make you feel safer investing in him, right? He would have told you the truth afterwards ... after he made you rich he would have explained it all to you. You trust him, right? Ask him, he will tell you. Aside from that I never did anything wrong. I didn't do anything wrong here except sit at your desk; you can't fire me for that.'

'You got the details of all my investments with Cognate,' Aunty Lee pointed out. 'I remember the other day you were talking about the McDonald's and I remember Darren telling me about the McDonald's so I know that that was really my account. You looked up my account details for him, right?' This made the others snap to attention.

'She accessed your confidential investment records? Aunty Lee, why didn't you say so earlier?' Mycroft, who had been sitting back and enjoying the show, was suddenly alert.

'Darren?' Miss Wong snapped at the same time.

'Not from me,' Darren said with absolute confidence. 'I went strictly by the book. You can see my call records.'

'She wanted to trust Jonny,' Eva wailed. 'She must have told Jonny about all her investments. He said she is one of those old aunties that only invests in what the bank tells her so if he wanted to help her he had to make her think that the bank approved of him! It's not my fault. I only tried to help!'

'Your bank people are very thorough,' Aunty Lee said comfortingly to Miss Wong, 'especially your Darren. I told him so many times already: "do what you want", "I trust you *lah*", but every time he does anything he must send me the report. By phone and then by mail. Waste so much paper.'

Then, with a jolt, Aunty Lee remembered Jonny Ho playing with a notepad made of her recycled investment updates in the café kitchen. She had had to replace that notepad, not thinking anything more of it till now. All her recent account transactions would have been there.

'Maybe Jonny Ho looked through my dustbin and found the

records that Darren sent me. I never gave him anything,' Aunty Lee said vaguely.

'You should get a shredder.' Mycroft was tapping something into his mobile phone. 'When is the last time this Jonny Ho contacted you?' His question was addressed to Aunty Lee but it was Eva who answered.

'I haven't seen him for some time. He told me he was going to be busy for a while, then I didn't see him. We're getting married but I haven't heard from him for over a week, and he doesn't answer my calls.' Eva tearfully dabbed at her face with a tissue, and Aunty Lee noticed she had glitter patterned nails that matched the glitter floral earrings she was wearing. Eva Tan would land on her feet.

'You still have to go,' Miss Wong said.

'Not yet,' Mycroft said. 'The police will want to interview her.'

Eva's wail of 'It's not fair!' came at the same time as Aunty Lee's murmur how 'Young girls always getting taken advantage of. Luckily nothing serious happened.'

'Mrs Lee will not be taking any further action,' Mycroft said.

'But the police will have to be notified,' Miss Wong said.

CHAPTER TWENTY-ONE

Housebreaking Gang Caught

SS Panchal had come round to the shop to pick up some tea snacks for the office, and to tell Aunty Lee (unofficially) that the stalking and harassment charges against Inspector Salim had been dropped after Nina told them she had not made, and had no intention of ever making, a complaint against Inspector Salim.

Of course, Aunty Lee made her sit down with a cool glass of homemade barley water while a fresh batch of 10-spice chicken wings was fried up. And, of course, Aunty Lee had to tell her all about what had happened at Cognate the day before.

'That man should be charged for trying to cheat you!' Panchal echoed Mycroft. But Aunty Lee, who had never been at any real risk of being cheated, had her mind on other things.

'So is Inspector Salim back at work yet? Now that they know the man who complained about him is a liar and a swindler they should say sorry to him and bring him back, right?'

Because, although Nina was back, she was still keeping Salim at a distance. Now it was because she blamed herself for everything that had happened to him. To Nina, even the disgrace of Salim's suspension was her fault. If there had not been so many unanswered messages from Salim on her phone, Beth's spiteful complaints would not have got him into so much trouble.

'No, the Inspector's not back at the office yet,' Panchal told Aunty Lee. 'But he's aware of everything that's going on.'

'So, what is going on?'

It was unofficially understood that Aunty Lee could be told what they had got from the phone she had handed in to the station. Not just because it had come from her, Panchal suspected, but because more might come from her. Even in modern Singapore there remained respect for the old village wise woman.

From fingerprints found, the phone that Nina had found hidden behind a drawer in the tiny room at the top of the stairs was identified as Julietta's secret phone. Seetoh verified it was the phone that he had given Julietta, and the number matched the one she had given Fabian. The police found long conversations with Seetoh, which incriminated him in their eyes. They had obviously had a relationship, and Seetoh had been trying to get her to run away with him. Aunty Lee felt bad that the police were now looking for Seetoh, but she was (almost) certain he would never have hurt Julietta, and once Salim was back on the job everything would be cleared up.

There were also messages from Fabian, some of them angry, complaining that Julietta was avoiding him and not answering his calls. Fabian had wanted Julietta to give evidence against Jonny in a police report he was making. Fabian alleged that Jonny had stolen jewellery, cash, and art pieces belonging to his late mother, and needed Julietta to find proof. In short, he wanted Julietta to find or manufacture evidence that Jonny Ho had sold valuables belonging to his mother and late father and would pay Julietta to do so.'

'Is Fabian in trouble? He could just have been joking, *what*,' Aunty Lee pointed out.

Panchal did not want to talk about the amount of trouble Fabian might be in. There were other secrets in Julietta's phone, most significantly a photograph of Patricia Kwuan-Loo's will. According to this will, dated the day after Helen Chan's house had been burglarized, Fabian was his mother's sole beneficiary, aside from the sum set aside for Julietta's children.

'There's also a big difference in the money she left to Julietta.'

'No, there isn't. It's one of the few things that doesn't change.'

'In the old will, the money was to be sent to pay their university fees with an allowance for books and living expenses.'

That was wise of Patty, Aunty Lee thought approvingly of her dead friend. She wanted to do good but she was no fool. Had she been concerned about Julietta's children or Julietta herself? Even bills for study materials were to be paid through the lawyer's office. Why then did the new will pass the money for Julietta's children directly to her?

'Do you think Julietta's children will still get the money? To be fair it should go to them, right? They'll need it even more now their mother is dead.'

'Did she tell Julietta to photograph it?'

'Very possibly she showed it to Julietta to show her that her children would still be provided for. But Julietta took it the wrong way. We spoke to her son in the Philippines who told us that Julietta said Patty changed her mind and only wanted to give them money if they were clever; if they were stupid they could go and starve. Her son said she was very angry with her boss and was going to fix it.'

Because Julietta had come to feel she and her children were entitled to the money, what Patty might have intended as incentive had been seen as judgement.

Aunty Lee thought Fabian's sense of entitlement had warped him. It seemed he had not been the only one.

'I think after Patty told her that she was going to the lawyer to make a new will, Julietta took a photograph of her rough draft and showed it to Jonny and Beth, to warn them. Even though she had been working for Patty for some time, Julietta's first loyalty was always to herself and her family. She was angry with Patty because she had expected to get money for her children when Ken Loo died; her son had been counting on that; but now, instead, she had to wait for Patty to die too, and even then her son would not get any money unless he went to university. I don't know whether Jonny Ho sweet-talked her with business propositions or if he seduced her, but you know he has always had a way of talking women around. I don't think Julietta expected them to do anything to Patty.'

'Julietta could have said something to the police. She never did.'

'Maybe she couldn't. It was only after Patty died that Beth became so strict about not giving her time off and not allowing her out of the house alone, remember?'

'There was nothing to be left to the new husband?'

'What she was leaving the new husband and the old sister was the interest that they wouldn't have to pay back to Fabian. She made a note of it there, as though she expected her lawyer to ask about it. Because that was the draft she was going to bring to her lawyer. Remember, all Patty's previous wills were drawn up by her lawyer. She might have had good sharp business sense, but being married to a lawyer for so many years made her realize that what somebody intends doesn't count as much as what is written down and properly signed and witnessed on paper. She would never have written that new will in private.'

Also interestingly, as Panchal told her (after all, hadn't she handed the phone over to them), there was a sound recording on the phone of what appeared to be Jonny romancing Beth.

'What you mean "romancing"? You mean like saying, "oh you are so pretty" romancing or "I want to have sex with you" romancing?'

'I think more the second,' Panchal admitted.

Aunty Lee remembered Jonny Ho smiling at her, placing an arm around her shoulders while walking, and his hand over hers at the table. It had never occurred to her that he might be flirting with her, but a policewoman might think so. 'Sometimes that is a misunderstanding,' she said. 'After all, he is not from here. You know how French people auto-maniacally kiss everybody and

American people auto-maniacally grab everybody? Maybe Jonny Ho auto-maniacally flirts with everybody.'

'Automatically,' Panchal said faintly, after a moment. 'And not all Americans do that.'

But Aunty Lee was already on to the next thought: 'And the fact that the phone was behind the drawer in her room shows that she was around the house when she was killed. Because if she was sneaking out somewhere she would have taken it with her. And she used the phone to contact Seetoh – that means she didn't sneak out to meet him, right?'

'Seetoh is the chief suspect now.'

'No, *lah*! How can? Have you talked to him?'

'We haven't been able to find him. His Dispatch Office has no idea; he's not responding. The other drivers say they don't know who he is. Looks like they all covering up for him.'

'*Alamak*. Have you talked to Jonny Ho again?' Aunty Lee felt a twinge of guilt remembering Selina's warning not to make trouble for KidStarters. Still, getting the police to investigate one of the KidStarters' partners before he got the school into trouble might be seen as positive.

'He's another one that's dropped out of sight. Beth Kwuan says she hasn't seen him for days. Apparently, he told her he was going to Hong Kong for a business meeting, but the Immigration and Checkpoints Authority has no record of him leaving the island.'

'What's wrong?'

'Why should anything be wrong?' SS Panchal looked taken aback. But something in the young police officer's voice alerted Aunty Lee, and she wasn't going to let go so easily.

Producing dishes was all about getting the balance right. Of course, having a finely honed sense of taste and smell helped, but all Aunty Lee's senses were finely honed and she could tell there was something wrong here. She had watched SS Panchal mellow from an officious, self-righteous go-getter and relax into a reliable, committed police officer who wasn't above accepting the occasional snack and sharing an occasional titbit, and she could tell something was wrong.

A terrible thought struck her: 'That man, that Jonny Ho, did he come back and *kachiau* you? Since that time you all interviewed him here?' As far as Aunty Lee could see, Jonny Ho flirted with all the women he came into contact with, and a police uniform would be no barrier.

Panchal's snort of disbelief reassured her. 'That racist? No way.'

Aunty Lee believed her, but there was still something wrong. 'So, what is it?'

'Nothing to do with any of this. I've been thinking about getting married, that's all. But you look at the kind of men available ... this Jonny Ho comes along and charms so many women because there are no alternatives. My parents tell me I should think about it but they don't do anything to help me. They say they are too modern to arrange anything for me. They are the ex-hippie generation.'

'What would you want your father and mother to do?'

'I don't want an arranged marriage; I suppose I just want them to take an interest.'

'Then do it yourself. You are in the police; you should know how to check up on a man's background better than your father, and you have seen so many couples fighting so should know how to tell what makes a good husband better than your mother. And then once you decide on somebody, if you end up marrying him, the most important thing is to forget everything you learned about him before. Because this is a new start.'

'Thanks,' Panchal said. 'I don't think I will ... but thanks anyway. And, by the way, I don't believe Inspector Salim did anything wrong. Nobody here believes it. People always come and make complaints.'

There had been times ... were still times ... when SS Panchal did not see eye to eye with her station Inspector. And all too often it was Inspector Salim's easy-going relationship and bending of rules with the residents that Panchal objected to. But since his suspension the number of people who had written letters, posts, and started petitions in Salim's defence had taken the force aback. Never were the police so popular as when one of their number came under attack.

'But proper procedure must be followed,' Aunty Lee said in her best wise voice.

It was so peaceful in the café with the voices of Cherril and a subdued Nina occasionally coming through from where they worked in the kitchen. The doorbell jangled and Aunty Lee called out 'Welcome! Come in!' as she usually did to customers, before she saw that it was Beth Kwuan.

'I've been hearing so much about your place here. I thought, since I wasn't doing anything special for lunch, I would come and see it for myself.'

Panchal excused herself and left, collecting her chicken wings from Cherril. Nina had started to come out with them, but disappeared on seeing Beth.

'Nina told you about my café? She always says I try to do too much. But running a place like this, there is always something to do!' Aunty Lee felt guilty that she had been caught sitting and chatting with a friend rather than hard at work next to the helper she had taken back by force. 'Have you applied for another maid yet?'

Beth brushed off the question. It seemed she wasn't there to talk about her maid problems.

'About Jonny Ho ... '

I was right! Aunty Lee thought with glee. Beth has finally seen through Jonny Ho after watching him being mean to Fabian!

'He's got good ideas and he's got a lot of organizational and managerial skills, but he isn't very easy to live with, if you know what I mean. He's from the "little emperors" generation, an only son of two only children, so even though his family was not very well off they gave him everything they could. He's used to getting his own way, and when he doesn't he gets these temper tantrums. He can't understand how Fabian can sit around all day staring at his phone,'

'Are you trying to get him to move out of Patty's house?' Aunty Lee asked. 'Or buy him out of KidStarters?'

'What are you talking about?' Beth raised her voice involuntarily.

'You were telling me how difficult Jonny Ho is, *what.*'

'I was telling you why Jonny and Fabian don't get along. It's men like Jonny that have what it takes to succeed. They have a drive and a commitment to work and take risks. Our parents' generation, the pioneer generation in Singapore, had it, but after that, with the easy life, everybody here grew soft. Someone like Fabian is a prime example. That's why we need people like Jonny Ho in Singapore.'

There was a fervour in Beth's voice that reminded Aunty Lee of a woman who had once gone from table to table in the café trying to sell CDs for her church.

Beth Kwuan had come on a mission. Was she trying to palm off her poor nephew or was this another attempt to exonerate Jonny Ho? Aunty Lee was on the alert.

'Jonny Ho got a girl at the bank to impersonate her boss and lie to me,' Aunty Lee said. 'I felt sorry for the girl. She thinks that she loves him and he is going to marry her. But he has so many women in love with him, and she has only one job. Now she's lost it.'

Aunty Lee did not tell Beth Eve had later told the police that Jonny had nude photos of her that he threatened to send to her boss if she did not do what he wanted. And the girl still thought herself in love with him? Aunty Lee did not understand young women. 'The police are going to talk to Jonny Ho about it.'

Aunty Lee poured them cups of tea from the glazed porcelain tea pot that had appeared on the table.

'That's not very nice of you,' Beth said. 'You should have asked Jonny for an explanation before going to the police.'

Beth's fingers unfolded a table napkin then re-folded it with precise attention to the folds, running a fingernail along the crease to sharpen the mark. Aunty Lee was momentarily distracted by Beth's manicure ... shiny nails in graduated shades from dark red thumbs to pale pink pinkies. If Beth had got them in different colours rather than different shades she could have used her nails to teach colours to her pre-schoolers, Aunty Lee thought. It was a strange contrast ... the nails straight, cut short, and the fancy manicure colours over them. Like a little girl playing dress up. And was the woman wearing lipstick? It was hard to tell.

Beth raised her voice slightly, pulling Aunty Lee's attention back. 'He's treating the house like a hotel. Whenever I see him he's hunching over his phone whispering. I don't know whether he has a girlfriend or boyfriend or what!'

'Jonny Ho?'

'Fabian!' Beth said impatiently. 'My own sister's boy in prison. Maybe even worse. Singapore, they still hang people, right? *Aiyoh*, imagine my own sister's son getting executed for murdering her husband!'

'Why are the police questioning Fabian?' Aunty Lee felt cross with Panchal for not telling her that.

'It's obvious, isn't it? Everybody knows how much Fabian hated poor Jonny. Even when my sister was still alive he would phone and tell me how much he hated him. He was already making threats. And since coming back this time he told me that he was not going to stand for it anymore. He was going to make sure that Jonny Ho got what was coming to him. And now Jonny has disappeared!'

'You told the police all this?'

'I had to. They are the police. I can't keep it to myself and get arrested for withholding evidence. They got so angry with me for not reporting Julietta's disappearance, so I called them as soon as Jonny went missing. But they are not taking it seriously.'

'I'm sure they will find him,'

Had Beth just come to vent? Aunty Lee could not tell. It could not be easy for her: losing her sister then her maid, and now her shady business partner was on the run.

Of course, Beth's Julietta might not have been as close to her as Nina was to Aunty Lee ... Aunty Lee felt a pang at the thought of losing Nina. She did not grudge her helping out at Beth's, not at all, now that she was safely back at Binjai Park. But Aunty Lee had missed her sorely ... even though she had proved her independence by surviving. And perhaps it was time to shine light on the other plan lurking in the dark reaches of her mind, while her *compos* was still relatively *mentis*.

'So you see,' Beth's words pulled Aunty Lee's attention back to her. 'So you see, I can't possibly tell the police that without making it look as though I suspect my own nephew!'

'Tell the police what?'

'That after Fabian left the house that day, I saw him talking to Julietta outside. That was the last time I saw Julietta. And he tried to phone Julietta. He must have got her to meet him.'

'Did you see her leave with him?'

'I don't know. I thought I heard two taxis so maybe not.' Unfortunately, the presence of a second taxi suggested Seetoh might not be in the clear either. Given his possessive, suspicious nature he may have followed them ...

Aunty Lee blinked at the woman. Beth's smile was fixed expectantly on her but without giving any clue as to what was expected. Aunty Lee fell back on the Psychiatrist's Solution: 'What do you feel you should do?'

Beth's smile tightened slightly. 'I told you. I think the police have to be told the truth. I just cannot bear to be the one telling them.'

Ah, there was the request. Unfortunately, Aunty Lee still had no idea what she was supposed to tell the police.

'Look … ' Beth opened her handbag, 'I made some notes for you, just to help you keep it straight.' Still the schoolteacher, Aunty Lee thought.

'Let me find my spectacles.'

'No need. I'll read it to you.' Beth's suppressed impatience broke through. 'Fabian told the police that he was at my place all afternoon yesterday. He's staying at my place, yes. But he was ranting and rambling on and on, and he gave me such a headache that I had to go and lie down just to get away from him for a while … '

'Why didn't you just tell him to leave? Or keep quiet?'

'Rosie, he's my poor dead sister's only son. How can I ask him to leave my house? Anyway as I was saying … '

'Even if he was your own son you can ask him to leave your house if he's giving you a headache, *what*. I'm sure Patty wouldn't expect you to … '

Beth raised her voice. 'Anyway, as I was saying, I went to lie down in my room. When I came out later Fabian wasn't there anymore so I didn't think anything of it. Only, later I found out that he had gone and told the police that I could swear he was with me; I got worried. Look, all you have to tell your policeman is that I told you I wasn't feeling well and slept all afternoon. Make sure you tell them I have no idea what time Fabian left. That's all you have to say. Let them figure out what they want to from that.'

Aunty Lee looked at Beth. Of course, it was entirely possible the woman did not realize she was as good as handing up her nephew as a prime suspect in her partner's disappearance.

Beth was not bad looking, Aunty Lee thought. Even now she could have made something of herself if she wanted to. It was not a question of adding make-up or new clothes (which Aunty Lee herself was hopeless at). Beth would look so much better if only she could drop the superior condescending way she was looking down at Aunty Lee right now … Aunty Lee decided the best thing to do was nothing. Sometimes when you left something to sit for a while the fats and the facts rose to the surface and could be skimmed off.

Her phone rang.

It was Helen Chan's number, and Aunty Lee answered, ignoring Beth's resentful sniff.

'Helen? I'm with somebody right now ... '

'Rosie! It worked! Our plan worked! Omigod I can't believe it! We can become detectives! Is Fabian with you? I can't reach him ... if he's there, tell him he was fantastic! He should become an actor!'

'I never expected the burglars to make their move in broad daylight, though looking back it makes perfect sense. Neighbours would report anything suspicious at night, but who looks twice at construction workers in the daytime, right?'

To test Aunty Lee's theory (that Patty had suspected her new husband of passing on information to the housebreakers), Fabian had deliberately told Beth and Jonny that Helen and Kok Peng's house would be vacant when they were in Bali. Helen had booked herself and her husband a staycation at the Oasia Novena hotel and set the house alarms to alert the police silently. And the housebreakers had taken the bait ...

'They tried to break in about an hour ago, in a construction lorry with planked sides and fake work order. Fabian was there; he posted a phone video. He must have been hanging around outside the house waiting since last night. Everybody's looking for him to interview him. They interviewed me and I told them it was all Fabian's idea, like you said. Oh! Fabian's video is on NewsAsia now! Turn on your TV! *987 Live Online* wants to interview him but he's not answering his phone. It must be Jonny Ho, right? How else would they know! Everybody is looking for him! Do you know where Fabian is? He's a hero!'

'Why are you asking me? Why should I know?' Aunty Lee turned to ask Beth whether Fabian had gone back to her house, but Beth was gone.

Cherril turned on the television on the wall in the kitchen, and they watched a clip of the shaky video. It had obviously been taken through a hedge from the garden next door. Aunty Lee wondered whether Fabian had asked the homeowner's permission. And she saw why Salim had not been at the Bukit Tinggi Police Post. He was there, dressed in gardener's outfit and shabby cap, confronting the housebreakers as soon as they were inside the house. The housebreakers had not paid any attention to him. Aunty Lee hoped it did something to make up for what Jonny Ho had put him through. But where was Jonny Ho? Squint as she might at the iPad on which they played and replayed the scene, Aunty Lee did not see him.

Nina stared at the screen, watching and re-watching the 'gardener' easily disarm two men as his backup team appeared, blocking their vehicle. Her eyes were shining with love and longing.

It was painful, Aunty Lee thought, it was a painful waste. Aunty Lee, who knew all too well the importance of precise timing when it came to eggs and love, was tempted to break her resolution and phone Salim to come over right away. But Aunty Lee had promised herself not to meddle in anyone's love life anymore.

But where was Fabian? It was strange that he had disappeared in his moment of triumph. Aunty Lee had thought Fabian thrived on attention, and publicity was the very essence of attention.

'The last I heard, he was going back to the house to change his clothes before being photographed,' Helen Chan told Aunty Lee. 'And then nothing. Do you think he dropped his phone in the WC? That keeps happening to me. And apparently "water-resistant" means they can survive in the rain but not in the toilet.'

'I need to think,' Aunty Lee said.

Mr and Mrs Guang came in and she got them seated and accepted the bouquet of *kesum* leaves Mr Guang handed her.

'What would you like to eat today?'

'Whatever you would like to cook today, Chef!'

They were rapidly becoming her favourite customers. Aunty Lee went through to the kitchen. She would prepare their lunch herself because she always thought best when she was cooking. The more effort required, the harder she thought. 'Order some more prawns. Today's special I will make for them *Masak Lemak Nenas & Udang!*'

'Madam?'

'Prawn & pineapple cooked in coconut sauce,'

'Use frozen prawns, okay, Madam?' Xuyie asked. They had started using frozen prawns because Nina had not been around Aunty Lee to choose her own fresh prawns. 'We still got quite a lot.'

'Okay,' Aunty Lee said. Sometimes you had to be flexible.

She kept one eye on the television screen but there was no sign that they had found Jonny Ho. She checked her phone. There was still no word from Fabian.

'Finish all the frozen prawns,' Aunty Lee instructed Xuyie. Maybe she would get Nina to bring a special lunch treat over to the police post. But a look at Nina's still wan face changed her mind. If not for Aunty Lee, Nina would not have spent days being treated as a prisoner. Aunty Lee would not interfere again. After all, the police seemed (finally) to be winning over the bad guys.

CHAPTER TWENTY-TWO

Fabian?

The burglars caught breaking into Helen's house had all come into Singapore on tourist visas. None of them were foreign work permit holders who Singaporeans were so quick to blame when anything went wrong. The seven Chinese nationals had signed up to come to Singapore on a robbing rather than shopping spree, organized by a Chinese gang. They were all well off enough to have paid an agent for Business Class return tickets to Singapore and rooms in a rented apartment. The package had promised them access to easy burglary targets. Instead of shopping for souvenirs, they would steal them and transport them back home to sell. What they made would cover their expenses and leave them a good profit.

Jonny Ho was their contact person in Singapore. He had provided them with construction worker clothes and information on rich Singaporeans' houses and apartments that would be easy targets. None of the men captured seemed to know very much about him, but then they were tourists. All they knew was that Jonny Ho had offered to help them move money, goods, and even people in and out of China. It also seemed that all his business deals were fake. Poor Beth, Aunty Lee thought. But she couldn't suppress just a little satisfaction, remembering how Beth had looked down on her own messy business practices.

'Thank goodness they stopped them before they did their business everywhere like they did the last time.' Helen Chan was crowing with delight when she phoned Aunty Lee to tell her how well Fabian's plan had gone.

'That was the worst of it. I made them do DNA tests on the pee and poo the last set of burglars did, but apparently none of them match. And there's so much online. Like how Jonny Ho got Julietta to use her contacts to get men from the Philippines to supply fishermen to overseas clients like Taiwanese tuna ships.'

'You cannot believe everything you read online,' Aunty Lee said, even as she scribbled 'online news' on the ingredients needed list. Nina would know how to find these news sites. It was so good to have Nina back.

'You know the newspapers here aren't allowed to publish the really juicy stuff. That Jonny Ho and Julietta were working together! He never had a registered maid agency. He got Julietta to get other Filipino maids in Singapore to recruit from their home towns. The men would be promised high wages and asked to pay thousands of dollars in processing fees and for a plane ticket to Singapore, and they would come in on tourist visas, so no need papers. They found a whole lot of them locked up in a tiny room in Chinatown. And they have photos, but you have to pay to join the site if you want to see them so I didn't pay. The room was full of urine and shit because they had been locked in there by a Filipino manager and his Chinese boss.'

'And the police searched the office space that Jonny Ho was renting in an industrial building at 1 Commonwealth Lane and found Jonny's buddies were making drugs there! Can you believe it? That one I saw the photos. But no big deal. It looked like one of those modern kitchens, or a laboratory. Full of glass bottles and heating equipment. Three men were picked up there.'

It was just incredible enough to be true, Aunty Lee thought. Singapore was so safe and conservative on the surface that most people didn't bother about what their neighbours were doing.

And because Singapore was so hungry for money from Chinese entrepreneurs and cheap foreign labour, nobody looked too hard at where the money and the labour came from.

That was probably what had drawn Jonny Ho to the island, how he had been able to use his looks and smooth business talk to get lonely women to trust him, Aunty Lee thought. She had not trusted him herself but she had felt sorry for him and might well have indulged him if she had been alone and lonely. Something still didn't feel right. She felt Jonny Ho was a smooth-talker and small-time con man, not someone who could oversee drug kitchens and human trafficking. He had not even managed to set up a convincing front at KidStarters! Poor Beth, Aunty Lee thought, her dream school was going to sink along with its native Mandarin speaker. And he had not even been a very good speaker of Mandarin, according to Mr Guang!

But facts were facts. Jonny Ho must have started by targeting the houses he was invited to with Patty. If Patty had suspected what he was doing, that would explain why she had stopped going out altogether.

Unless, of course, Patty had confronted him ... what would Jonny Ho have done if Patty accused him of robbing her friends and demanded a divorce? Had Patty chosen to avoid her friends or had Jonny Ho drugged her and kept her stupefied until he could get rid of her ...

'Did you actually talk to Patty?' Aunty Lee interrupted Helen's excited narration. 'Last time. When she said she was too busy or not feeling well enough to meet up. Did you talk to her yourself?'

'Sure I did. Until right before the end when she was in hospital. But by that time she wasn't talking to anybody. Why?'

'Just wondering if that Jonny Ho was stopping her from going out.'

'You remember what Patty was like ... nobody could stop her from doing what she wanted! But yes, I spoke to her, or to Beth. Poor Beth. I wonder how she's taking it? Fabian said Beth only found out something was wrong when the police went to the house to look for Jonny; it must have been such a shock for her!'

'He wasn't there?'

'No sign of him. His car, his passport, all gone. Missing. Fabian made sure the police checked out the whole house before he went back. He wanted them to take all Jonny's things away; cheaper than calling a disposal company,' he said. Helen's giggle was girlish.

Aunty Lee hoped Helen was not getting a crush on someone young enough to be her son. 'But the police refused. You haven't heard from Fabian, have you? He said he was going back to the house to wash up and dress up because of all the reporters who wanted to interview him. But they've been calling me because they can't reach him. He hasn't been answering his mobile, and I don't want to phone the house in case Beth answers.'

'Maybe he changed his mind about being interviewed and turned off his phone.'

'That must be it. Funny, though. He was so excited.'

Everyone was so happy the house break-ins had been solved, they seemed to have forgotten about Julietta, Aunty Lee thought. It was assumed Julietta had been a victim of either the China tourist gang or the still missing Jonny Ho. But it didn't feel right to Aunty Lee. Burglar tourists didn't make a special trip to kill a domestic helper. And why would Jonny kill Julietta whose help he needed? Either Fabian or Seetoh would have much better reason, though Aunty Lee didn't want to think so.

But if your meat is rotten, it is always better to know the worst than end up with food poisoning.

'What's wrong?' Nina asked.

'Fabian went back to the Jalan Kakatua house to change clothes, and he isn't answering his phone. Helen is worried. But he should be all right because the police already went to search and Jonny Ho is not at the house.'

'Madam Beth is there?'

'Probably.'

'Madam Beth does not like people using phones,' Nina said quietly. 'If Madam Beth does not want people to go out, she will lock the doors.'

'Maybe we should go over there.' Aunty Lee tried to think of an excuse. 'I should congratulate Fabian on his idea working. And it must be such a shock for Beth; I should bring her something … soup, maybe … '

'I will make the soup,' Nina said. 'You should tell Inspector Salim if we are going there. Just in case.'

It was the first time since her return that Nina had mentioned Salim's name. Aunty Lee wanted to ask whether something had changed, but Nina left to get soup stock out of the freezer. Aunty Lee phoned Inspector Salim on his mobile phone. There were things she wanted to ask him, and she was glad when he answered.

'Aunty Lee, what's up?'

'Nina told me to tell you we are going to Jalan Kakatua to look for Fabian. Have you had lunch yet?'

'Should be no problem. I have somebody there watching out for Jonny Ho. Just keep your eyes open, okay?'

'One more thing. Since those tourist-housebreakers were not in Singapore when Julietta was killed, who do you think did it?' This was a wild surmise on Aunty Lee's part, so she presented it with all the more gusto. 'And there was no reason for Jonny Ho to kill Julietta, right?'

'We will be sure to ask Jonny Ho when we get a chance. But we are still looking for this Seetoh. Those obsessive types are dangerous.'

'You shouldn't automatically suspect the boyfriend, you know!' Aunty Lee's guilt over not telling the police about Seetoh earlier bubbled over. 'He hasn't done anything except get worried about her! He is a nice man.'

'Seetoh has failed at two business start-ups. He borrowed money from his parents to get his taxi licence, and instead of trying to earn enough to cover his taxi rental, he's driving around trying to find out what happened to a girlfriend his parents didn't approve of. Wouldn't you call that suspicious?'

'Did his parents disapprove because Julietta was a domestic helper and they were worried he would never be able to marry her?'

Salim chose not to answer this. He changed the subject. 'Anyway, you might as well know Seetoh's Dispatch company provided us with his taxi's GPS records. Yes, he was stalking Jonny Ho, but he only started five days after Julietta went missing. On the night Julietta disappeared, Seetoh was driving a tourist couple around Sentosa. But we still have to talk to him.'

'So, apart from Jonny Ho, your main suspect is Fabian Loo,' Aunty Lee said. 'Why haven't you got somebody watching him? Are you going to arrest him? Can I bring him back to my place for lunch?'

There was a pause. Aunty Lee got a strong impression Inspector Salim was laughing silently.

'What's so funny?'

'I've missed you, Aunty Lee. Of course you can feed him lunch. He's at his aunt's house in Jalan Kakatua. He got back three hours ago and hasn't left.'

Nina drove Aunty Lee over to Jalan Kakatua. Aunty Lee had offered to take a taxi, in case Nina was uncomfortable meeting Beth again, but Nina ended the discussion by walking back to the house and driving the car over to collect Aunty Lee.

Very little progress had been made to the renovations since the last time Aunty Lee had seen the house. She wondered if all Jonny's 'workers' had been robber tourists. As she pushed open the unlatched gate, Beth appeared at the door, seeing off a young man.

The man was not in uniform. But the easy grace of his well-developed musculature and attitude of respectful authority suggested he was a policeman. And a moment later, Aunty Lee was delighted to recognize him.

'Timothy Pang!'

During a previous posting to the Bukit Tinggi Police Post Timothy had been part of the team that solved a major murder case with Aunty Lee's assistance (or interference). That, and commendations from Inspector Salim, had contributed to his rapid rise and promotion, which Aunty Lee naturally also took fond credit for.

'Timmy Pang! Why you so long never come see me?'

'Aunty Lee!' Timothy Pang's cautious surprise was replaced by a broad grin. 'Long time no see! And Nina! I miss you guys. What are you doing here?'

Aunty Lee had forgotten how handsome Officer Timothy Pang was, but now it made her suspicious. 'You are not related to Jonny Ho, are you?'

'Not as far as I know. But Miss Kwuan here just asked me the same thing.' Timothy Pang nodded to Beth, who was glaring at Aunty Lee. 'There must be some resemblance. I look forward to meeting this gentleman.'

'So what are you doing here?' Aunty Lee asked him.

'I was going to ask you the same thing,' Beth said to Aunty Lee with a smile that was more than halfway to a sneer.

Timothy Pang glanced at her but answered Aunty Lee. 'I'm in international affairs now. Just checking out something for our colleagues in Hong Kong. And you? Are you two ladies friends?'

'Mrs Lee was a friend of my late sister. She lent me her servant for a few weeks. Illegally, of course, so please don't tell and get her into trouble. Now I'm wondering whether that was to spy on me!' Beth said with a little laugh. 'And Fabian told me you manipulated him into coming back to stay in the house. You did, didn't you? Told him to give this address to the police? He just landed on our doorstep with no warning.'

'He had no more money,' Aunty Lee said, 'and this is his parents' house, after all. Where else is the boy supposed to go? Where is he? I want to take him out for lunch.' She turned to Timothy Pang. 'Have you eaten lunch yet?'

'Fabian is not a boy. He is an incompetent, irresponsible adult with anger issues. His parents spoiled him and let him get away with everything under the sun but I'm not going to!'

'Where is he?' Aunty Lee asked again.

'Asleep. Sleeping off all the nonsense he got up to last night. He doesn't want to be disturbed. You better leave now. I'm busy.'

'Maybe his door is locked,' Nina whispered urgently to Aunty Lee. 'She likes to lock doors.'

'Get out of here! All of you!'

'Just a minute.' Officer Timothy Pang's voice was still low and reasonable but now the authority in it was unmistakable. 'I would also like to have a word with Fabian Loo before I go. Please?' He smiled at Beth, who stared at him. 'We won't bother you here. Maybe we can take him out for lunch.'

'Yes, yes! I *blanjah* you all lunch!' Aunty Lee said eagerly.

But Beth turned away stiffly.

'Just go away. I already told you he's sleeping and doesn't want to see anybody. I'm going to complain about you! I'm going to report you for harassment!'

This reminded Aunty Lee of Beth's report against Inspector Salim. Had that really been at Jonny Ho's instigation? Beth seemed only too ready to do the same to Timothy Pang.

Timothy Pang turned back to the house he had just been shown him out of.

'You can't come into my house without a search warrant!' Beth shouted, pushing the policeman's arm away and standing with her back to the door. She didn't trust him not to push past her if she opened it to let herself in.

'I am not searching your house, Miss Kwuan,' Timothy Pang said with professional patience. 'I am looking for Fabian Loo. He is a person of interest in our investigations.'

'He is sleeping. You'll have to come back another time. He told me he doesn't want to be disturbed! I don't want to make him angry!'

The shrill alarm in Beth's voice made Aunty Lee wonder what Fabian had done to her. Was there another side to the self-pitying, self-centred young man?

'It is for your own protection.'

Timothy Pang had clearly heard the same thing. 'Where is Fabian Loo's room?' He addressed the question to Beth, but it was Nina who answered: 'Top of the stairs on the left.'

Officer Pang stopped to tap a message into his phone before gently pushing Beth aside and going into the house.

Officer Pang knocked gently and called through the door: 'Mr Loo? Can I have a word with you?' There was no answer.

'He's asleep, I tell you!' Beth shouted. 'He didn't get much sleep last night so he took something. Don't disturb him!'

Beth's harsh voice was more likely to disturb Fabian, Aunty Lee thought. She made her way up the stairs as fast as she could, Nina staying a protective step behind her. Timothy Pang, after knocking again, tried the door handle. The door was not locked. Timothy went in, followed by Beth, who was still fussing.

But, as Aunty Lee reached the landing ...

'Don't come in!' Timothy Pang backed out of the room, pulling Beth along with him as he reached for his mobile phone.

Aunty Lee ducked under his arm and into Fabian's bedroom. Fabian was lying on the floor next to the bed. There was vomit all around him. Behind her she heard Timothy Pang requesting an ambulance: 'Yes, he's alive.' She thought she heard Fabian moan softly as the police officer came to her side.

'Should we put him back on the bed?' Aunty Lee suggested. 'More comfortable.'

'Better let the experts move him. Do you have any idea what he took?' This last was to Beth, who just wrung her hands help-lessly. 'Might be food poisoning.'

'He had a weak stomach,' Aunty Lee said.

'Lucky for him,' Timothy Pang said grimly.

As they waited for the ambulance Beth said: 'He may have done it on purpose. I was always worried he would.'

'You mean suicide?' Aunty Lee said. 'Nah *lah*. Why?'

'Guilt,' Beth said flatly. 'He and Jonny got into a big fight last night. I didn't know what it was about, but Fabian was gloating and Jonny was angry. And then Jonny stormed out of the house and didn't come back.'

Fabian hadn't been able to resist telling Jonny the police were onto the Chinese housebreaking gang, Aunty Lee thought with a sinking feeling. That was why Jonny had not been caught with the others. Once Fabian told him, he had run away and abandoned them.

'The police are sure to find Jonny Ho. Even if he got up to Malaysia before they started watching out for his car, look how they caught Mas Selamat, and that one was much cleverer than Jonny Ho. But that's hardly any reason for Fabian to get upset.'

'Actually, it's not out of character for him,' Beth said. 'Even as a boy, everything would be going well and then he would get these depressions. Just like his mother. I was always afraid that he would end up like his mother. Fabian may have tried to copycat his mother's suicide.'

It took Aunty Lee awhile to become aware that her mouth was hanging open. She felt the dryness on her tongue when she snapped it shut. 'What suicide?' Her voice sounded strange to her. 'Patty died of cancer.'

'Fabian may have been trying to copycat his mother's suicide,' Beth repeated. 'We told everybody that Patty died of complications but she had been depressed for some time. The pain was getting worse; she knew she was never going to get any better. She overdosed on sleeping pills and whisky.'

'I didn't know that. Nobody told me.' Aunty Lee had thought

that, in the course of his talks, Fabian had said everything he had to say on his mother, with repetitions. But he had never mentioned this.

'We didn't want Fabian to know but, during that last fight, Jonny got angry and told him. Obviously, that sent Fabian over the edge.'

'Don't say that!' Aunty Lee said quickly. 'We still don't know what really happened, *what*. It might have been an accident. Nowadays all these young people whole day taking powders for protein and fibre and slimming, so easy to get mixed up with drain cleaner and fungus powder, especially when you don't use the whole packet and you transfer to a bottle, and you mean to label it properly but then the phone rings and you forget!'

Beth seemed to have some difficulty following Aunty Lee. She shook her head and dismissed the thought.

'Thank you for coming,' she said with a sudden sweet smile. 'Things have been so stressful I don't know what I'm saying anymore. If you hadn't come to look for Fabian, we might not have found him in time. Thank you.'

Beth Kwuan was another puzzle, Aunty Lee thought. For all Beth's claims to distrust her sister's husband, she had continued living in the house with him, even going into business with him.

Jonny Ho had told Aunty Lee he took care of Beth because, according to Chinese tradition, he was responsible for his dead wife's sister. But Beth Kwuan was hardly a helpless damsel with bound feet. She had been a schoolteacher for years, and anyone who could survive hormonal teenagers and their tiger parents was a survivor.

Aunty Lee remembered Fabian's mysterious talk about plans guaranteed to make Jonny Ho confess, and her heart sank. Why hadn't she forced the stupid boy to tell her what he was planning? '*Alamak*, that Fabian so *goondu*! I am going to shake him … ' The look on Timothy Pang's face stopped her. She might not have a chance to shake Fabian. Poor silly Fabian.

Aunty Lee was suddenly furious with everyone who hadn't believed Fabian's suspicions that his mother was murdered … including herself. But given he believed that, why would he try to kill himself the same way as her fake suicide?

But Beth was speaking again. 'You don't think Jonny or Fabian could have killed Julietta? Julietta might have found out something about one of them he didn't want to get out … I told you she was behaving strangely after Patty died … that's what you're thinking, isn't it?'

Aunty Lee did not remember Beth mentioning Julietta's strange behaviour. Maybe she had mentioned it to the police in her statement. 'No. I think that Jonny Ho is a con man and a cheater but he doesn't seem like a killer.'

'The ambulance is here!' Nina shouted. She led the men upstairs, and two more police officers joined Timothy Pang and started clearing a path through the construction debris to the ambulance outside the gate. 'Might be food poisoning from the look of it.' Aunty Lee heard Timothy tell them, which made her angry with him. Why did everybody automatically blame food poisoning for everything? After what seemed to her an agonisingly long time, Fabian was carried down the stairs with a drip in his arm and an oxygen mask over his face.

Aunty Lee bent over the stretcher at the foot of the stair and squeezed Fabian's limp, cold hand. 'You get better, Fabby, okay? We will work out everything. Just get better.'

Beth's strange steady gaze followed Aunty Lee through half-closed eyes.

'Still no sign of Mr Jonny Ho?' One of the newly arrived policemen asked Beth.

'He took his passport and international driving licence. I don't think he's coming back.'

'Master Jonny used to park his car in the next door garage,' Nina said. 'The neighbours moved out because of all the renovation noise and dust. Temporary, they said. They took their cars with them so Master Jonny used to park his car there when he wanted to hide it, so people didn't know he is here.'

It didn't seem likely. The homeowners had been away long enough that weeds were flourishing on the pebbled driveway. And not only were the garage doors closed, the fancy metal gate was protected by a padlock and chain. 'The owner's a lawyer,' Beth explained. 'Very security conscious.'

'I smell something funny,' Aunty Lee said, sticking her head between the upright rods of the gate. 'And look. But a car must have driven into the garage because it flattened some of them. See? Starting here, near the gate, see where that patch of goose grass got one flattened strip through it? That one grows so fast, must have just happened. Very good for women after having babies, you know. And for making tea if you got worms ... ouch ... '

As Aunty Lee withdrew her head with more care for her ears, she heard Timothy Pang saying: 'Get me a search warrant. Now.'

CHAPTER TWENTY-THREE

Quiet Women

Fabian Loo's sensitive stomach had probably saved his life. If he had not vomited up a good part of his last meal, he would have been dead instead of in a coma. But even apart from his coma, things didn't look good for him.

The police found Jonny Ho's shiny blue Subaru hidden in the garage. It was unlikely Jonny Ho had hidden it there this time, because the police also found Jonny Ho dead in the boot. Jonny Ho had been drugged. And when he was unconscious, someone had shot him three times in the back with a nail gun. It was probably the same nail gun that had killed Julietta. But because Jonny Ho had been shot in the back instead of in the head, it would have taken him much longer to die.

Had Fabian killed Jonny before trying to kill himself? Jonny had been killed the same way as Julietta, with a nail gun. And the police found a nail gun hidden in the toilet cistern of Fabian's bathroom.

'But Fabian solved the housebreaking case!' Aunty Lee protested. 'Jonny Ho was going to be arrested! Why would he go and attack Jonny Ho for?'

'Fabian came back to the house and found Jonny getting into his car with his bags,' Beth said. 'They started arguing, shouting at each other. I was afraid they were going to start fighting. I couldn't stand it anymore. By the time I came back, Jonny was gone. I saw him getting ready to leave earlier, so I thought he just left. I asked Fabian what had happened, but he just said "wait and see" and went upstairs. When I asked him where he was last night, he told me to mind my own business, that he was tired and fed up and wanted to sleep.'

That sounded exactly like the Fabian Aunty Lee had known over the past few weeks. But surely his big coup would have cheered him up? Helen had said Fabian was looking forward to talking to the reporters, even wanting to get dressed up for photographs. But then Fabian had wanted revenge against Jonny Ho more than anything else, so he couldn't have cared less about some Chinese gang getting apprehended if Jonny Ho had got away. When he went back to the house for a change of clothes, Fabian had probably been thinking about what he would tell the reporters about how he had exposed the man who married his mother. Instead, he had found Jonny Ho about to make his escape.

Aunty Lee liked Fabian Loo. He was, after all, her old friend's son and the right age to have been *her* son. But she had seen enough of him to recognize his obsession with his stepfather. Fabian was the sort who got an idea inside his head and wouldn't see things any other way.

And Fabian had come back to Singapore to challenge his mother's will and demand her house and all other property. Aunty Lee had herself heard him ranting against Jonny Ho, and Beth had heard him threatening him.

Aunty Lee didn't want to believe Fabian could have killed one, possibly two, people. But the police would say he had both motive and opportunity. His attempt at suicide might have come from shock at what he had done or be an attempt to escape justice. Even if he survived, Singapore still had the death penalty as well as laws against suicide.

At least Nina was back. Looking back, Aunty Lee thought how silly she had been to be so worried about Nina.

'You are right. I missed you so much,' Aunty Lee said to Nina as they started home after locking up the café for the night. Nina looked surprised, then smiled sadly.

'I also missed you,' Nina said. 'It is good to be home.'

They were walking back to the house. It was a slow, easy walk in the relative cool after sunset. The street lamps were bright through the trees lining the road, and the lighted windows showed glimpses of cosy domesticity ... parents sitting in front of television sets and children sitting at computers. It had not been a particularly busy evening, but Nina still looked worn down after her time working for Beth. And Aunty Lee was still shocked by Jonny Ho's horrible death and the suspicions against Fabian, who was still unconscious.

'He was a stupid man,' Aunty Lee said. 'Just because he was so good-looking did not mean he can go around flirting with old women. But he also did not deserve to end up like that.'

'Jonny Ho flirted with everybody, not just old women,' Nina said. 'Except Miss Beth. Miss Beth is the one who was always trying to flirt with Jonny Ho.'

'What?' Aunty Lee stopped so suddenly that Nina thought at first she had tripped. 'Beth is far too prim and proper to flirt.'

'Not when there's nobody around.' Clearly servants didn't count to Beth. 'I was there, remember? I saw her. And Master Jonny saying, "don't sit so close", "don't touch me like that". So funny. What are you looking for?'

Aunty Lee was fumbling in her purse. 'My mobile phone ... ah, here it is.'

'Madam, we are almost back home. Why not go home then phone?'

But Aunty Lee was too caught up trying to sort out the thoughts ... and sudden panic ... Nina's words had triggered. 'Helen? Are you still at the hospital? Is Beth there? What? If she comes back don't leave her alone with Fabian. Never mind why. Just stay there with him and let me think.'

'What's wrong?'

'Maybe nothing. Beth was at the hospital but left when Helen arrived. That was about three hours ago.' Aunty Lee started walking homewards again, much faster this time.

'Your friend is very worried about Master Fabian,' Nina observed to Aunty Lee's back as she followed her.

'It's all your fault that my Jonny is dead. You are the one that ruined everything. My school, my life, my love. It was all finally coming true. I worked so hard for it and you just came in and messed up everything!'

Aunty Lee was still blinking in the sudden glare of a torch in her face when Beth swung a stone lotus flowerpot stand at the side of Nina's head and knocked her down.

'Unlock the door,' Beth Kwuan ordered. 'And get inside. Leave her.' She was still speaking in her genteel mission school prefect voice, and Aunty Lee obeyed. Her hands were shaking, and it was understandable that she had some trouble unlocking the door. Nina moaned softly but didn't get up. She would be better off outside, Aunty Lee thought. Beth might forget about her. Or she might wake up and go for help. On that thought, she got the door open.

'Come on … ' Beth Kwuan yanked Nina to her feet and pushed her at Aunty Lee who supported her. 'Inside.'

Beth followed them in and switched on the lights, putting down her torch.

'Would you like a drink?' Aunty Lee asked. It was absurd given the situation, but came out of her as automatically as the 'Have you eaten yet? Please don't take off your shoes,' that followed. Phrases that were triggered by anyone coming into her home.

Beth did not answer. She also did not take off her shoes. Aunty Lee hoisted Nina inside and eased her onto the upright hall chair and pulled her hand down to look at her head. There was going to be a nasty bruise. Beth darted into the kitchen, and Aunty Lee wondered whether to run for help. The problem was, she could not run and she did not want to leave Nina alone with this madwoman.

'Can you walk?' Aunty Lee tried to get Nina back on her feet.

'Move away from her.' Beth reappeared with a knife and a glass of water. 'Further. Get over there by the wall.'

When Aunty Lee reached the wall, Beth held the knife against Nina's neck as she drank the water. When she finished, she aimed, then threw the glass at Aunty Lee. Luckily her left handed shot was unsteady and the glass smashed against the wall an arm's length from Aunty Lee. Aunty Lee squeaked in alarm, which made Beth laugh.

'Now you know how it feels to have people attacking you, throwing things at you!'

'You killed Julietta,' Aunty Lee said, because she had nothing to lose. Beth meant to kill Nina. Beth probably meant to kill her too, but somehow that felt less important. She had put Nina in danger by letting her go to Beth and now by bringing her home. She saw that Beth was quite mad. Mad as in insane, crazy 'cuckoo' as they would have said in school. If only she could distract her until someone came …

'Julietta was a shameless slut,' Beth said. 'Totally shameless. She threw herself at Jonny. The poor man didn't know what to do. Just like Patty. They had husbands of their own, you know. But they were greedy.'

'Patty's husband was dead,' Aunty Lee pointed out. Nina looked dazed but Aunty Lee hoped she was recovering. 'Patty didn't even meet Jonny Ho until after Ken died.'

'Patty took whatever she wanted without any consideration for anyone else. Right from the time we were children she was like that. I was only one year older but I was supposed to look after her. When she did anything wrong, my parents blamed me for not looking after her. I told them they shouldn't have favourites, but they didn't care. They spoiled her. She was always the centre of attention, and she loved getting attention. I was studying hard and doing what I was supposed to and she just didn't care, but she always got away with it!

'All I ever wanted was to be appreciated for myself. To be acknowledged, just once, for what I do. Is that too much to ask? All of you say it was so romantic that Patty was got married so soon after university. Her parents paid for the wedding dinner; his parents paid for the fancy honeymoon. What's so romantic about that?'

'It was romantic because she was the first in our year to get married, and they were a couple all through university!' Aunty Lee protested, caught up in Beth's grievances.

'Do you know, I met Ken Loo before she did? Ken and I were in the same class in the National Junior College. He came over to our house to work on a group project but Patty came along and distracted him, and he just abandoned the rest of us and spent the whole afternoon talking to her! I went and told him that if he didn't do his share of the work I would make sure he didn't get any credit. But Patty just laughed at me, and Ken said "okay Teacher". He made a laughing stock of me! I was so embarrassed. And the rest of the group refused to back me up. I went and told the tutor I couldn't work with them anymore.'

'That was over forty years ago,' Aunty Lee pointed out. 'I can't even remember people who were bad to me last week! And Patty wasn't just flirting, they were happily married for so many years!'

'I will never forget the humiliation. The deliberate humiliation. That was what Patty was really like. That was the side of her that friends like you never saw.'

'Did Patty know you had a crush on Ken Loo?'

Beth sneered. 'You think that would have made any difference to my sister? The day before the wedding, she said to me, "If you tell me you love him I'll let you have him and get someone else!"'

'What made her say that?'

'What difference does it make? She didn't mean it and, of course, I told Patty it was wrong and immoral of her to talk that way about the man she was marrying. And, of course, she wouldn't have. She was just looking for a chance to humiliate me further. I refused to attend the wedding. Patty always took everything she wanted and everything that anybody else wanted.'

'Your parents said you had measles.' Aunty Lee remembered.

Beth waved that away. 'They covered up for her, of course. In spite of all that, when Ken died and left Patty all alone, I said to myself, I have to do my sisterly duty and go to keep her company.'

Beth had been quite as alone as Patty, Aunty Lee thought, but said nothing. Beth, carried away by historical grievances against her dead sister, had lowered the knife and she didn't want to recall her to the present. Why didn't anybody come? But who was there to come?

'She was selfish and self-centred all throughout our girlhood years. And then, of course, when we met Jonny Ho in China, it started all over again.'

'You fell in love with Jonny Ho,' Aunty Lee said. Of course she had. Jonny Ho had been the sort to flirt with every woman he encountered, and poor Beth, being lonely, inexperienced, and hungry for any attention, had fallen for him.

But, of course, Jonny picked the rich widow over the poor spinster.

'I met him first, you know. I was the one who arranged the China tour, who found a guide who could speak English. Patty wasn't even interested. She just said: "Whatever." I had to make all the decisions for her, always.'

The hand holding the knife dropped to her side. 'Even the end. Patty had cancer, you know. She would have gone sooner or later and in much more discomfort.'

'She asked you to give her an overdose?'

'Patty was already sick. She just had a fight with Jonny. She accused him of telling his contacts how to break into her friends' houses. I gave her some pills to calm her down. Then when she was groggy I just gave her more pills. Dr Heng may have guessed, but I told him that Patty had been depressed about the diagnosis and he came to the conclusion that she killed herself. But he's the one who signed the death certificate as natural causes. Because he knew that if there was no hope of recovery for her, it was better than going through all the chemo and the pain.'

It wasn't your decision. Aunty Lee felt anger mixed with guilt stirring inside her. Beth had decided what was best for her sister much as Aunty Lee tried to decide for Nina and Salim. Because she was sure that her way was better for them.

Julietta had known ... or suspected.

'That was when Julietta started becoming difficult. Mocking us and dropping hints about what she could tell the police if we didn't make her happy. Julietta knew Jonny was getting desperate. Patty hadn't left as much money as we expected. I had a feeling that Jonny had expected even more than I did. Patty had been making donations to the SPCA and the Pelangi Pride Centre and I don't know what else without us knowing. And Jonny didn't know the Singapore market, so it was taking him longer to get started.'

For all his talk of being an experienced investor and entrepreneur, Jonny didn't know the most basic rule about entering a new territory ... he had charged in without studying the terrain. Perhaps his gung-ho attitude and youthful brashness had served him well up to this point ... it had got him a wife and her money and the right to stay and make profits off Singaporeans, but once he had collected all the low-hanging fruit he had no strategy to get him further. He knew nothing about planting and growing trees for the future. He may even have cut down the tree that might have supported him well for years, desperate for the fruit on its highest branches. Surely even Jonny Ho wouldn't have been so short sighted? To her surprise, Aunty Lee felt sorry for the

229

man. And why not? He was dead after all, unlike this madwoman in her living room.

'That was when I had to start locking her up,' Beth continued. Now she had breached her silence, words were gushing out of her like water out of an inflatable pool. 'I couldn't have her running around and saying things to people. She was even sucking up to Fabian, you know.'

'So you killed Julietta. Jonny knew?'

'Jonny got rid of the body for me … after all, he couldn't have the police nosing around. Aside from that he didn't care. He was so busy sucking up to his China connections, trying to prove to them he was useful to them.'

'But why did you kill Jonny Ho?'

'Can you imagine him, that luxury-loving free spirit, in prison? It was for his own good.'

So Beth had killed Jonny for the same reason she killed her sister. For his own good. *If we get out of this alive*, Aunty Lee promised the portrait of M. L. on the wall behind Nina and Beth, *I will never again do anything for anybody's good!*

There was a sound outside. Was it the gate?

'That must be my taxi,' Beth said. 'About time too.' She raised the knife against Nina's neck. 'Relax. It will hurt more if you struggle. People kill goats and cows like that all the time. And I've got to do your boss next.'

But at that moment Mr and Mrs Guang stepped in through the French windows from the garden. Aunty Lee stared in disbelief, wild hope surging.

'Excuse me, Aunty Lee,' said Mr Guang with his usual formal politeness, 'are you ready to join us on our evening walk?'

'Get out!' Beth shouted. 'She's not going anywhere!'

Beth might just have been able to kill one stunned maid and one tired aunty with one knife, but what use was a single knife against four people? Even madness must face up to reality sometimes.

Aunty Lee only hoped Beth would not slash Nina in frustration ... 'No!' she screamed as Beth, seeming to read her thoughts, raised the knife.

What followed seemed unreal to Aunty Lee. Little Mrs Guang stepped swiftly and silently across to Beth. Blocking the thrust of the knife with her outer forearm, she rolled her arm over Beth's so that Beth's elbow was locked in her armpit. At the same time, her other elbow hit Beth's chin hard.

'My arm!' Beth whimpered as Aunty Lee's seven inch Misono 440 Molybdenum Santoku knife landed on the floor. Mrs Guang grabbed a firm handful of hair on the top of Beth's head and held her in a half clinch.

'Are you all right?' Mr Guang asked Aunty Lee.

'What was that?' Aunty Lee wondered if she was dead and dreaming of a martial arts movie.

'*Chisau* or push hands. It is t'ai chi. My wife does not often get a chance to practice as she does not believe in competition.'

CHAPTER TWENTY-FOUR

Menu Planning

The Guangs had been in Aunty Lee's Delights when a woman came into the café looking for Aunty Lee. She was a friend, she said. Avon had given her Aunty Lee's address and directions to her house.

'We thought, if she is a friend of yours, surely she would know your home address,' Mr Guang said. 'And if she was not a friend of yours, she should not get your home address without you knowing. So my wife and I decided to take our evening walk. We saw her at the side of your house watching for you. So we waited. If you saw her and said, "Wonderful! My friend is here!" then we would have gone home.'

But, instead, Beth had hit Nina on the head. So the Guangs came into the garden and watched the drama through the French windows. They had not been able to hear what was being said, Mr Guang explained, but the knife at Nina's neck did not look like a friendly gesture.

The Guangs could watch people in the café all they wanted, Aunty Lee decided. And all the free tea and free *laksa* they could drink and eat.

By the time the police arrived, Beth was her genteel schoolteacher self again. She had been calling on an old friend, she told them,

232

when two mad people burst into the house and attacked her with a knife. She stood there in her beige cotton shirt and brown skirt that ended at where her calves were thickest and said: 'Rosie, tell them it's just a misunderstanding!'

Even Aunty Lee might have been convinced. But her legs were still shaky from the terrors of the last hour. 'She tried to kill us,' she said firmly, 'and she killed her maid and her sister's husband, who she was in love with … '

Aunty Lee could hear herself being incoherent. Luckily the first two police officers to arrive knew her and knew that it was her house. They took Beth in for questioning. Nina was sent to hospital and made to stay overnight for observation though she insisted that she was all right. True to her promise to herself not to interfere (and against all her instincts), Aunty Lee did not phone Salim to tell him that Nina had been hurt and was in hospital. Anyway, she knew he would see the reports.

Aunty Lee closed the café for a small home party when Nina was allowed home. This meant that, in addition to those she had invited over, any customers who turned up were invited to join them as guests … but had to eat whatever Aunty Lee decided to cook. Helen Chan was not there. Fabian had finally surfaced from the drug-induced coma, and she was at the hospital.

'We'll have a bigger party when Fabian gets out of hospital,' Aunty Lee told her.

Aunty Lee served up bowls of hot *bak kut teh soup*. The excitement had left Nina's stomach too ready to lurch and retch, but she could drink the hot, spicy pork rib soup even if she didn't manage to eat much. The fragrant ginger in the nutritious soup was soothing and calming from the inside out. It never does any good to force your body to eat what it is not ready to digest.

Aunty Lee had invited Salim and his mother. They could not eat the pork in the soup, but Aunty Lee had also made *nonya chap chye* or vegetable stew. All Singaporeans know to have at

233

least one vegetarian dish at every party, since there will be Muslims who don't eat pork, Buddhists who don't eat beef, and possibly Christian fundamentalists who don't eat shellfish. Salim introduced his mother to Nina, but as they sat down, Commissioner Raja drew Aunty Lee firmly away to another table.

'I want to talk to you.'

'I wasn't interfering. Not this time.'

'No. All you did was go home.' Commissioner Raja sat down beside her with a small grunt. The once slim muscular athlete had put on some weight since his days on Singapore's Olympic yachting team. But the years had also brought a dignity and he wore them well.

'Early or late, love tends to be blind. But another love that can be even more blind and irrational love is parental love.'

They looked from Salim's mother to Selina, whose pregnancy was just starting to show. She was ordering Mark around for the good of 'the baby'.

'Did Beth confess?'

'Not a confession so much as a justification of why she had to do what she did, given the unfairness of everyone ... you and her parents included ... making her sister the favourite.'

'Still, Patty left her the house in her will ... '

'Only according to the will that Beth and Jonny passed off as Patty's. There are photographs of another will on the camera Nina found. This one is witnessed by Patty and Julietta. It looks like Patty drafted it after she became aware of Jonny's involvement with the housebreakers. It's very close to the earlier one that she left with her lawyer, leaving everything to Fabian with some money to go to Julietta's children's university fees, to be paid directly to the university. And she wrote down the amounts of money that she invested in Jonny and Beth's projects and says that they are to pay the amounts back to Fabian, without interest, until 2020 and, if not fully paid back by then, at five per cent interest from then on.'

Aunty Lee sat back. Clearly Fabian had had no idea of this will or he would not have been so angry with his dead mother. Someone had deliberately made Fabian think that Patty had died angry with him when, in fact, she had made sure that everything of value that she had would go to him. 'I don't know how anybody could have been taken in by that stupid fake will!'

'People often change their wills after they get married.' Mycroft stopped at their table bearing a tray of condiments, guided by Cherril with baskets of *kropok*. 'I did.' He looked at his wife and smiled. 'But don't worry, I don't have that much to leave anyway.'

Aunty Lee thought Mycroft and Cherril very likely had very different ideas about what 'that much' might mean. Even her two stepchildren, born and brought up in the same environment, had drastically different ideas about money and what they were entitled to.

'Didn't your husband leave everything to you?' Cherril teased as she arranged the little dishes on their table. 'Mark always gives the impression that he was cheated out of a fortune when his father married you and left you everything.'

'That's different,' Aunty Lee said. M. L. had indeed left her a life interest in all his properties. But he had also made clear (as had Aunty Lee in her own will, as Mycroft would know) that it would all be divided between his children when she died. Indeed, Mark had already borrowed heavily on his anticipations to fund his various business ventures. If Aunty Lee had not been topping up the family investments from her profits, there would have been a lot less left than Mark so confidently expected, and the one who would suffer unfairly would be Mathilda …

Commissioner Raja fished a strip of Panadol out of his pocket and swallowed two tablets with his Homemade Cloudy Lime Juice. Despite the happy (at least in Aunty Lee's eyes) ending, Commissioner Raja looked as though he was having a headache. And he was. This was going to be a public relations nightmare. Already half the social media activists were shouting that it was the consequence of allowing too many Mainland Chinese to set up businesses in Singapore too quickly, while the other half were ranting about how badly Singapore dogs treated entrepreneurial true Chinese businessmen.

But all that could be taken care of later. For now, there was food on the table and friends to share it with.

'Has Salim forgiven you ... the police ... for suspending him?'

'Nothing to forgive. He understands the procedure. Rules are rules. If you don't want to follow them, you either get them changed or you get out.'

'Yes,' Aunty Lee said. She made her decision then. It hurt, but it was right.

'I was saying I'm ready to come back to work.'

When Aunty Lee went over to her table, Nina was trying to clear her own plates but Cherril and Salim were making her stay seated while Puan Aisyah laughed.

'I am terminating your contract,' Aunty Lee said. 'When you feel well enough to travel, I will arrange for you to go back to the Philippines.'

Nina's mouth opened and shut several times before she said, in a strangled voice, 'it is not my fault, Madam. I did not want to go to work there; you sent me to work there.'

'Like Madam Beth said, I'm the boss and you should do what I tell you instead of talking back.'

'But, Madam, I ... ' Nina was on her feet, sounding stricken. Salim, also on his feet, looked poised to act. But it was not physical action that was needed here. His mother watched Aunty Lee with calm, clever eyes that knew there was more to come. 'I am sorry I made you angry! Please don't send me away! You need me!'

'Nina, if you are not in Singapore when Salim applies for permission to marry you, you will have a better chance. They may still say no. But if you start your own business and come back to Singapore as an entrepreneur ... ' like Jonny Ho, Aunty Lee almost said, but stopped, 'you can apply for PR and then apply to get married.'

A voice inside Aunty Lee's head said, *Thought you weren't interfering anymore?* It was so clear that Aunty Lee looked up at the photo of her late husband. It was his voice. 'I'm Not interfering, I'm strategizing,' she said firmly.

Nina and Salim had sat back down and were talking together in what was clearly meant to be a private discussion. Aunty Lee looked at the other woman at the table. She was suddenly aware that Salim's mother had every reason to be angry with her. For once she had nothing to say.

Fortunately, Puan Aisyah did.

'Your potato curry puffs are very good,' she said. 'Did you make the filling specially?'

'Oh yes. I thought of making them because we had a lot of leftover potatoes. But then, with so many things going on, I forgot. So in the end I threw them out and cooked a new batch. Wasted, I know.'

Puan Aisyah nodded. 'Sometimes you cannot help it.' She smiled.

Sometimes you just have to start over from scratch.

Acknowledgements

I want to thank so many people, especially my super agent Priya Doraswamy, Lucy Dauman who first welcomed Aunty Lee to the UK and the wonderful team at Killer Reads: Kathryn Cheshire, Sarah Hodgson, Janette Currie and Micaela Alcaino

CPSIA information can be obtained
at www.ICGtesting.com
Printed in the USA
LVHW04s0128180818
587241LV00010B/53/P